Beautiful Butterfly

Look, look, butterflies everywhere
On my shirt, socks, finger and in my hair
They remind me of my past history
The early days, right after my injury
When I felt broken and off-beat
Like a caterpillar, ugly and incomplete

But we are different, the caterpillar and me
It didn't have to work to be set free
While I had to learn to live a new way
By putting all that I learned into play

I had to accomplish many seemingly simple tasks
Like holding up my head without being asked
To use one hand, instead of two
Is not an easy thing to do
To get around, since I can't walk
To communicate, since I can't talk

But my transformation is not yet complete
I still have many goals to meet
And as I work and persevere
I hope my problems disappear
Then, like the helpless caterpillar in a cocoon
I'll become a beautiful butterfly soon.

Bari Lynn Dizengoff 1999

ANOTHER DAY OF INFAMY

A Novel

Diane Saks

iUniverse, Inc.

New York Lincoln Shanghai

Another Day of Infamy

iUniverse books may be ordered through booksellers or by contacting:

iUniverse
2021 Pine Lake Road, Suite 100
Lincoln, NE 68512
www.iuniverse.com
1-800-Authors (1-800-288-4677)

This is a work of fiction. All of the characters, names, incidents, organizations, and dialogue in this novel are either the products of the author's imagination or are used fictitiously.

ISBN: 978-0-595-42635-5 (pbk)
ISBN: 978-0-595-86962-6 (ebk)

Printed in the United States of America

To the MossRehab Drucker brain injury center, the MossRehab Clubhouse, Bari Lynn Dizengoff and especially to Mr. Jamie Hogan who may not know each other and were not involved in the 9/11 crisis.

CONTENTS

Preface

This is not just another book about the World Trade Center tragedy. I wanted to make two points. The first one is that I chose to write a personal view about a couple who worked in one of the twin towers, what their life was like before, during and after the incident. There are relatives of the dead and survivors of the World Trade Center plane crashes who still are trying to heal. I decided to write something that might relate to those people.

My second point is one of my characters suffered significant brain injury. I don't want to put down productions like _The Miracle of Kathy Miller_ which was about a girl on the brink of graduating junior high school, who was hit by a car while crossing a highway. She suffered head injury from windshield impact and was comatose for months. In about a year or two after her accident she recovered about 95%. It was a good movie and was a true story. However, there are far too many brain injury stories like _Kathy Miller_ which suggest that brain is short-lived and nearly completely curable. For some people it is. It doesn't always happen that way. I don't know how long Matt Cobel, one of my characters, will have the effects of brain injury. The families of anyone with a brain injury don't really know how long or short, temporary or permanent the effects of brain injury will last. I take him into two years past the World Trade Center experience and he still isn't as far along as Kathy Miller was two years since her accident.

Since my subject matter is about the 9/11 and World Trade Center crises, I made it a point to see _United 93_ and The World Trade Center. Neither film took my viewpoint. I was happy about that. What I am not happy about is that both films may have contributed to saturating the writing industries with stories about the World Trade Center and airline hijackings of 2001.

United 93 focused on an airline being hijacked by terrorists. It failed to show that side of why the plane was being hijacked and why the passengers were being murdered. The film only showed passengers talking on plane phones, saying goodbye to their families. It also showed air traffic controllers discovering many aircraft which was off the designated routes. The film showed the two airplanes that crashed into the twin towers. When the first one hit, people thought it was an accident of some type unrelated to terrorism.

The second film was <u>The World Trade Center</u> that promised to be personal about people involved in the disaster and their families. What I saw were several firemen going into the elevator shaft of a tower that was collapsing. Falling debris and such had caused two men to be injured and trapped while several others were killed. The film showed the families of the two firefighters as they waited, worried, and hoped, wondering when and if these men would be returned safely to their families. My story of The World Trade Center is nothing like these films so I hope you will give this book a chance and enjoy it.

Acknowledgements

I would like to thank my writer's group, the Writer's Circle, who have helped me with this book for the past two years. I would also like to thank the therapists and many of the participants of Moss Rehab in Philadelphia, a couple of them who I have mentioned by name. Others include Cynthia Nesmith Williams, Dallese Frasier, Beth Ann Sinott, Maddie DiPasquale, Stephanie Wingate Gardener, Roberta Brooks, Lorrie Robinson, Walter Lewis, and all the other people, staff and participants alike whom I have had the pleasure to know.

CHAPTER 1

▼

FREE WRITE.

Before she drifted off to sleep, Bari Lynn wondered to herself, "Why do the terrorists think that they will be honored by God for murdering people? Why would anyone want to blow up an airplane of innocent people when they themselves would be instantly killed?"

Aside from the glow of the street lamps, only the lights of the jet airliner could be seen drifting through the dark sky over the North Jersey neighborhood of ranchers. Suddenly, the aircraft seemed to deliberately head for one of the bedroom windows. At the sound of broken glass, the plane, hanging from the window frame, spewed flames and smoke. As usual, Bari Lynn, looking like she had climbed into bed after a hot shower without drying off, sat up in bed. She looked over at the window where the attack had been, only to find that everything was intact. The sheets felt as though they had been placed on the bed directly from the washing machine without a visit to the dryer. The fatherless daughter peeled off her bed clothes. The teenager's skin was chafed for the third time this week. She didn't scream as she had the first time it happened. Bari Lynn pulled open a dresser drawer, yanking out night clothes like a magician pulling scarves out of a top hat. The former cheerleader stopped when she grabbed onto a sheer nightgown. The teenager sighed as she ripped the pillow cases from the pillows and stripped the sheets from the bed, flinging them to the floor. It was the middle of the night and Bari Lynn was too exhausted to think about getting fresh bed linen this time around.

She sat at her lap top and booted it up. The high school senior tapped the pointing element until it clicked on MS Word 2000. Over on the far right side of the screen, Matt's sister manipulated the element until there was a hand with its index finger pointing out the "why I want to enroll in your therapy program" document. Bari Lynn brushed her damp dark hair away from her eyes as she stared at the blank screen. "Hey Matt, what do you call it when you combine a series of actions into one single command and how to you do it?" She paused, "Oh I forgot!"

Free write she typed. *My name is Bari Lynn, which is pronounced Barry Lynn.* She started to type something else. *The Boy Named Jacob. He saw everything a boy could in a dark 98.6 degree moist world. He took food through a tube that led to his stomach. He spent his entire life in that world.* "No, he really spent most of his life in an incubator." Bari Lynn wiped a ticklish sniffle from the edge of her nose as she read what she had typed. *Matt once spoke with a softness that could melt the heart of any cheerleader. Now he speaks with the clarity of a crinkled audio tape as it plays.* She sniffled again. *That's why I want to enroll in the therapy program. I want to help people like Matt get back their lives from whatever terrible thing has happened to them. You see, Matt is my older brother and he and my family have a tragic tale to tell.* The teen turned around and noticed her bedding strewn on the floor and the contents of her pajama drawer lying on a damp mattress cover, soaked over a previously dried round pale yellow stain. The high school senior wondered whether to remove the mattress cover and throw the entire thing in the trash.

Thinking back over the essay she was writing, *I wonder if they will understand what kind of a therapist I want to be. I want to be a brain injury therapist, like the ones who are helping Matt everyday when he goes to rehab. I read up on it. I can either be a brain injury therapist/case manager that will require that I get my masters and have two years of experience with the brain injured community. I could also be a brain injury therapist/job coach which requires I have a bachelors degree in psychology and vocational counseling and one year of experience with the brain injured community. I don't suppose hanging around with Matt since the incident will qualify my requirement for experience with the brain injured community. I could go for the first type and if I can't find a job I can always go back to school for two more years. I visited him there at the center when they had their Christmas parties, and end of the summer parties. A therapist for the brain injured. There were people who have suffered from strokes, car accidents, and incidents as strange as Matt's ordeal. They say that every cloud has a silver lining and that you should make your worst day your best day. Before it all happened, I didn't know what I wanted to do with my life. All I cared about was volley ball and wanting to be head cheerleader in my high school. My grades were average.*

My best friend since elementary school is Nicole, who I call Niki. We must be as tight as Gayle King and Oprah Winfrey. She has a sixth sense when it comes to people, especially boys. I was lucky to have a friend like that when I was finally old enough to date. Bari Lynn looked over at her N'Sync Poster, particularly at Lance Bass. *I remember when I first put that poster up on my wall a couple of years ago, Niki was with me. She told me that Lance Bass looked gay to her. She is usually a good judge when it comes to boys in our life, but this is stretching it a bit. She doesn't even know Lance.*

Except for Niki, things have changed so much in the past year I was only five-years-old at the time my father was killed and Matt was barely a teenager. He became "the man of the family," even though Mom hated it. Is this family cursed?

I was watching the History Channel the other day and I saw something on President Kennedy. I really identify with Caroline and John John. I wonder if there are anymore Greek shipping magnates left in the world. Maybe someone could fix my mother up with one of them. She laughed out loud. *Who am I kidding? If there are any I don't think he's looking to settle down with a hairdresser. Hasn't this family been through enough? Who are we? The Kennedys or the Cobels? I suppose I should be grateful that Matt is still alive. They say two out of three ain't bad, but what about one out of three? We still lost two other members in this recent tragedy. What kind of a life does my brother have to look forward to now? I suppose I am being negative. He has been making progress and you really never know. It has only been a year. September 11, 2001, another day that will live in infamy.*

CHAPTER 2

▼

THE BOSS' SON
JULY, 2001.

As she entered the office, Shauna felt like a two-legged ant making her way through the shag carpeting in the olive wood paneled room. That is, a small ant with red shoulder length hair. The young woman could have been a twenty-one year-old top model for a glamour magazine, but wasn't.

Seated behind the desk in front of tall book shelves sat a solidly built young man who looked like he had been working out with one of those home rowing machines. He looked like he had one of those bronze tans from sitting out on the beach all summer. His hair was as dark as tar. Shauna shook like a groupie entering a rock star's dressing room for the first time. She started to stammer, unable to get an audible word out of her mouth. The long haired thirty-three year-old wore a long white robe instead of a business suit, making him resemble a Middle Eastern cult leader like Bin Laden. Stroking his beard, "Hello Shauna. You're right on time." Shauna, feeling a chill in her short-sleeved knit and knee-length skirt, barely answered. She kept staring at him as though she were hypnotized. He spoke. "I made all of this myself. I'm a carpenter by trade."

"Somehow, I knew that," the first clear words Shauna could get out of her mouth. She spoke in an Irish brogue.

"My dad is very busy and asked me to meet with you. He's busy with a rather large assignment and wanted you to help." The young man handed Shauna a piece of paper. "Can you read this?"

Shauna spoke in Arabic as she read the paper.

"Stop being nervous. I'm just a carpenter, not a Messiah. You know where Asbury Park is? There's a stretch of highway and right beside it is the Atlantic Ocean. I want you to be there at 11 a.m. sharp. Here is what I want you to do."

*   *   *   *

Shauna Houlihan stood on the grassy roadside. She stood with her back to the tall leafy green trees and the beach that peeked out between the foliage. The young woman sang to amuse herself, waiting for her ride to show up. *I don't know how to love him ...* By the time the station wagon drove up she started to sing the lyrics *I never thought I'd come to this. What's it all what's_____it_____all"* The singing stopped as she went over to the car. She wrinkled her nose like a rabbit.

An old sky-blue Vista Cruiser Station wagon with sputtering motor and sawed-off shot-gun sounding exhaust pipe carried two couples. By the look of the dull body, the car appeared as though it hadn't been waxed in thirty years.

The passengers of vehicle were two dark haired men in the front seat and two swarthy women in the backseat. "Jesus_____" Shauna clasped her hand across her mouth as she peered into the car. The women's hair could not be seen because of the babushkas wrapped around their heads and tied under their necks. The female in the rear passenger side of the car wore gray wire-framed glasses.

The man in the passenger seat ordered the spectacled woman behind him to open the door and let the lady in. She obeyed in such a way that you would almost expect her to say, 'Yes Master.' Without saying a word Shauna sat down on the navy blue car seat, between the two women. The seat had so many creases and gray lines that Shauna expected a spring to come up and pierce her in the buttocks. The cruiser continued down the road.

Shauna was so tall that when she leaned her head back against the seat, her head brushed up against a large brown cardboard box. When Shauna turned around for a second she noticed in the box several brown paper bags of onions, carrots, cucumbers, potatoes and tomatoes. Thinking about the meeting the day before, *What's wrong with that guy? Everything here looks perfectly normal to me.* There was one bag that was filled with a large spool of copper wiring and about a dozen 9volt batteries. There was an aluminum cylindrical can about thirteen ounces without a label. It looked like it may have contained ground coffee at one time. *Broken buttons, but I can't tell because I would have to open up the can and this is not the time to go snooping. Maybe that guy yesterday was right, hmm.* One of the women turned to Shauna and she quickly turned to face front, trying to think of an excuse if someone asked. When Shauna sneaked another peek into the backseat she saw an old beat up vacuum cleaner. *Maybe what's inside that coffee can l be transferred into this vacuum cleaner.* She slowly turned around continuing to think of an excuse to use if asked. The man in the passenger side of the front seat turned around and noticed Shauna as she was turning her self around to face front. "Bagrad, please move the box towards the tailgate. It seems to be getting in our passenger's way. "Bagrad stopped eating her lunch from a green Tupperware container, turned around and gave a quick shove as the box made its way towards the back of the station wagon. "I'm sorry about the inconvenience. I'm Bagrad and this is my sister-in-law Reni," who was too busy reading the newspaper to Respond. "My husband Abdulad is sitting in the passenger side and Reni's husband, Salmi, is driving." Abdulad was too busy opening up the back of a boom box that rested on his lap, to respond.

"I'm Shauna Houlihan and I appreciate all of you stopping to pick me up." She leaned over and touched Abdulad on the shoulder.

He jumped as though he had his hand in a safe and he turned around. Consciously, slowing his breathing, "Do you want something?"

Shauna handed him the note. Reni looked up from her newspaper that was written in Arabic. Bagrad stopped eating her brown rice and beans. Abdulad took the folded note and read it. "Do you understand Arabic?" he asked Shauna.

"Yes, it's an address of a place located in Bergen County."

"I don't know why an address in Bergen County would be in Arabic," Abdulad answered. Abdulad refolded the note, handing it back to Shauna. "I can see that. Salmi, our guest needs to go to Morrow Drive located in Englewood in Bergen County."

"That shouldn't take too long."

Why don't you take a left on this upcoming street?" Shauna suggested.

"This street is more direct," Salmi responded

"A mile down the road is a roadblock," Shauna mentioned.

"I don't believe you, Salmi responded. Salmi continued down the road until he came upon the roadblock. It looked like a work crew was trying to fix a pipeline in the road. Salmi pulled the car over. Shauna found herself standing on the side of a residential street. The man with the long brown hair, beard and robe approached her, "Shauna there has been a slight change in plans."

CHAPTER 3

▼

NEW YORK CITY

Laura Daniels plopped herself at the café table for a lunch break. "Oh, Matt, why couldn't we have eaten at the Window of The World instead?" Even the red and white pinstriped umbrella over the white metal table didn't cheer her up.

"You know we have been saving that place for special occasions. I thought it would be nice to have some fresh air and a nice lunch. Usually we have lunch at my desk, too, and I wanted a change. They have great coffee. Sometimes I stop here on my way to work and get one to go."

"I forgot. It seems that every lunch is a special occasion when I'm with you. I'll be too tired to get back to work with all this walking." Laura waved away a fly that had attempted to touch down on Laura's napkin like an airplane landing on an airport runway. "I hope the food makes up for this."

"I think I can make up for this," remarked Matt, who started to fidget with something in his jacket pocket.

Shauna, wearing a waitress uniform, approached Matt and Laura. "Hello, I'm Shauna and I'll be your waitress." She noticed a small box partially sticking out of Matt's jacket pocket. "Should I bring some champagne over?" The waitress walked away. Matt thought to himself, Until *today I was so glad that the cubicle next to me opened up so that Laura could move there. Now I am not so sure.*

Noticing the annoyed look on Laura's face Matt said, "No I don't think that will be necessary."

Laura threw down her napkin and rose from the table. "That waitress makes me nervous."

"Me, too."

As the couple left the café and strolled north, Laura became inquisitive. "So do you really have something that warrants champagne? I had a feeling we should have gone to Windows of The World for lunch today. I could just feel it."

I'll tell you about it when we get back to the apartment," Matt winked.

Matt lived in a red brick apartment walk-up. There wasn't even a doorman. Once inside the one bedroom apartment, he turned on the 600BTU window air conditioner.

Laura placed her set of keys on the mahogany entry table that stood to the right of the door. She placed her purse on the table and removed a brush. Matt's girlfriend stood by the mirror brushing her long black hair, Matt walked over to the refrigerator-freezer. Opening the freezer door, "How do you like that waitress knowing my business?" Matt took a look at the frozen dinners.

"Matt don't worry about her. Anyway, I suddenly feel like going back to that café."

"Why?"

"Maybe she tells fortunes like reads tea leaves, tarot cards or reads palms. I could use a fortune teller right now."

"Oh Laura!" He changed the subject. "Look, I have three different kinds of frozen dinners. The first one is lasagna."

"Alright. How many do you have of that?" Laura put her brush away and strolled her slinky body over to the dinning room.

"I have two lasagnas. Look I just have enough time to put them into the microwave for ten minutes, and then we have got ten minutes to eat and then_____"

"OK OK don't get so nervous. We'll get back to work in plenty of time."

"Look why don't you read a magazine or something until I'm ready. By the way, why are you acting so nasty?"

"OK" she smiled snidely. "You probably are wondering why I am so ornery and why I tend to eat so much and I am always going to the bathroom."

"That's crossed my mind."

"I was afraid to bring it up, but this is the second month that I didn't get my period."

"You mean we have more to celebrate than I thought?"

"Don't tell my parents, please. My mother wants me to be this 'Jackie Kennedy image' though I wonder how pure she really was before she married JFK. My mother believes that girls who conceive out of wedlock are evil. She wasn't that thrilled with me getting together with a computer major."

"That is the wave of the future. It happens that the richest man in America got that way through computers."

"That's my mom."

"Are you sure it's what you think it is?"

"I'm going to see my gynecologist next week and then I'll know then. In the meantime don't tell anyone even if it turns out I'm right."

"That ski trip we went on back in April, you didn't forget to take your pills, did you?"

"I don't remember."

"You don't remember?"

CHAPTER 4

▼

MORROW DRIVE

The wood siding on the Cobel family North Jersey rancher grayed like the Asbury Park boardwalk. Caroline and her late husband bought the house from a retired G.I. soldier in the late 1960s.

More than a two scores later, Caroline shared the house with her teenage daughter, Bari Lynn and grown son, Matt, who lived there on weekends.

Bari Lynn entered the room wearing a red Y Camp T-shirt, white shorts, red ankle socks, and brand new New Balance sneakers. Pouring the batter onto the waffle iron, Caroline asked, "Your sixteenth is only a couple of months away. Have you given some thought about what you want to do for it?"

Bari Lynn went over to the cabinets to get a half bottle of maple syrup from the shelf. "I would really like to have pancakes today."

"We're having waffles and I asked you a question."

"I was thinking about a Sweet 16. I can't decide whether I want to have a dinner dance with boys and girls or a luncheon in a restaurant with just girls."

"I really wish that I could give you the Sweet 16 of your dreams, but the only choice we have is to either have the luncheon at a restaurant or have the gathering here in the house," Caroline replied as she took two plates from another cabinet and placed them on the light blue Formica countertop.

"I definitely don't want the party here. This entire place looks bogus. Everything in this place is from the 1950s. I'd rather have my party on the *Happy Days* set than here. That set looks better than anything in this house does."

"Well, nobody has used that set for years maybe I could consider looking into it," Caroline said, tongue in cheek.

"Really. In here you still have ceramic bathroom tile on walls. What's with the Formica? It has little yellow and pink and blue triangles overlapping on a blue background? The wall telephone has a dial on it and we sit on potato chip shaped table chairs. And how about that living room?"

"Bari Lynn, I 'm trying to juggle your father's pension and my beautician salary. When you go to work I'd like to see you do half as good a job having to try to handle the family budget. Besides that, your father loved this kitchen." The doorbell rang, "Bari Lynn answer the door I have to clean up the breakfast dishes."

Bari Lynn opened the living room screen door to find Shauna standing there holding her sandals in her left hand. Brunette, pigtailed Bari Lynn asked, "Who do you want to see?"

"Is this the Cobel residence? I'm Shauna Houlihan."

"This is the Cobel residence. Are you an interior decorator?" Bari Lynn asked as Shauna walked into the house carrying her sandals in one hand and a brief case in the other. "I was really supposed to be here yesterday, but my boss last minute had me make a sudden visit to New York City."

Bari Lynn left the room, "I'll be right back." As Bari Lynn spoke, her mother entered the room. Caroline, wearing a hairnet on her coiffed brunette hair, joined her daughter. Shauna fixed her eyes on the mother who was wearing an embroidered apron tied around her waist. "May I help you, Miss?" Bari Lynn's mother spoke.

"I'm here to see Caroline and Bari Lynn Cobel. It's like I told your daughter, I was supposed to be here yesterday, but my boss wanted me to make a quick trip to New York City."

"That's nice. My son works in New York City—the twin towers, World Trade Center."

"That's hard to miss."

"What exactly do you do?"

"You might say I am a Jill of all trades."

"Then you're an interior decorator", the teenager smiled.

"I'm not here for that. I was informed that you need a party planner for a Sweet 16."

"How could you know that? We just decided that a few minutes ago in the kitchen."

CHAPTER 5

▼

PARTY PLANNER.

"Did you meet my son when you were in New York?" Caroline asked as the threesome left the living room and dinning room area and entered the kitchen.

"Yes I did."

"I don't want to spoil something that Matt set up."

"He really didn't ask me to plan this party," Shauna sat down on one of the "potato chip" plastic chairs. Noticing Caroline and Bari Lynn's inquisitive stares, "I can't really give you my sources. I assure you I mean no harm. I 'm in the business of helping people, you might say." The visitor took out a notebook and a pen from the briefcase. She started to take notes.

Bari Lynn took a seat beside Shauna, "What kind of a person are you?"

"I'm Irish, actually. I was born in a suburb of Dublin."

"Can I fix you anything for breakfast? We just had waffles," Caroline interrupted. Bari Lynn frowned at her mother and then turned to Shauna.

"I mean it. You knew about the Sweet 16 before we even thought of it."

"I'm sure that Ms. Houlihan is being paid by someone to help us and we don't want to waste her time on idle chatter. We really appreciate your help. I don't think I could afford your services otherwise. I suppose the Government agency that takes care of my husband's pension is taking care of this."

"Well …" shrugging her shoulders, "I would really like to know what type of affair you are interested in." Shauna took out a booklet about different types of intimate restaurants luncheons.

"Mom she's a witch. How did she know I wanted to have the party out of the house?"

"Well, Shauna was a teenage girl once and she probably wanted her Sweet 16 in a restaurant," fishing for an answer while suspecting something herself.

"Thank you, Mrs. Cobel. No Bari Lynn I'm not a witch. Actually they didn't have Sweet 16s when I was your age. I never had one."

"I suppose it wasn't something that they did in Ireland," the hairdresser responded.

"May I have fruit cup?"

"Sure!" Caroline opened a cabinet and searched for a can of fruit cocktail. "We seem to be out."

The houseguest got up from the table, "May I try?"

"Well go ahead, but I really think we're out."

The party planner reached into the cabinet and pulled out a container of fruit cocktail. She yanked off the ring top. "This should do it. Where do you put the trash?"

"I have a paper bag under the sink." Caroline squinted thinking that she was sure there wasn't any fruit cup in there.

"I guess I didn't look there very well," the mother stepped aside as Shauna opened up the bottom cabinet to throw out the lid. She returned to the table. "I would really like you to read over the booklet to get an idea of what type of restaurant and food you want for the party. I also have some menus if you want to see any."

Bari Lynn suggested, "If we don't have any money in the budget for a band I can always bring my CD player and my new *Celebrity* album."

CHAPTER 6

▼

LAURA'S FAMILY

Laura was the daughter and only child of Mitchell and Sue Daniels who lived in a large two-story single stucco home on Long Island. It was a fifteen-year-old four bedroom home that was worth about $300,000. Laura's mother, Sue, made her living as an interior decorator. Mitchell was a car salesman. The house looked like it was worth three million dollars. The entryway floor was made of large white block marble. The tables looked like they were white marble topped and sitting on bamboo legs. Louver vent-like doors closed off certain parts of the dining room and the kitchen. The staircase banister up to the second floor was made of wood, painted bright yellow with a hint of Kelly green marbling. The staircase had five steps up and a landing then a slight left turn. There were five more steps leading to the bedrooms. Mitchell and Sue's bedroom was off to the left. The double bed frame was made of bamboo and the bedspread was made of many swirls greens, yellows, reds and blue colors. In spite of Sue's tropical taste in home furnishings, that marriage was no paradise. A frozen moody Sue would sit at her vanity brushing her hair with her baby blue nail painted hand. "Why Sue? Why did you betray our marriage?" asked Mitchell.

"I'm thinking seriously about asking you for a divorce."

"So you can run off and be with him?"

The Daniels' marriage had deteriorated into a brother-sister non-sexual relationship when they even bothered to talk to each other.

Mitchell was a car salesman who didn't aspire to be anything more than a car salesman. He liked walking through the showroom and the car lot showing off the new Saturn cars to prospective buyers. This was his passion.

Sue worked her way up as an interior designer. Her profession eventually got her noticed by politicians, athletes, singers, actors and the like. When Sue met Mitchell back when she was a student at a textile college, she never knew what it meant to be around men who truly aspired to build an empire. When the ambition bug bit her, she had tried to inspire Mitchell to become a mover, shaker and go-getter. It was at the college when he thought about being a men's clothing tailor. When Mr. Daniels couldn't find work in the field of tailoring, he took a job at a Saturn car dealership.

Chapter 7

───────────▼───────────

The Journey

The apartment was an efficiency type for one person. It was one large room plus a kitchenette. The entire apartment had square block black linoleum tile like many places had installed back in the 1950s and 1960s. The black tile had white streaks on them. Each tile was placed on the floor, alternating between horizontal and vertical. There was nothing on the floor except for a large area rug made from beige burlap. Four sleeping bags were rolled up in the corner of the room. Salmi sat cross-legged on the floor typing away at a laptop computer plugged into the wall. The internet was a dial-up type. Orbitz.com was typed in the URL. The family would be leaving from Jamaica, New York and going to Washington, DC. The departure date was set for Tuesday, September 11, 2001 and he needed an early morning flight for four adults for early in the morning.

In the kitchenette, although the apartment had a dishwasher, Reni stood by the sink washing her Tupperware container in the sink and started to cry.

CHAPTER 8

▼

INTRODUCING LAURA.

Bari Lynn took one look at the restaurant brochure and jumped out of her seat. "Oh my goodness!"

Caroline looked up at her daughter as though she were implying that there was something wrong with one of the restaurants in the brochure.

"I'm going to be late for Y Camp."

Caroline suddenly felt a warmness that she hadn't felt since she was a child playing on the beach. "I have some company coming soon, Shauna do you mind going with her?" inquired the mother. "I'm going to need to be here for them." Caroline wasn't the sort of person to leave let a stranger accompany one of her children anywhere.

"I don't mind."

"I've known you for a few minutes and I already feel comfortable with you, Shauna," remarked Caroline.

"So do I and I'm sorry about the witch remarks," Bari Lynn seconded, feeling the same warm glow coming over her. "I have to go to my room and get my stuff."

*   *   *   *

Shauna followed Bari Lynn into her bedroom. Slipped into the edge of the mirror above the dresser was a maroon school banner with the words Charles

Lindbergh High School. On the wall to the right of Bari Lynn's double bed was a picture collage of *NSYNC in all types of poses, in concert and at play. All the other walls were bare. "My mom told me only put a poster on one of my walls."

Shauna looked surprised at the remark.

"I figure I can wake up and see these guys when I stand at the mirror brushing my hair and applying makeup. Let's see," Bari Lynn pointed out each member, "We have J.C, Justin, Joey, Chris, and that one is Lance. The group is named by the last letter in each of the band member's names. The first is N for Justin. The S is for Chris The Y is for Joey. The other N is for Lansten, who is known as Lance. The C is for JC. I read that Justin's mother came up with the idea for the band name."

"Do you have a favorite or do you just like them all?"

"Justin Timberlake, but I probably won't ever meet him. It doesn't really matter to me." The teenager sat on her bed and gestured for the party planner to sit beside her.

"What does matter to you?"

The teen bent and reached under her bed's maroon dust ruffle for her duffle bag. She spoke as she grabbed for her bag. "I don't know. I really don't know. I just know that I want to try out for head cheerleader at the end of next month."

"You're a cheerleader now?"

Bari Lynn clutched her duffle sack, pulled it out from under the bed and stood. "I didn't make it in the ninth grade, but I tried out again in tenth. We're the Aviators"

"This year you're in eleventh grade."

"I have to try for head cheerleader this year because I'm signing up for Driver's Ed in school next year."

"You know something, Bari Lynn?"

"What?"

"I have a strong feeling that before this year is out you'll find your life's goal."

Bari Lynn felt like shaking Shauna, but resisted the temptation. "Please tell me what it is. I know you by now. You know something, don't you?"

"Alright."

"Don't be in such a hurry for the future."

They walked out of Bari Lynn's bedroom, "My school grades are a C average and that means I can still be a cheerleader," Bari Lynn boasted.

"Do you think a C average is good enough?"

"I don't believe that I'll be doing anything other than a good two-year college. I don't know, maybe I could do something in the clerical profession or something," said the teen, dispassionately.

As they walked up the street, a black four door late model Volkswagen Jetta drove down Morrow drive and made a left into the Cobel family's driveway. Matt Cobel was behind the wheel and his intended, Laura, was by his side. She got out of the car and looked at the house as though it were an abandoned haunted house instead of a wood sided rancher that needed a paint job. Despite the need for a paint job, the lawn was neatly cut and the flowers stood in their beds like neat soldiers.

The young couple walked up to the front door. The curtains on the living room window moved back and forth once.

They walked up to the front door and Matt knocked on the screen door. Caroline quickly rose from the living room sofa and went to the screen door. She was as excited as a television game show winner, grabbing onto her son and hugging him as he was about to enter the house. The mother, who came up to her boy's chin, calmed down.

"Mom, this is Laura and she's going to be …"

"We're engaged!" Laura blurted out.

Caroline jumped around and hugged Laura and Matt. "When is the wedding?"

"We don't know yet, probably next spring, One thing I know is that it will probably be at Saint Patrick's Cathedral," said Laura. "I'll have to think about where the reception will be held."

"Mom, aren't you still working at that hairdresser place? It's Saturday!"

Calming down, Caroline answered, "I got the day off because I knew that my son was coming home for an extended visit."

Laura looked around the living room. As far as she was concerned, the Cobel family could have made their home in a barn with the cows, pigs and chickens. In reality it was a neat well-kept living room with very inexpensive furniture. The floor was bare, a hardwood blond floor with a solid bluish-green rug in the center of the room. At the living room window was a fake blond wood framed sofa with light weight dark blue cushions, the type that one might put on a hard chair to make it more comfortable for sitting. It was the kind of a sofa that belonged in the family recreation room rather than in the living room. The coffee table at the front of the sofa was an empty long white plastic rectangular table about the same length as the living room sofa. Laura looked at it closely and found that it was dust free. Over in the corner near the bedroom hall entrance was a box filled with parts for a wall unit. "My mother would absolutely love this room!"

"Thank you for the compliment Laura. My daughter was just criticizing my tastes earlier today."

"My mother would just love this room. She's an interior decorator who works with room designs all day long."

"So I'm not so bad after all if I could make an interior decorator and her daughter happy with my furnishings. Matt, I was wondering if you could work on the shrubbery out front today?"

"I think that I could," Matt answered. "What about that over there," Matt pointed out the box of unassembled wall unit.

"Could you do that tomorrow possibly?"

"I think so."

"Can I get you something to eat for lunch?"

"I smell waffles, "said Laura.

"I'd love some waffles, too Mom."

Caroline headed into the kitchen.

"Top it off with ice cream if you can," requested Matt's friend.

"What kind?"

"I don't know. Do you have vanilla?"

"Vanilla it is," as Matt's mother headed for the kitchen.

"Are you nuts?" he almost screamed. Matt nearly jumped off the sofa.

"Shhhh. Keep your voice down," Laura replied. "You're acting like my father." There were vast differences between Sue Daniels and Caroline Cobel.

"You like this room?"

"My mother is an interior decorator and she would love this room because there are so many decorating ideas she could come up with. I really don't want your mother to hear. Since we're all going to be family, maybe if I bring my mom by sometime for coffee she could get to know your mother and…."

"I don't think my mother would be interested in doing over the room. She would be too concerned with the cost and she barely accepted my father's pension as it was."

When Laura was ten-years-old and Sue Daniels became an interior decorator to the stars, she was determined to have her daughter brought up like a Bouvier. What is a Bouvier? A Bouvier was one of the wealthiest if not the wealthiest family on Long Island. Maybe I should say Auchincloss after Jacqueline Bouvier's stepfather. Sue Daniels was going to raise her daughter like the Bouvier family raised daughter, Jacqueline. Those who know their Bouvier history know that

Jacqueline Bovier married a politician who became President of the United States, and she became First Lady. Some people wonder if it's more than coincidence that Sue Daniels' one and only child bares the same first name as the current First Lady, Laura Bush. Laura Daniels, who was really named for the author Laura Ingalls Wilder, went to private schools in Europe where she tried to learn five different languages. She's lucky to speak one language fluently and two languages just so-so. She couldn't even stand before a crowd of Italian descendents on Columbus Day and give an entire speech in Italian. It was ironic that even though Laura's namesake, Laura Ingalls Wilder married a farmer, Sue wanted her daughter to marry the son of some dignitary. Hopefully, a Catholic dignitary. Matt's girlfriend had a coming out party when she was eighteen-years-old. After the celebration, Laura was a little embarrassed because two of her closest friends told her that coming out parties were outdated.

"Why do I sound like your father?" Matt said, opening the garage door.

"He never wanted to try anything new. He's just content to stay in that car salesman position of his."

Laura's fiancé reached for the garden clippers from the nail on the wall. "Did you ever think that he was happy dong what he was doing?"

"Well I'm not asking you to consider another career."

"Thank God. I like being a computer programmer." Matt pulled the trash can out and rolled it outside along side his mother's car, parked in the driveway.

"Customer service representative."

"So are you. After I get a few promotions I'll be a computer programmer."

"We could make it a congratulations mother-in-law present."

"Trimming the bushes?"

"The redecorating of course."

"My mother wouldn't like it."

For the past ten years, Caroline Cobel had been a poor, but proud woman who frowned on any kind of financial help. "How would you know? Did you ask her?"

"After my father was killed I went down to the newspaper office and got a job as a paperboy."

"You mean one of those boys with the bicycle and the sack of papers?"

"Yes that's what I mean, "Matt responded defensively.

"Alright," Laura backed down.

"When my mother found out what I was doing, she made me quit."

"Why?"

Matt sat among the flowerbed and Laura handed him the clippers.

"It was like I told you; she doesn't like anyone trying to help her financially."

"Especially a son with a paper route? How did she find out what you were doing to help the family expenses?"

"When she opened up my sock drawer to put away freshly cleaned socks, she found my paycheck. I told her that I kept the money there so Bari Lynn couldn't get at it. She was in kindergarten at the time."

"You hid the check so that she wouldn't find out that you were hiding the money?"

"She confronted me with it and asked me about it. She had a look on her face that eventually got the truth out of me."

Suddenly there was a slam of the screen door.

Shauna dejectedly and slowly entered the house looking down at her leather sandaled feet. For all that energy Shauna lacked, Bari Lynn had an anger that almost caused her to break furniture. A red and white tornado seemed to fly through the room.

A door slammed.

Matt and Laura looked at Shauna in curiosity across the yard as they saw the screen door slam shut as though from a big wind. Caroline poked her head into the room, "What's going on in here? I just heard a loud bang." She walked over to the screen door, opened it up and poked her head out.

"Well, the waffles and ice cream are on the table and you can both help yourselves."

*   *   *   *

Shauna knocked at BariLynn's bedroom door.

Bari Lynn was sitting at her laptop computer that was on at the desktop page. There were tiled pictures of Justin Timberlake lined up like a large page of postage stamps. He had his bleach blond permanent and bare chest. His strong biceps stood out as he stood with arms bent and hands on waist. The tattoo on the left upper arm could not be missed. It looked like a kind of a crucifix that could have been drawn with a black marking pen.

"Go away. I'm never going to come out," Bari Lynn sobbed.

"Are you mad at me, Bari Lynn?"

"Yes!"

"Would you please tell me why?"

"You didn't put a magic spell on the team to make us win the Volley Ball game."

"Would you please open this door so that we can discuss this?"

"No!"

Bari Lynn reluctantly opened the door, and Shauna walked in.

Bari Lynn turned her computer chair around and faced Shauna who stood beside the desk.

"So you lost the game today."

"I don't like to lose games."

"Winning wouldn't mean very much if you didn't lose every now and then."

"I'm so angry I don't know what I'm going to do."

"How do you feel about building things … putting pieces together?"

"Do I have to?"

"You can stay in your room and feel sorry for yourself or you can come out and do something constructive. Your mother needs some yard work done."

Bari Lynn got out of her computer chair, "I have to power down my computer." She pressed the start menu on her keypad and selected shut down from the Microsoft Me operating unit menus.

CHAPTER 9

▼

THE MOTIVE.

Like a mule hauling a heavy wagon, Reni dragged her metal grocery cart up the community driveway in back of the apartment complex. When she got to her building, she pulled the cart up a flight of six concrete steps. The woman hauled the cart up another flight of steps, through the doorway, down the hall, until she reached her apartment door.

"Salmi, open the door!" Reni cried. Salmi sat in the back of the room behind a partition, watching television. Bagrad, who had been washing a sink load of dishes, left them to answer the door.

"What a day I had today," said Reni who not only wore her babushka around her head and neck, but also had her nose and mouth covered. She lowered scarf. "Those Americans don't know how to raise their children. I was at the grocery store. One little boy came up to me and asked me why my nose and mouth were covered. The mother grabbed him and pulled him away from me. I think she was afraid of me."

"I don't understand these people either," answered Bagrad, her hands dripping soap suds. "They don't wear anything to cover up their faces and they even walk around with their legs and arms uncovered," said Reni as Bagrad moved the cart over to the kitchen area. She started to unload the cart, placing the grocery bags on the counter. "The last time I was in one of their stores," said Bagrad, "I noticed they were playing music. In our country, the leader would have closed down the store and beheaded the owner. The things they get away with in this country. I could have sworn that a woman was running the checkout when I went over to pay. You know that our government would never let a woman run the checkout."

"I know what you mean?" answered Reni. "I saw a woman talking back to her husband today."

"We'd get slapped if we talked back to our husbands like that," answered Bagrad.

Salmi, sat on his mat, reading an article in a recent Arabic newspaper about Osama bin Laden's criticism of The United States. According to bin Laden, Americans accused Palestinian children of being terrorists. The youths had no weapons and have not yet reached maturity. America was allegedly siding with Israel because of all the help and support that the United States government was giving.

Salmi and his brother moved to America in order to work as civilian government employees in North Jersey. At first, he never really believed what Osama bin Laden said about Americans. Salmi wanted to move to the United States in order to find out for himself. He would quickly change his mind about Americans.

He read another article. A blind shiek made his home in Jersey City. Omar Abdel Rahman became politically involved with bin Laden and the February 26, 1993 bombing attempt in the parking garage of the World Trade Center. The article went back to Rahman's involvement of 1982. Salmi read about Rahman's history of terrorism. He had allegedly taken part in the assassination of Egyptian leader, Anwar Sadat, who supposedly mocked the Muslims. Rahman slipped through American and Egyptian justice.

Ramiz Yousef set the 1993 bomb in the World Trade Center garage, killing six people. Yousef's friend, Eyad Ismid, apparently drove the van that carried the powerful bombing device. To understand the role of all of these men is to think of it like a Chain of Command office setting. Bin Laden could have been like a corporate executive. Rahman was like a Branch Chief. Yousef's role in the bombing resembled a section supervisor, and Ismid likened an employee. Bin Laden, Rahman, Yousef and Ismid worked for the Al Queda, Murad organization. Murad wanted Ramiz to come to America and locate an important landmark in the country that would upset people if it were destroyed. And so, in the summer of 1992, plans to blow up the World Trade Center were underway.

He wasn't living long in America when Salmi learned some negative things about the country. In such newspapers like *USA Today*, *New York Times*, the internet, and the Asbury Park Tribune, Salmi read many things about the American government that angered him. For example, in Waco, Texas there was a man named David Koresh who ran a cult group called Davidians. Koresh, a self appointed comrade of God, believed in brainwashing those who joined him. Originally named, Vernon Wayne Howell, he was born in 1959 to a fifteen-year-old single mother. He never knew his natural father. Koresh was dyslexic, a bad student and a high school dropout. The leader had musical ability and strong interest in the bible. The head of the Davidians failed his original pursuit of a rock music career and went to Waco, TX in 1981 to start on a new dream. In 1990, he became the official leader of the Branch Davidians and legally changed his name for "publicity purposes." Howell changed his name because he saw himself as the reincarnation of King David and Cyrus. Cyrus is supposed to be a form of the name Koresh. Like most cults, people who joined them were dissatisfied with society and Koresh wanted to be a power over people. The American government believed that Koresh, committing harm to people, had to be stopped. Salmi could not understand the charges brought against Koresh and his people. The leader of the Branch Davidians was considered dangerous and armed. Salmi was thinking about becoming an American citizen. Not only was it the right of the Muslims to have arms, but it was also stated in the Second Amendment of the United States. He felt that Americans were being hypocritical about the core of their beliefs.

Salmi couldn't understand the American government's problem with polygamy. It was a natural way of life for the Muslim community. Osama bin Laden had three wives and thirty children. It seemed that if the leader of the country Salmi called home could have many wives, what was wrong with that? The Qur'an stated that men could have no more than four wives, even though many Muslims had only one wife. Salmi and Abdulad would have had more than one wife if they could afford it. Koresh, an American, had sixty wives and eighty concubines. It didn't even faze the Muslim that some of Koresh's wives and concubines were underage for marriage according to American law. Attorney General Janet Reno and the army came to the Davidian compound. Eventually, David Koresh, some of his followers and their home were destroyed. Many Americans themselves thought the government was wrong getting involved with David Koresh in the first place.

One of the Americans angered with the government for getting involved with Koresh, was thirty-something Timothy McVeigh. The administration accused McVeigh of bombing a Tulsa, Oklahoma government building, two years to the day after the death of David Koresh to avenge the leader. The bomber was recently arrested and being considered for death by injection. McVeigh saw himself as an army of one doing something that was no more wrong than any war the United States was a part of. McVeigh referred to his victims as "collateral damage." This Muslim family believed McVeigh was in the right to defend his beliefs. Salmi was surprised McVeigh wasn't "one of us." Terry Nicholls originally planned to work with McVeigh, but at the last moment decided to drop out. Salmi drank in all of this news in the many months he lived in the states. He put down his newspaper and walked around the partition towards the front door. "Where are you going?" asked Reni.

In a depressed mood, Salmi answered, "Just out."

CHAPTER 10

▼

WE'RE HAVING A PARTY

Middle July on a late Sunday afternoon Caroline, Shauna and Bari Lynn stood by the driveway as Matt and Laura loaded the their suitcases into the trunk of their Jetta.

Caroline said to them, "Thanks for all your help you two."

"We appreciated it," answered Matt who had his arm around Laura's waist. The couple took turns embracing Caroline and Bari Lynn.

Bari Lynn spoke, "You'll be here in September for my Sweet 16?"

"Sure, "Laura answered. Her eyes turned upward as a loud hum came from up above. She eyed a small airplane as it appeared to be flying too close to the telephone wires and looked as though it would crash into the trees. She ducked.

Bari Lynn had a big grin on her face as she noticed the airplane making its way by the telephone line and tree tops and soon out of vision. "I just can't wait for spring."

"Me either. I think we better be going now if we want to rest in time for work tomorrow." Laura opened the front passenger's door, and slid into the car. Matt got into the driver's side. Shauna, Caroline and Bari Lynn watched as Matt backed the car out of the driveway. He made left into the street, turning down the street until the car was out of sight.

"Now," Shauna said, "what kind of theme did you decide on for your Sweet 16?"

Bari Lynn looked back up at the sky, smiling, and then looked down. "I don't know what the theme is, but I know one thing is for sure." Shauna and Caroline had their heads cocked and focused on Bari Lynn.

*   *   *   *

While driving down to the George Washington Bridge, Matt discussed his plans with Laura. "What would you say if I told you I've been keeping articles about the people involved in the bombing of the World Trade Center?"

"Why?"

"I think with careful planning I may be able to help prevent the next attack to the World Trade Center."

"Do you know when it is supposed to take place?"

"Well, no, not really, but I've been making plans."

"What kind of plans, Matt?" Laura answered, beginning to squirm, as though she had ants crawling up her leg.

"Well, what I find is if I can sneak myself into one of the organizations …"

"I'm afraid to ask; wouldn't the Muslim organization be suspicious? I mean you don't look like a Muslim."

"I have an idea."

"Don't involve me. I would really like to discuss the plans for our wedding. Don't you care about that?"

"Don't you want to save the World Trade Center? If we save the WTC, then we can assure a world for us and our family. So, I do care about our wedding."

"Why don't you leave it to the Secret Service? Besides that I do want to save the World Trade Center. I want to have our wedding dinner at Windows of The World restaurant.

"I might as well tell you about it."

Laura reached over and poked Matt in his lower rib. "All you care about is this espionage stuff you aren't even listening to me. I said I would like to have the wedding dinner at Windows of the World restaurant."

Ignoring Laura, Matt continued, "With all the articles and pictures I have on people like Osama bin Laden, Omar Abdel Rahman and his young friend, I think I know what they look like."

"No!"

"Alright, then I'll stop off at the costume shop right after work. Once you see everything I have planned you'll want to be a part of this, too."

Laura groaned, her face paling as though she had seen a ghost. "Didn't you hear me?"

"There is no place for people to dance there. I don't even know if you can arrange to have affairs there."

"We could ask."

"We could also save Windows of the World for Valentines Day and our wedding anniversary."

"And the anniversary of the day we met. Our first meal together that day in line when you handed me crazy line."

*   *   *   *

Shauna followed Bari Lynn into her bedroom and sat beside her at the laptop computer. "Let's think, Bari Lynn, would you like a futuristic sort of Jestons theme to welcome the new millennium?"

"Too babyish."

"The soldiers from Desert Storm?"

"Too depressing."

Bari Lynn logged onto her VH1 homepage and typed into the search block, the word "Airplane".

"I know you don't want an airplane theme for your Sweet 16?"

"Not really. Hey! Stop reading my mind."

"I'm sorry. It's an old habit with me."

A listing of everything that had to do with airplanes came up. Bari Lynn browsed the list, frowning.

"If you had asked me I would have told you that what you are looking for is not under airplanes."

"Why wouldn't it be?"

"It's too general."

"What else do you know?"

"I know you would like to have the party at that lovely French restaurant we ate at yesterday. Don't you think tying the airplane bit into the French restaurant affair would be awkward?"

"What would you suggest?"

"I think I'll go into New York on Monday and see if I can arrange something."

*   *   *   *

On Monday afternoon after work, Matt walked into a costume shop. He saw shelves filled with many costumes of vampires, super heroes, and others. The store sold plenty of masks of George W. Bush and Saddam Hussein, capes, wigs swords. There was a display case filled with costume accessories like fangs, belts, wands, crowns, etc. The shopkeeper walked from the storeroom over to the display case in the front where Matt stood. Matt's eyes widened when he saw the shopkeeper. "Shauna!" You work here?"

"Can I help you?"
Ready to walk away, Matt said, "I don't know now."
"Broadway producers come here all the time. They know we have more costumes than anyone else in New York. I can't promise you'll find what you want elsewhere."
Matt followed Shauna to the back of the store, but stopped at the doorway of the storeroom. "It's getting late and I waited seven years to do this, anyway."
Shauna came back in a minute. "None of the other costume shops have this." She held in her hand a clear plastic box with a fake dark beard that could just cover the chin. "I have special glue and a glue remover I can show you." This reminded Matt of Stephen King's *Needful Things*, a book about a shopkeeper who had everything anyone wanted.
"I can assure you I am nothing like the shopkeeper in that book. I also have some special hair dye that washes off. The bottle is a three-month supply," Shauna winked at Matt.
"Do you know something you're not telling me?"
"I'll get you the hair dye." Shauna slipped back into the storeroom. In a minute she came back with the black hair dye.
"If you know something you're not telling me ..."
I can give you fifty percent off everything." Shauna headed for the front of the store and to the cash register. "Will this be cash, charge or debit?"
"I want you to tell me why I only need a three month supply!"
"If you need another three month supply you can come back. Do you have ten dollars on you?"
"I did have one more thing to tell you."
"Yes, but I'm not leaving here until you tell me what you know about the next three months. Shauna's sea green eyes stared into Matt's hazel eyes.

"I've got one more thing to tell you."

"Now we are getting places."

"You're going to need some contact lenses, dark brown if you want to carry this off. Don't worry I'm still not going to charge you more than ten dollars for the whole package. And don't wear any robes or turbans because you're not of some special political order. The Muslim men are trying to fit into the American society by dressing more like us."

"There is something strange about you. I didn't even tell you I wanted to disguise myself as a Muslim."

"Ten dollars please or I'll have to charge your credit card."

"Somehow I believe that." Matt reached into his wallet and pulled out two five dollar bills. Shauna took the bills, rang them up on the cash register, and put the items in a plain brown paper bag. She walked Matt to the front of the store. "It's a pleasure to serve you. I put the instructions in the bag. Enjoy!"

∗   ∗   ∗   ∗

Matt and Laura were now living together in his apartment. Tonight was Laura's computer class at New York City College. Matt entered the apartment with his plain brown paper bag in hand. He entered the bathroom. Matt sat down on the edge of the bathtub and placed his bag on the closed toilet lid. There was the box that contained the easy washout black "No-Frills brand hair dye, some special glue for the mustache and beard, some de-bonding cream and finally a case filled with brown contact lenses. Noticing he overlooked something for his lashes and eyebrows, Matt opened the medicine cabinet looking for Laura's black eyebrow pencil and black mascara.

"Let me see. I can start with this hair dye, opening the box and finding fifty packets of hair dye—"I wonder what I'm supposed to do with this." He took out one packet and read it.

About a half an hour later Matt was combing out his newly dyed black hair. "Now I'll put on the black beard and mustache. He dropped the opened case in the sink. "All I need is for this to go down the drain."

Five minutes later Matt looked in the mirror and saw a man with black hair, matching beard and mustache with brown eyebrows, eyelashes and hazel eyes. "*So far so good,"* opening the contact lens case and taking out the brown lenses. Matt had a good half an hour fight trying to get the contact lenses in his eyes. He pulled down the lower lid of his eye with his second finger of his right hand and tried to insert the lens with his index finger. The lenses were soft; they turned inside out on his fingertip, landed on his eyelid. *"I should have never gotten soft lenses."*

In less than two hours, Matt walked out of the bathroom looking like one of Osama bin Laden's followers. He sat in the arm chair by the pole-lamp and started to read the newspaper.

Soon he heard the sound of a key turning in the lock. Laura walked in. Matt put down the newspaper. Laura shrieked, opening the coat closet.

"It's me, Laura, **Matt!**"

Laura reached for a broom in the coat closet. She tried to hit him over the head with the brush part, but Matt blocked it with his hands. "You even colored that gorgeous wavy light brown hair."

"Laura, will you come to your senses?"
Laura propped herself on the broom as if it were a cane. Still upset, "You scared me half to death, you nut. Do you realize how many Muslim terrorists there are in this city and you're playing Halloween?"

"I'm not playing Halloween. I'm going undercover."

"What about the eyebrows and eyelashes_____"
"Oh my God you didn't use_____"

"I'll pay you the money they're worth."

"You better. Now where are you planning to wear this costume?"

"I'm going to one of those Muslim fellowship places."

"Terrific," Laura sighed. "I hope Omar Abdel Rahman doesn't decide to come after you like he came after Sadat."

"I'm not trying to make fun of anybody. I'm trying to save the World Trade Center. Maybe I'll learn something at those meetings."

*   *   *   *

The next day, Matt looked like his old self again. They were in the kitchenette having breakfast, a whole grain grape nut cereal. "Laura, you remember that lady who was over the house last week?"

"I'm trying not to. She frightens me."

"Maybe she works for the Muslims."
"Look Matt, I'm not going to one of those Muslim meetings so don't try to find any disguises for me."
"I won't."

*   *   *   *

On Saturday Shauna and Bari Lynn walked down the street towards the shopping center. Bari Lynn said, "I was thinking of having the party on September 15th."

"That's not a good idea."
"Why?"
"On September 15th I have another assignment and I won't be available. How about September 8th? We still have a little more than a month to plan for the party."

"O.K. I suppose so. I still don't have an idea for a theme."

Shauna and Bari Lynn walked through the parking lot to the concrete walkway of the strip mall. They strolled to the door of a gift shop. "Here we are, Bari Lynn, the shop I wanted to show you." The shop was called Maxine's Gift Shop.

Noticing the sign on the window, Bari Lynn said, "It looks like it is going out of business."
"You can get party supplies here at a deep discount."
"But will I want what is left to choose from?" asked Bari Lynn.

Most of the shelves in the store for greeting cards, wrapping paper, paper gift bags, party decorations and more were empty. Bari Lynn couldn't help noticing a small, portly graying woman trying to get just the right crepe paper for her gift bag.

"Do you have any yellow crepe paper to go with this lemon yellow bag?" the woman asked a saleswoman.

"I'm sorry," the lady replied, "everything we have left are on the shelves, but perhaps I can make some suggestions."

Bari Lynn turned to Shauna, "Can we go to another store?" I'm afraid we won't find what we are looking for."

As Shauna and Bari Lynn strolled down the greeting card aisle, all the display shelves were bare except for a few shelves that had several cards, but mostly mismatched envelopes. There was a sign there that said any *five cards for one-dollar.* "I think what we're looking for is right at the end of this aisle, Bari Lynn." At the end of the aisle was the party section. Shauna found a white sign-in board about a yard long and wide. There was a two-pack of black washable ink pens tied to the board with a twister seal. "This is perfect for the party." Shauna looked at the back of it. "And look, it has one of those flaps you find on the back of framed photographs so it can stand on the table." Shauna and Bari Lynn walked down the aisle and found some rolled up blue and white crepe banner around the entire circumference said, *Happy Sweet 16.*

"We're almost done, Bari Lynn."

"Would you like some candles for a candle lighting ceremony?"

"Are there any left and if so, are there enough?"

Shauna picked up a box of blue and white swirled party candles. "I think this will do."

"If this shop had customers as good as you are they wouldn't be going out of business."

"Thank you Bari Lynn."

"I still don't know what theme to use. A French theme would be too obvious."

When it was time to get in line for checkout, Shauna and Bari Lynn found themselves standing behind the woman who was looking for the yellow crepe paper. She stocked up on assorted paper gift bags and one pack of orange crepe paper.

The lady took her bag of gift wrap paper and left the store after she was waited on. Shauna and Bari Lynn moved up to the counter, placing the sign-in board, candles and crepe streamer up on the counter for the sales lady to ring up. "I thought we were out of these sign-in boards."

After Shauna and Bari Lynn left the store, the party planner remarked, "How about that, all of this for only five dollars?"

"How about that?"

*   *   *   *

A mother and her strawberry blonde daughter walked into the Shear Delight Beauty shop where Caroline worked. The mother walked up to the cashier who asked, "What would you like done?"

"It's not for me; it's for my daughter."

"Name please?"

"Her name is Allie."

"Is there anyone special you want for will you take any hairdresser?"

"I would like Caroline if she is available."

"That will be a fifteen minute wait."

Caroline was in the back shampooing a customer's hair at the sink tub in the back of the salon.

Allie and her mother sat on metal framed vinyl upholstered chairs near the cashier. They started flipping through fashion magazines and pointing out different looks to each other.

A portly lady with raspberry looking short hairdo asked, "What's the occasion?"

"Allie is having her Sweet 16 this coming Saturday."

"If you need to buy some more decorations don't go to Maxine's Gift Shop."

"Oh you can forget about that they hardly have anything left to buy there. I was there last week and they didn't even have one sign-in board left for a Sweet 16. I had to go someplace else."

"What are you gong to do for the affair?"

"We're having Allie's friends over at our weekend beach house in Asbury Park. We're having a clambake. It's supposed to be a Hawaiian theme."

The cashier said, "Mary, we're ready for you."

The lady with the growing out raspberry hair dye got up from her seat. She followed a hairdresser dressed in a light blue smock back to the sink tubs where Caroline was working.

CHAPTER 11

▼

THIS TAPE WILL SELF-DESTRUCT

Laura entered the apartment after attending another session of computer class. She found Matt seated at the dining room table with a pile of library books. "What are you doing with those?"

"The best way for me to find out more about the plans to blow up the World Trade Center is to become a Muslim, myself."

"How do you know they want to blow up the World Trade Center? They already tried once and all they did was blow up a garage and kill six people. Maybe they gave up after all these years."

"I don't think they're going to give up any time soon. They've probably spent all this time trying to refine their plan."

"Oh No this can't be happening," Laura put her right palm up to her forehead as she had a headache.

Not understanding or wishing not to understand, Matt responded, "this is part of my undercover work. I'm not really going to convert to Muslimism. I just found out they believe in bigamy. The Quran' says Muslims are allowed to have four wives at one time. They believe in no show of public affection."

"I don't see how they can show public affection to four wives at one time."

"After a sneeze 'Al-Hamdulliah' is what they say instead of bless you or *guzend-heit.*

You must speak to someone in a calm polite manner. Pride comes before fall, so they don't talk in boastful manner. They remove shoes after entering a mosque. That's what they call a church. They also use their left hand to wipe private parts after using the toilet."

"Maybe that's why they don't have public shows of affection," Laura said as she walked away without expression.

"Wal'laikum Sallam, Laura," Matt called out. Laura began chanting as she walked into the bedroom and closed the door. "Oh please God help him."

Matt yelled, "THAT MEANS 'AND UPON YOU BE PEACE!'"

Matt looked over his stock of books, *"The Teachings of Muhammad Introduction, The Five Pillars, The Mosque, The God of Islam, The Prophet of Islam, The Presence of Islam In The 20th Century."* Matt looked through the teachings of Muhammad. "Hey Laura, did you know they call God, Allah?" There was no answer. Matt just kept on reading Five *Pillars of Islam.* "The essential duties required of every adult who is mentally able." There was the sound of a loud "HA!" that came from the bedroom.

"For your information, Laura, they take converts, what do you think of that?"

"HA!" Laura called out from behind the bedroom door.

Laura left the bedroom and entered the dining area. "And what happens when they find out you're a spy? I'm scared for you Matt. I really am." Not listening to what Laura said he continued.

"I have to learn all this very quickly and then find a mosque. Soon I'll be able to save the World Trade Center."

Laura's arms were crossed and she let out a heavy sigh. She returned quietly to the bedroom and closed the door behind her.

Matt called out after her, "Does the night school you attend have any classes on the Muslim religion?" There was no answer.

*   *   *   *

Laura was lying on her stomach across the double bed with the phone receiver in hand, against her ear, "No Mom, he doesn't want to convert to Islam. He wants to find out about any future plans to destroy the World Trade Center so he can save it before hand," Laura paused and listened for a few seconds. "He's worked there for over a year now. He wasn't there when the garage was blown up." Laura was silent again. "No I don't want to leave him, especially now. I think he has really lost his mind this time and if I don't help him he might lose his life." Laura was still. "I know he's one of those impulsive people who get into things without thinking them through. I knew that when we first started dating this past February. I actually thought it was cute. Oh," she whimpered, "I should never have called you for advice; you're no help at all." After she slammed down the phone, *No wonder I hardly share anything with you.* Laura opened up the closet door and took out a yard stick. *I hope this works.* She went over to Matt's desk, opening and closing drawer after drawer until she located a lined writing tablet. There was a homemade pencil holder decorated with felt and construction paper in the likeness of an upright basset hound, filled with pencils and pens. *This will have to do. I worry so much about you. I don't know what you would do without me to hold you back from some of your wild ideas.* She looked around the room at the low and high boy dressers they bought together, and the double bed. *I'll never be able to stick another dresser in here and where will the crib and changing table go? Oh Matt you don't even care about the baby. All you care about is this Muslim stuff. I really have a feeling we're going to have a son. I can just feel it.* Laura turned on the television set in the bedroom to a cable network which ran an old rerun of *I Love Lucy.* Lucy and Ricky had their new baby Little Ricky. Lucy wanted to find a bigger apartment so there was a room just for the baby. Ricky kept telling her they couldn't afford it and he would have to stay in their bedroom. Laura sighed. She turned off the television set. "We don't even have enough room for the baby to share our room. If we don't find a bigger place by February he may have to sleep in the living room, if we have room in there."

The next evening, Laura was down on the floor on her knees in the living room, holding on to Matt's legs. She pleaded, "Oh Matt please don't go," like a small child pleading with a parent. "You'll get hurt. Stay home and forget about this. You can't do anything to save the World Trade Center. I want the baby to know his father."

"I'm ready to go to the mosque and there is nothing you can do about it so let go of me."

*　　　*　　　*　　　*

The mosque outside looked like no church that Matt had ever seen before. It was a hot August evening. Matt wore brown contact lenses, dyed black hair, fake black beard and a turban on his head. He was dressed in a long sleeved white cotton button-down shirt and a gold sleeveless vest. Matt entered the mosque that inside looked less like any church than any church he had ever seen before in his life. If someone had blindfolded Matt, brought him into the chapel and then taken off the blindfold, he would have thought he was in an empty office somewhere rather than in a religious chapel. There was no pulpit, no church pews and nothing on the walls to indicate Jesus, God, or even angels. The walls were white and bare except for a few small photographs of some important Muslims.

When the congregation wanted to sit down, they knelt on the floor. The leader stood up before the congregation and called Matt up to join him. Matt professed that Allah was the true God and that he accepted him. Matt was beginning to feel sweaty and it wasn't the way he was dressed, either. As he walked back to his spot and kneeled down on the floor, Matt began to wonder if he was doing the right thing after all. Maybe Laura and her mother were right that he had to be crazy trying to become a Muslim, even if it was for undercover purposes. When the congregation got up to leave, he followed them out. Matt heard the theme from *Mission Impossible*, playing in his head, but this time it was so strong he could swear he was really listening to the theme from *Mission Impossible*. He'd seen reruns of the show on FX. In his head he envisioned the fuse string lit and burning shorter. Matt saw himself as an agent listening to the assignment on one of those old table reel-to-reel model tape recorders. The assignment should Matt choose to accept it would be to stop the people who were planning to bomb the World Trade Center. "In a few minutes this tape will self-destruct." Smoke came up from the tape recorder. The tape recorder and the mechanism were fine, but that tape has vanished. In Matt's mind he thought about being spotted by his "fellow worshippers." *What if he meets one of them on the street when he is out of costume? What would Jim Phelps do in a case like this? Jim Phelps would have other agents helping him and letting him know when danger was on the rise. Jim Phelps would have other agents helping him and letting him know when danger was on the rise. Jim Phelps would have been training so he knew how an agent should act on the job. That is what Jim Phelps would do.* "Am I in too deep?" *Matt felt alone and abandoned just like Timothy McVeigh God forbid. Matt didn't want to blow up any agency, he* wanted to save the World Trade Center. Matt wondered if it was really healthy for him to go on believing he would succeed. It wasn't fair. Timothy McVeigh succeeded in bombing the Oklahoma Federal Building. Sure McVeigh was caught, given a trial and put to death by lethal injection, but the mission was accomplished and a lot of innocent people were killed. Matt loved his country and wanted to save everyone's lives. He cherished the World Trade Center. A large chance of failing was eminent and it just wasn't fair. Matt finally reached his apartment garage and pulled in looking for his assigned spot. *"I have to think I am on the right path. If I could only befriend these Muslims and see if they can tell me anything or lead me to anyone. Oh I wish I knew how long we had left. Damn that Shauna. I know she knows something she is not telling me.* The theme song from Mission Impossible was playing so distinctly Matt could swear it was real. He was shaken out of his dream world, slipped his hand into his side pocket and pulled out his cell phone. "Darn it Laura, I told you not to call me here It's a very dangerous time."

"It's important. I want to discuss what we are going to call the baby."

He pressed the off button on his phone and returned the phone to his pants pocket.

✳   ✳   ✳   ✳

During lunchtime the next day Matt, dressed as his American male self, went up to the guard who stood at the entrance of the north building and started a conversation. "Nice day Pete, isn't it?" Matt asked.

"Can I help you Matt?" the security guard responded.

"I was just thinking about the bombing in the parking garage of this site about eight years ago."

"Well, you have nothing to worry about. He was caught and arrested and is now in jail." The guard had a way of holding a conversation with Matt and also keeping an eye on anyone who came through the door, checking for I.D. badges.

"Don't you worry about another attempt? I know I do. Do you realize if he had succeeded in blowing up the entire building everyone could have been killed in these buildings? Let me ask you something. Have you been working here in 1993?"

"Yes I have. I was here then. One of the six people killed in the garage was a personal friend of mine. How long have you worked here?"

"About a year, but I'm concerned."

"There is nothing to worry about. We have stepped-up security and so far it has worked."

"I am in the process of working on penetrating into the Muslim religion, hoping to find out any information about the next attack?"

"I don't think so. My job is just to guard this building. I'm not trained in undercover services. How do you penetrate the Muslim religion?"

"I have this whole outfit that I got from a costume shop and from a thrift shop. I put on my makeup and I dress up like a Muslim, and I just paid one visit so far to the local mosque, that's a church."

"I think you are biting off more than you can chew. Speaking of that, you better get some lunch and leave the safety of the World Trade Center up to me and the other security guards".

"What about undercover agencies?"

"They won't do it unless you have a suspect in the area. Since those who bombed the garage are in jail now, there isn't anyone else."

"Maybe if I can find some kind of a lead in a mosque?"

"Finding a lead in one of the mosques is like trying to save Ireland by becoming a Catholic in an American church."

"What do you mean?"

"Just because someone happens to be a part of the Muslim faith doesn't mean they have connections with Osama bin Laden. The men who were involved with bombing the garage of this site were from Islam and they had intimate connections with Osama bin Laden. It's just like if someone in another country was a part of the same religious faith as George W. That doesn't mean the members of the religious order have connections to George W."

Matt walked out of the building thinking, *"I wonder."*

He headed off to lunch.

"One word of advice," the guard said.

"What's that?"

"Don't talk about this to any other guard or they might run you in."

"I won't."

"I hope not."

Matt quietly walked off thinking to himself, *"I wonder ..."*

CHAPTER 12

▼

THE COMING
OF AGE OF BARI LYNN

It was around 11:30AM on Saturday, September 8, 2001. A white Cadillac Eldorado stretch limo pulled in front of La Jolie Bella Restaurant. Bari Lynn sat in the backseat of the limousine among her family and best friend. Laura and Matt spent that ride trying to decide where to hold the wedding. Laura thought "their place" the Windows of The World restaurant would be the idea place. Matt didn't like the idea, "I told you before there's not enough floor space for people to be able to get up and dance. That restaurant was just for dining, not for parties."

"Oh, but you're wrong. I checked with them just before we left to come here. They can arrange everything. I can have the reception right in the restaurant if we book them. I'm thinking that maybe around Christmas time I could call them and make arrangements for the spring. I CAN'T TELL YOU HOW EXCITED I'M GETTING. I just have to figure out when we can have the wedding and where the ceremony will be." They arrived at the restaurant. Laura was the first person to step out of the car. Hunched over even when she was outside, "OOOH! My aching back," she complained holding the small of her back.

"What kind of pain?" asked Caroline, who followed her out.

"The hurting kind!"

"I mean is it dull or sharp?"

"Is it possible to be a combination of both?"

Once inside the Bergen County, New Jersey French restaurant, the group walked over to the entrance of the dining room where the luncheon would be held. There was an old mahogany table with many place cards in the center of it. It was easy to see some of the cards had been removed. Off to the left side was the sign-in-board labeled "Happy Sweet 16 Bari Lynn" written in script. There was a felt tip pen which hung down so people could write messages.

"They look great!" exclaimed Bari Lynn as she looked at the place cards. Except for her brother, only females were invited to the party. Instead of numbers on the cards there were names of six flowers: roses, daisies, poppies, tulips, lilies and violets. Bari Lynn looked over at the sign-in-board. On the upper left hand corner, a wallet size of her last year's school picture was displayed. She read over the birthday greeting and poems which guests had written for her on the board. Bari Lynn noticed most of the guests even misspelled her name.

There were six square dining tables; five of them were small enough to hold four people. One table, the Rose table, held six: the family, best friend, and the honored girl. Those who had arrived before the family, shouted "Happy Birthday!" even though her true birthday was September 4th. The Rose table was lined with white paper roses. On the other tables were plastic flowers, as centerpieces and a name the represented the table. At a small table near the Rose table, there was a round cake with sixteen candles waiting to be lit after lunch. The birthday cake had white icing trimmed in pink with white, pink, red and yellow sugar roses. Across the top of the cake in pink script was Happy Sweet Sixteen Bari Lynn. Bari Lynn entered the room which looked like the kind of a place Napoleon Bonaparte might have dined at during the days of the Battle of Waterloo. All eyes were on the Sweet 16 girl as she walked slowly down the middle of the room towards the Rose table. She had her dark brown hair up on her head in a bun. Rather than looking like an old woman, she could have passed for one of George W. Bush's almost twenty year old twin daughters. The birthday girl wore a pale pink strapless braless gown, almost like Britney Spears may have worn to the Grammies. She was thinking that if Justin Timberlake could see her now, he would leave Britney Spears for her. Caroline, Matt, Laura, Shauna, and Bari Lynn's friend, Nicole, discretely walked over to the table where the sign-in-board was. Caroline picked up the felt tip pen and squeezed her message in a small spot near the top of the board. *Bari Lynn, I'm proud of you and I love you darling. Happy Sweet 16 Love Mom!* Laura, Shauna, Nicole and Matt were also able to find small spots to squeeze in messages of their own. After she took her strut down the aisle, Bari Lynn sat down and took her seat as though she were one of those classic European charm schooled teenagers. She even drank her cranberry flavored tea, holding the cup handle with her right pinky hanging out.

The meal started with fruit salad in a light cling juice. As the waiter served the meal, Laura sat in one of the mahogany straight back chairs, back against a cushion.

Matt spoke about his career plans. "I want to put in for one of those computer programming jobs which just opened up at work. I've been there almost a year and since I already have my foot in the door."

Laura added, ""I've been looking at one of those nice New York City apartments with an elevator, central air and heating, and a guard out front." With that she placed her napkin on the table and got up. "Excuse me I need to use the bathroom."

After finishing a teaspoon of fruit cup Bari Lynn said, "Mom, you're beautiful!" and to Shauna, "You rock!" As Caroline and Shauna thanked Bari Lynn, the croissant and butter arrived. Laura returned to the table. The soup arrived: butternut squash soup with a dollop of crème franiche', followed by eggs Benedict and crepe Suzette with choice of toppings, maple, and blueberry and apricot syrups. The butternut squash soup was a yellow-orange color with a swirl of white. It looked like one of those swirls which make you dizzy when you stare at it.

"Are you alright?" asked Caroline.

"Don't worry about me. I'm fine."

Caroline put the back of her hand against Laura's forehead only to be shoved off. The future mother-in-law realized her son's intended had a slight temperature. As the waitress went to collect the soup cups, Laura said "I'm not sick and I don't want anything to ruin this for Bari Lynn," diving into the eggs Benedict as though she were running a race. It looked like two egg McMuffins with yellow Hollandaise sauce over the bread. Changing the subject and between bites.

"I can tell you things I can't tell my own mother. If I told her about my receptionist job she just wouldn't understand. This wasn't supposed to happen to me. It is a disgrace to be dismissed from a job. She always worries about what other people think."

"Because you lost it?"

"Because I got it and then I lost it."

"That sounds petty to me. It sounds like you can't win either way."

"I like customer service a lot better than any job I ever had. Things are going so well I was told I should consider putting in for team leader."

"I think your mother might be proud of you if you get that position."

Before Laura could comment, the waitresses brought over the crepe Suzettes, thin pancakes which she cooked in pan over a fire beside the tables. She dipped the delicacies into confectioner's sugar and served them. Matt nudged Laura who was wiping her plate with the last of the bread. "Slow down, the waitress is watching you!" The waitress stood in front of Laura waiting until she was sure she was finished before she moved the plate to the side and served the pan cakes. She walked away and summoned some busboys to collect the empty dishes from the earlier course. As the busboys worked on another table, the waitress returned with sodas: ginger ale, lemon-lime and colas all brought over with a parasol topped straws for anyone. There were diet sodas for guests who requested one, but not caffeine free diet colas. Laura inhaled her ginger ale in one breath. By the time a busboy came by to clear the empty dishes, she requested a refill. By the time the crepe Suzette dishes were collected, there were four empty soda glasses with parasols lined up two on each side of the plate.

It was time for the candle lighting ceremony. The waitress took out a cigarette lighter and lit one of the bright blue candles. Bari Lynn went over to the cake table where the cake was, followed by the rest of the Rose table. She took an unlit candle and held the wick against the lit candle, then placed it in the cake along side the other candle. Each person took turns lighting a candle. One by one other people were called up to light the remaining twelve candles. By the time the candles were all lit, Bari Lynn closed her eyes blew out the candles and made a wish. After she was done, the waitress came over and whisked the cake into the kitchen to be sliced up, put on plates and topped with French Vanilla ice-cream for dessert. When she opened up her eyes she took a deep breath. It was as though *NSYNC had some to the party.

It was the cheerleading squad. In August, Bari Lynn had just tried out for head cheerleader. The girls entered wearing their maroon and white uniforms with the aviator mascot on the front. The squad assembled in front of empty table which once held the birthday cake. One of the cheerleaders mentioned to the audience that the Charles Lindbergh aviators had a surprise for Bari Lynn. Bari Lynn walked from behind the empty table towards the girls. "I'm sorry I didn't invite you girls", embarrassed. She covered her face with her hands for a second and then placed them down at her sides.

"That's alright because, Bari Lynn," the girl spoke like a prize announcer on a television game show, "You're now head cheerleader for the years 2001 to 2003." Bari Lynn clutched her chest as though she were having a heart attack. She started to hyperventilate trying to say, "This is the first time my birthday cake wish came true." The cheerleader handed her a brand new set of pom poms "Don't die on us; we need you for the football game next Saturday." When the waitress came out of the kitchen with a plate of chocolate chip birthday cake alamode, Bari Lynn said, "I hope we have enough cake and ice-cream for the cheerleader squad. The cheerleaders stood up and did a special cheer for Bari Lynn. Caroline noticed that on their feet they wore what looked like low white sneakers called Asics Tiger instead of the black and white saddle shoes from her day. "You spelled my name right. I have an idea why don't you stay and join us as I teach everyone how to do *the Electric Slide.* Someone had brought along a CD player and played an album of dance tunes including *the Electric Slide.*

"Come on up everyone. Put your legs apart. Put your legs together. Take your left foot and place it behind your right foot." The music stopped and everything went silent until someone let out a scream. "Someone tripped over her right foot and fell."

CHAPTER 13

▼

THE CONFESSION

Caroline took a damp wash cloth and wiped it gently across Laura's forehead as she rested in Matt's bed. "I feel I should call your mother up and let her know what happened."

"Please don't do that," Laura said weakly.

"Why not?"

"Please don't. I'll tell you a secret that Matt and I were sharing."

"Don't do that."

"We were trying decide on what to name the baby. We won't know the sex until I'm in my second trimester."

"That's why you're not showing."

"We were thinking of Emily if it's a girl and Jacob if it's a boy. Those are supposed to be the most popular names."

"But if they are supposed to be the most popular baby names, why don't you_____"

Laura fell asleep and Caroline left the room.

*   *   *   *

Meanwhile:

Nicole took out her party favor which was a small purse size bottle of French perfume. "This must have cost a fortune buying one of these for each of the girls."

Shauna said to Nicole, "Don't look a gift *cheval* in the mouth."

Everyone laughed.

Bari Lynn came in wearing a yellow T shirt, faded jeans and a pair of New Balance sneakers. "I hope you weren't laughing at me now that I am casually dressed."

"No it has nothing to do with you. I made a joke," replied Shauna.

"Mom seems to still be in with Laura. Is she going to be alright?"

"I'm sure she will be."

"I want to discuss Laura's bridal shower plans with you. You did such a fantastic job with my Sweet 16 that I think you would do a super job."

"We can discuss that at a later time, after all, the wedding isn't until spring, isn't that right Matt?"

"We haven't exactly set a date." Changing the subject, Matt said

"What happened to that lovely woman we spent the afternoon with?" quipped Matt.

"Very funny."

"I was going to offer you a ride back to New York tomorrow, but now I'm not sure about Laura," Matt said to Shauna.

"After what I have to tell you, you may not want to drive me anywhere."

Looking at the stares, Shauna continued, "I'm an angel." Soon amber light surrounded Shauna.

"I knew there was something about you!" exclaimed Bari Lynn.

"Then maybe you can tell me what the fate will be of the World Trade Center?"

"I can't because I don't exactly know. Angels don't have the ability to perform magic unless the Father lets us. Mortals are made to make their own decisions and so we'll have to see what happens with the people who are involved in the plans."

"I thought you were from Dublin?" asked Bari Lynn.

"I do come from that area," answered Shauna.

"Do you know who is involved?" Matt asked about the World Trade Center incident.

"I only know they are involved with Osama bin Laden and that is all I know. I'd like to tell you a story about my first assignment which took place back in 1921 when I was only twenty-three."

Matt thought for a second, "You aren't 103 years old, are you? I don't believe that. That's just fantasy."

"But you do believe I am an angel?" asked Shauna.

"Wow! 103 years old; you look great for that age. Can I hear about your first assignment?" asked Bari Lynn

"It was in September, 1921 and I was assigned a nursing assistant's position at New York's Presbyterian Hospital. It was there I met the former assistant secretary to the Navy. I helped assist the physical therapists in trying to rehabilitate Mr. Roosevelt. He and his family had been vacationing that summer at Campobello Island, New Brunswick not far from here. He was taking some time off from his corporate law practice."

"Did the therapy do any good?" asked Bari Lynn.

"He made some progress in his neck and his upper back. He reminded me a little of you Matt."

"How?"

"No matter how many times people told him it couldn't be done' he was determined to have his dreams come true."

"You mean run for President of The United States?" asked Caroline, who had just entered the living room. "I couldn't help overhearing."

"Not right away. He wanted to walk again. He tried to walk on crutches while carrying along those heavy steel braces on his legs. He kept that dream alive right up until his death in 1945. Franklin Roosevelt tried everything he could think of to regain the use of his legs: electric currents, ultraviolet light, massage and mineral baths. I knew he would never walk again. If he was talked into believing he would never walk again, he would have probably given up on life and not fulfilled his prophesy to help this country through World War II."

"I thought he was confined to a wheelchair?" asked Caroline.

"Practically all the time," answered Shauna.

"What was he really like?" asked Caroline.

"Well, when I knew him he lived with his five children—four sons and a daughter, Eleanor and his mother. He was always being told what to do by his mother, but he was also helped by Eleanor. His mother wanted him to stay in his house and be treated like an invalid. Eleanor was at odds with his mother because Eleanor wanted him to go on with life as usual even though he was disabled."

Laura entered the room. "Are we going to experience a tragedy in the very near future?"

"I really don't know. I have some advice for you, Laura and Matt."

Laura and Matt looked at Shauna as if to ask about the advice.

"Matt, don't try to be a superhero. Why don't you think about the place where you work and figure out emergency escape routes and things like that? If anyone else is interested get them involved in your plan. The best way to save lives is to teach people how to handle themselves in an emergency."

"We'll certainly try that. Nothing else worked," mentioned Matt.

"You mean the undercover work you were up to?" asked Shauna.

"How did you know about that?" responded Matt. "He thought for a second and remembered the salesperson who waited on him at the costume shop.

"You mean …" Laura began.

"Tell me about him?" asked Laura.

"You're doing a good job, Shauna," said Matt.

"I appreciate that."

"Escape plan, huh?" Matt asked.

"Yes."

"I didn't get anything out of those Muslim church meetings."

"Don't say that. I'll bet you learned a lot if you think about it."

"The most important thing I learned was those people knew nothing about any plans to attack The World Trade Center. I'm sure glad I met you, Shauna."

"How old were you when you died?" asked Bari Lynn.

Everyone except for Shauna stared at Bari Lynn as though they just learned she was a psychic.

"I was never alive. I just showed up as a young woman," said Shauna.

"Did you ever work with any other famous people?"

"Bari Lynn, it's been a busy day. I'm sure Shauna wants to get some rest along with the rest of us," Caroline winked at the angel.

"Matt I need to see you for a few moments, alone." The two walked into his bedroom. "I've needed to talk to you."

"What is it?"

"I've been on the internet trying to look up a name for the baby. I can't name him after the guy who designed the World Trade Center."

"Why not?"

"He's Japanese and that doesn't go with Cobel. Then I looked up any assistants and I found some guy named Antonio and that doesn't go with Cobel either."

CHAPTER 14

▼

ANOTHER DAY OF INFAMY

Matthew Cobel, with Styrofoam coffee cup in hand, sprinted out of a nearby coffee shop. It was only 8:40 on a clear Tuesday morning. He had gone by the north tower just long enough to hear someone on the PA system urge the employees to "stay inside." By the time he entered the south tower he heard an explosion and the ground rattled as though New York City were experiencing an earthquake. Matt bypassed the elevators which he was planning to use and headed for the stairwell. He checked out his watch which read a quarter to nine. Prior to that day the building used to sway a little and gently swing back as though it were waving in the breeze. The blinds used to clap as they moved back and forth gently. The employees seemed to have gotten used to it, but this time the structure didn't swing back right away. It righted itself, but didn't return.—at least for several seconds. That was when many of the employees headed for the same stairwell Matt used to get to his office. Opening the stairway door, he headed for the second floor landing on his way to the tenth floor. By the time he reached the fourth floor landing, the entire stairwell started jolting south and snapped north as though it were being shaken by some gigantic baby playing with a toy building. Loud footsteps like an elephant stampede sounded in his ears.

*   *   *   *

Laura ran into the ladies room. A woman passing by shouted to her, "You don't have time for that, we have gotta get out of here."

"I'll only be a second. Why is it so dark?"

The lady didn't answer. "OK, but don't say I didn't warn you," she shouted back at Laura.

Laura felt her way into one the bathroom stalls and kneeled over the toilet bowl. There was a wham wham wham sound which gradually made its way, in a domino effect, from the 107th floor to the first floor. It didn't even faze Laura the lights in the restroom started to flicker and buzz on and off and then completely off One of the building's volunteer fire marshals—a male—ran into the ladies' room, carrying a flashlight, after he noticed Laura being warned. He ran into the room and banged hard on the bathroom stall. The marshal yelled "GET OUT OF HERE NOW!"

Laura yelled back "YOU'RE A MAN YOU CAN'T COME IN HERE."

He yelled back. "THIS PLACE IS ON FIRE. YOU'LL DIE IF YOU DON'T LEAVE NOW!"

Laura got up from her stooping position with some vomit still on her lips. She tried to wipe it away with the back of her hand and flung open the door. He grabbed her, lifted her up and carried her out in the corridor. The lights were out. The marshal stepped over ceiling tiles, nearly tripping over buckled floor tile. He tried to jump over fallen cable wire, fearing electrocution because one didn't know if the wire was still live. The walls were torn and jagged as though someone could tear the walls apart like paper covering an open doorway. The building shook as though it were moving and there was nothing for him to grab onto. The two headed for stairwell A. The marshal headed there because it was the one less traveled, but little to his knowledge it was the furthest from the impact point. During the trip outside the building, Laura began to have breathing problems that were not just the mere result of her body fluids.

*   *   *   *

The footsteps got louder as stairwell C started to resemble the subway during rush hour. The volume of the tramping seemed to drown out what sounded like they were inside a popcorn popper. There were also sucking sounds, like being near a giant glass of soda and drinking straw, from their building exploding. The group came down these regular stairs out of habit from what they have learned from a fire drill. Matt felt as though he was in the subway terminal heading away from the trains when the others were going towards them. Suddenly everything went black and he felt hot liquid pour onto his suit. From the back, his suit was soaking wet as though he had been lying in a gutter somewhere. Water gushed down like a heavy rain storm, but was only wetting the stairwells. It was a mixed blessing for Matt. Once those people got to the building exit, they started to run as though King Kong were chasing them, but sadly Matt was unconscious on the stairwell of the third floor.

*   *   *   *

"Paging Doctor Velps wanted in emergency. Dr. Velps wanted in emergency." The call over some PA system kept going.

Bari Lynn and Caroline strolled down the hospital passage as television sounds from patients' rooms talked about the World Trade Center disaster. Some stations carried news that the white house was even under attack by terrorists, except the plane crashed into the Potomac River and there were no survivors. The airline carried local New York City school students, on a class trip to see the White house and state capitol. Also on the plane were two husband and two wife Muslims who also perished in the flight. Both mother and daughter thought, *"I don't know how they can play that thing all day long."* They remembered the destruction of the twin towers was all that could be seen on television that day since all the other programming had been pre-empted.

Caroline could remember watching the second half Good *Morning America* only to have the local news come on and take over the rest of the morning. She canceled work as the newsbreak came on. Mrs. Cobel drove by Charles Lindbergh High school to pick up Bari Lynn. Caroline could have rushed into a burning building to rescue her daughter, she ran so fast into the foyer of the school. For all the times she had been to the school, suddenly she was clueless about which way to turn until a teacher passing by approached her. "Something wrong?"

"My daughter," barely being able to get the words out. "I have to have my daughter."

"It would help if I knew who your daughter was," the teacher beckoned Mrs. Cobel to follow her into the administration office. The next thing she knew a call went out to Bari Lynn's second period class. The teacher answered the phone. Caroline began breathing heavily as thought the minutes it would take for Bari

Lynn to get to her were hours. The receptionist there said, "Why don't you put your head between your thighs and that will make you feel better."

The dark haired pigtailed cheerleader appeared in the doorway, "Mom?"

Caroline sat up straight in her chair, "You have to come with me now."

"I have cheerleading practice after school."

"Now come with me Now!"

"But I'm the head cheerleader and it's my first practice as head cheerleader."

"Now!!!"

Bari Lynn started to sound as rushed as her mother. "Like this?"

"There's no time to change you have to come with me." A wave of depression swept over the teenager like a monsoon as she walked out with her mother.

Mother and daughter slipped into the car. Caroline took a few breaths. "I owe you an explanation. I was watching *Good Morning America* this morning."

"You took me out of school for something you saw on *Good Morning America?*"

"There was a news report. An airplane crashed into the building next to where your brother works and then as I was riding on my way to pick you up, another one crashed into your brother's building."

"Is he dead?"

"I don't know anything. "I'll be calling some hospitals to find out."

"What about Laura?"

"I told you that I don't know."

While driving to New York City, the concerned mother spent almost the entire drive on her cell phone trying to find out if Matt was checked into any of the hospitals. Many reports would continue for perhaps the rest of the year.

The Cobels didn't want to be reminded of their ordeal through listening to the news. There was a theory someone could have planted a device in the buildings themselves to make them collapse because the structures of the buildings were too sound to be brought down by an airplane crashing into them. The buildings were constructed between 1972 and 1973. They were so high, at 110 floors, that they exceeded the Empire State Building which was formerly the tallest building in New York City with 102 floors. It was constructed between 1930 and 1931. The new homeland security was working on collecting a list of suspects who worked behind the scenes, arresting them and getting the facts. Were the airplanes crashing into the towers, enough to make them cave or was it a bomb that had been preset? Caroline and Bari Lynn were too concerned with

Matt to care about how the towers happened to fall. The answer to that question would not fix Matt.

The young women entered Matt's room to find him hooked up to all kind of wires, including his right arm being fed intravenously. Bari Lynn couldn't help but stare at the plastic pouch that hung upside-down from what looked like a metal coat rack. The clear liquid level ebbed as it slowly slipped into a thin plastic cord which led into Matt's arm, secured to a splint with white tape. His right index finger was wrapped in that same white tape to a piece of plastic with a white tube leading to the vital sign equipment. Bari Lyn thought to herself, *what is that hanging from his finger.* Matt was sound asleep. His head wrapped in bandages made him look like a fortune teller in a trance. Under his nose on his upper lip where a man's mustache usually is was a clear thin wire stretched across. There were what looked like two small clips leading from the line into his nostrils Bari Lynn noticed the wire led to an oxygen tank. "Mom, do you know if people in comas can dream?"

"I don't know. We would have to ask the doctor, I suppose." Matt would be in a coma for three days.

Matt's thoughts take him back to the month of February. When he made it to the 106th floor, he strolled down the corridor that led to the famed Windows of the World restaurant. He could see a tall willowy woman with hair dark hair down to her waist peering into the glass door. As he walked closer, she turned and walked in the opposite direction. He could see her long hair swaying along the back of her mid-length camel coat like branches dancing in the breeze. "Oh beautiful one I want to rent bicycles and ride through Central Park, along Strawberry Fields, forever.' He was too far away for her to hear him. Matt's eyes slowly eyed down the coat, the belt and the back of her legs clad in sheer black panty hose. *Is she a model? Because she ought to be. Matt looked through the same restaurant door the young lady previously glanced through. He saw a roomful of round tables with red upholstered leather wood framed chairs. Each table had a white table cloth with a green striped print which seemed to mimic the way the rays of the sun poked out from the sphere. He noticed the fancy china cups and saucers plus the white linen cloth napkins which were set beside them. What was that small yellow booklet that was placed at each setting? I'll have to eat here some time.* Someone dressed in a white uniform; probably a busboy came over and held up ten fingers. He mouth the words "Go away we don't open until ten." Matt walked back in the direction he came from towards the elevator.

*   *   *   *

A man wearing tie-dye blue, yellow, and red scrubs and matching cap entered the hospital room. He introduced himself to Caroline.

Bari Lynn replied, "Oh like that Mr. Phelps from *Mission Impossible.*" She turned to Matt, and slowed her speech, "we used watch that on the FX channel. It was his favorite show."

"It's Velps, Dr. Jamie Velps, V-E-L-P-S. And you," he pointed a finger towards the door.

"It's all right Doctor, she just turned sixteen a week ago."

"I would really like her to leave the room for a little while anyway. I want to discuss your son's condition with you. I would appreciate it if you could meet me in my office. I want to show you something. Maybe Bari Lynn could go into the visitor's lounge while we speak. He's been through a lot. The paramedics had to brush off broken pieces of dry wall which covered his body when they placed him in the ambulance. If you are looking for his clothes, we had to cut most of it off of him. The jacket is ruined from dry wall and the dirty water from the building's sprinkler system."

*   *   *   *

"LAURA DANIELS!" Sue Daniels cried to the nurse at the reception desk.

The nurse looked up the name on her computer. "Uh huh. She was just admitted and the doctor wants to see you."

"He wants to discuss her prognosis?"

"What's wrong with my daughter?"

"You have to discuss that with her doctor and he won't be able to tell you anything without the test results. We need some saliva samples and hair samples from you."

"That's the craziest thing I've ever heard. What about my husband being tested?"

"If we need to we'll be in touch with him. First I would like to get some information from you about Laura that we didn't get when we admitted her."

*   *   *   *

Four Days Later: Dr. Velps' office.

"I don't know why Matt keeps saying 'My baby my baby 'over and over unless it is a pet name for Laura.'"

"He also calls out for Laura."

"She's his fiancée. They're planning to be married this spring, but I guess we'll have to wait and see."

"The good news is that Matt is over the first hurdle and we already operated and relieved some pressure which was on his brain from the concussion. The brain is a complicated and not very predictable organ. He really suffered a jolt. We had to drill a hole in his skull to relieve some pressure and then we had to add a shunt in order to drain some fluid. It's called intercranial pressure."

"Is he going to be all right?"

"That's hard to tell. I never liked doctors who think they know everything. Many patients have surprised their doctors by exceeding the medical expectations."

"You mean like Christopher Reeve who claimed he could move his fingers and the doctors said he wouldn't be able to."

"I've been in this business a long time and I've seen everything. Matt could stay the same, make some improvement or he could walk out of this hospital as if the whole incident never happened."

"We can only hope."

"He suffered some trauma to the frontal lobe which could affect his short term memory. If a person is going to have a head injury that's the best place to have one. Brain injury anywhere could be temporary or permanent. He suffered a contusion."

"What's a contusion?"

"It's the area of the brain that swells and bleeds."

Are you familiar with TBI?"

"What's that?"

"It's traumatic brain injury. It's any injury to the brain caused by trauma to the head. The most common cause is motor vehicle accidents, but in your son's case only twenty percent happen in acts of violence."

"What are the symptoms?"

"It is difficult at this time to tell if Matt has all the symptoms. After three days he still showed signs of loss of memory, slurred speech, and trouble with concentration when we worked with him yesterday. It's only four days. Four days ago he was in a coma and now he is awake."

"That's a beginning. You said he could recover completely and walk out of here as though nothing ever happened."

"That's true, but each patient is different. His cerebrum is in shock."

"Cerebrum?"

"It's located in the back of the brain. Don't be alarmed by his speech. When there's some damage to the cerebrum, it can cause the way he speaks to sound somewhat garbled."

"His beautiful voice? Gone?"

"I've been telling you that there's no way to know. He'll be with us for some time and we're going to do our best to give him as much therapy as he is capable of. Rome wasn't built in a day."

"How could a frontal lobe problem cause problems in the back of the brain?"

"He fell down several flights of steps and was kicked all the way. He's lucky to be alive"

"What can we do about it?"

*   *   *   *

"Hello, Mrs. Daniels, I'm Dr. Hucktable, I'm handling your daughter's case," entering the office and closing the door. They shook hands.

"Dr. Huxtable, like on the Cosby Show?"

"No. It's Dr. Hucktable. Dr. Henry Hucktable." He sat down and was silent trying to fish for words.

"If she needs to be rehabilitated. Money is no object."

He shook his head. "That won't work. You see, we needed to conduct tests so that we could complete the autopsy."

"Autopsy? You're sure it was her?"

He handed her a donor card which was found on Laura. "She was rescued from the bathroom of the south tower. Well, the smoke got to her and," he shook his head and paused. "We found some sort of white dust in her lungs mixed with saliva and traces of mashed toast."

"She must have thrown up," Sue suggested while still looking at the donor card.

"She was alive until we got her on the examining table. Her heart must have given out over all of this."

"I understand," Mrs. Daniels got up thinking over what she might do about the organ donation.

"Don't leave yet. There's more."

"More?" *This would never have happened under Mario Cuomo. He was twice the governor George Pataki is.* She moved her thoughts to the national scene. *Damn butterfly ballots.*

"I have some good news for you."

"My daughter is dead. What good news?"

"The baby survived."

"What baby?"

"Your grandson. He was entering the second trimester."

"My daughter was not pregnant. You must have made some mistake."

"We had to perform a C section. He's rather small and his lungs aren't very developed. I could take you to see him. He might scare you all hooked up to wires and all taped up. He's in Intensive Care in an incubator."

She wiped a tear from her eye and shook her head.

"I'm sorry Mrs. Daniels."

"How did she die?"

"Smoke inhalation and we think she suffered a heart attack as a result."

"The truth is I haven't seen my daughter in months. I guess she didn't want to tell me she had conceived out of wedlock. I suppose she was going to tell me after the baby was born. We were going to have a wedding shower for her and I suppose I would find out sooner or later." Her emotions were playing a tug of war between sadness and happiness. "I always dreamed of Laura giving me a grandchild, but I certainly didn't want to find out this way."

"This is one of the things about being a doctor that I don't like, especially this week. I have so many patients and family members that I need to deliver bad news to."

"I don't know. I don't even know what to call the baby. It's hard because I've been planning the wedding shower for two months and now I have to plan her funeral. How long can you keep her body? I can talk it over with my husband and let you know tomorrow."

"That will be fine. I'll let the morgue know."

CHAPTER 15

▼

GROUND ZERO

Bari Lynn and Caroline walked down the hospital hallway as though they were prisoners of a concentration camp. They entered the elevator and took it to the garage which was adjacent to the hospital. Caroline was thinking about what she had just heard. Matt's doctor really gave them a rundown on the many tests which were done on Matt. Every time the doctor mentioned something about Matt's treatment, Caroline thought *Harvey I wish you were here. What will I ever do about Matt?*

The doctor told Caroline, "Matt cannot walk, sit, feed himself or do really anything else except talk. First we did what was called the Glasgow Comas Scale which was to see how he functioned now that he was out of the coma. We tested him three days ago and again this morning and he is getting better. He scored about a 10."

"Is that good?"

"He's marginal."

"We also asked all sorts of questions like 'Where do you live?' 'What is your name'? 'Who is the president of the United States?' 'Any family?'"

"How did he do?"

"He knows his name and who you and his sister are. He knows George Bush is president of the United States, but he thinks the president killed his father."

".Sometimes I'd like to forget the other George Bush, too. He was in Florida when this whole thing happened."

The doctor laughed a little. "We asked him which one and he looked at us strange and then he said 'George Bush killed my father.'"

"Well, you said that his memory could return."

"I wanted you to know how the questioning went. Like I said, his long term seems to be alright."

"Does he remember anything about a pregnancy?"

"Know about the pregnancy? I guess so."

"Laura was expecting their baby."

"He thinks he still works at the World Trade Center and he and Laura are getting married in the spring."

"I guess he hasn't heard the news. Would it help if he went to the funeral?"

"I don't think at this time he would realize that it was his fiancée's funeral and not someone else's. Perhaps in time he will be able to understand that Laura and the World Trade Center are no more."

He kept calling for Laura. The doctor told him nobody knew where Laura was or what happened to her, yet Matt kept asking for Laura. It was September, yet the earliest Matt could come home would be Thanksgiving and that would just be for the weekend. Caroline and Bari Lynn got off at the red level of the parking garage. As they walked off the elevator, the next thing to do was to look for the Geo Metro. It wasn't hard to find; it was the only electric blue Geo Metro with beige and black New Jersey state tags on the entire red level, if not the entire parking garage. When she opened the door she noticed Bari Lynn's cheerleading uniform and accessories neatly on the backseat. "What's all this?"

"I decided that I'm too busy with other things to be a cheerleader."

Caroline picked up theAsic Tigers. "Are these part of the uniform?"

"We are supposed to wear these shoes with the uniform."

"Even in the cold weather or rainy weather."

"Yeah!"

"I remember when we used to wear black and white saddle shoes with our uniforms. I thought we'd always have cheerleaders and saddle shoes."

Bari Lynn looked at her with the same blank stare as Matt had these days.

I thought a lot of things would stay with same." Beginning to cry, "Let's get into the car. Oh Harvey where are you when I need you the most."

Caroline backed the car out, nearly hitting the back of another car which was parked in the space located behind her. She quickly slammed on the brakes. "Mom!"

Caroline sighed, "I'm sorry about that, but I'm just …"

Bari Lynn said, "I know what you mean," in a weary sigh.

"You know that I haven't really been someone to ask for help, but now I don't know what I'm going to do. I feel like I've learned new values. I think we are both going to have to live differently now."

"Yeah," Bari Lynn said in another weary sigh.

✳   ✳   ✳   ✳

Caroline drove into the parking lot of Matt's apartment complex and found a parking space. Caroline and Bari Lynn got out of the car and walked up to the apartment building. They entered through the main door. There was some type of vestibule with rows of buzzer boxes labeled for each person who lived in the building. Caroline tried to walk by the buzzer boxes and ignore them, but Bari Lynn spotted the one which was marked *Matthew Cobel*, and a tear started to fall from her left eye. She knew if she pressed the buzzer to talk to Matt, all she would get is the answering machine with his voice telling her nobody was available and to leave a message.

"Come on Bari Lynn," nagged Caroline who was almost a second away from grabbing Bari Lynn by the scruff of her shirt collar. The doorman, a tall domineering figure, stopped Caroline and Bari Lynn before they entered the building through a second door which led inside. Caroline had to show him her driver's license before she was able to enter. "I was told there wasn't any doorman in this place."

"There is now as of this past Wednesday."

There was a radio playing in the background. A newscaster described the anthrax terror. "The mail was written with large capital letters trying to resemble that of an elementary school child writing to a politician or a television newscaster. The first letter was written to United States Senator Tom Daschle from South Dakota, postmarked Trenton, New Jersey and addressed to his office in Washington, DC. In 2004, he would be the first U.S. Senator in fifty-two years not to be reelected. The envelope contained a white powder which caused rashes and eventual death to anyone who came in contact with it. There was note which read '09-11-01, THIS IS NEXT, TAKE PENACILIN [*sic*] NOW, DEATH TO AMERICA, DEATH TO ISRAEL, ALLAH IS GREAT.' There was no return address. It is suspected that whoever wrote these notes is somehow involved in the World Trade Center crisis." Caroline felt as though she had felt a strong winter chill and quickly moved away from the sound of the radio as best she could.

Once they were inside in the foyer Caroline said, "After I see about the mail we can go down stairs to the garage." She ignored the possibility that one of those letters described on the news could possibly be in Matt's mailbox.

"Why Mom?" Bari Lynn also ignored the recent radio news report.

"I want to see if Matt's car is there."

"And what if it isn't?"

"We won't worry about that just yet." Across from the staircase was a large mirror, large enough to cover the entire wall. There were two openings on each side of the mirror. Both openings led to the mailboxes of the residents that could only be opened with the same key which opened up the apartment door. There was a pay telephone with a metal ledge that had white paged and yellow paged phonebooks. There was a large wastebasket filled with special newspapers from the supermarkets, pharmacies and clothing stores advertising their sales. Caroline opened up the mailbox labeled with the white label and black print, *Matthew Cobel.* There wasn't anything in the box except for circulars and cards advertising food, clothing sales and a pamphlet for Michael Bloomberg's mayoral campaign. Caroline took a look at the mail and tossed everything in the trash including the pamphlet about the upcoming mayoral election. As special as Rudy Giuliani was during the Ground Zero crisis, he had served his two consecutive terms in office already and now he had to step down.

Rudy Giuliani went down to Ground Zero wearing one of those cotton nose-mouth masks to keep the dust from the explosion out of his system. Caroline had seen those same ones worn by manicurists in her salon to keep out the smell of nail polish and polish remover. She wished she had remembered to stop by the salon and brought a couple of masks with her. Within an hour or so of the explosion, there he was on the scene comforting the scared and the crying. Mayor Giuliani was the man, the savior of the September 11, 2001 terrorist experience. Mayor Giuliani was destined to become *Time* Magazine's man of the year and *Biography*'s biography of the year.

Caroline and Bari Lynn walked toward the down staircase and they headed for the basement. The basement was in good condition, freshly white painted walls and pool carpeting. There was even a soft drink vending machine there. They were empty because the vendors hadn't been there in over a week to refill them. To the left of the staircase was a door which led to a large garage with two sections. The garage wasn't very different from the red level parking garage at the hospital. "Bari Lynn, do you remember what number Matt's car would be parked at?"

Bari Lynn shrugged her shoulders and said, "No, but I think it was over to the left in that section of the garage." She reached into her jean pocket and pulled out Matt's cell phone which she had found in the night stand drawer in his room.

Caroline and Bari Lynn looked around the section to the left of the garage and found a black 2000 Volkswagen Jetta parked. "Could be his car?"

"Do you have the car key Mom?"

"Yes, let me see if this works, but what if the car alarm should go off?"

"Just try it and I'll be your witness."

"Thanks a lot."

Caroline inserted the key into the lock and the door opened. The alarm was set in valet mode which meant it wasn't set to go off. "O.K. Bari Lynn we'll leave the car," the mother said as she closed the door and locked it, "for now and go up to his apartment." The two walked from the garage to the staircase. "What's that in your hand?"

Bari Lynn pressed a button on the cell phone and then manipulated the buttons until she could access his ring tone. As the phone played the theme from *Mission Impossible*, Bari Lynn said, "It's Matt's. I found it in his hospital room. It still works."

Caroline grabbed the phone away from Bari Lynn, and threw the phone in a nearby wastebasket over by the staircase. "What if someone finds it and uses it?"

"I'll have the service disconnected as soon as I get to his apartment."

They took the stairs to the third floor. When Caroline unlocked the apartment door there was a sense of emptiness, sadness and strangeness. It felt as though Matt had died. In one way he may have died, but not literally. When Bari Lynn and Caroline entered the apartment, the first thing they noticed, the sports section of the September 11, 2001 *New York Times* was still opened up and covering half of the kitchen table. Caroline walked into the kitchenette and opened up the dishwasher. She found dried on cold cereal soiled bowls, juice glasses with dried pulp residue and milk spattered spoons left in the dishwasher for almost one week. Caroline started to gag. Quickly turning away from the dishwasher, she opened up the cabinet under the sink, grabbed the powdered dishwashing detergent. Mrs. Cobel opened up one of the two compartments on the inside of the dishwasher door, and poured the powder in. She quickly shut the compartment and the dishwasher door. The mother pressed a button and started the dishwasher. She turned to Bari Lynn who sat at the table and looked as though she were trying to read the sports section of the paper upside down. "Now let's see, what's next? Suitcases! Bari Lynn, would you go into the bedroom closet and see if you can find any suitcases?"

It's alright Mom. It was a week. Matt could get better." Bari Lynn walked into the living room. She noticed a pile of magazines like *Parents Magazine, IKEA,* and there was a large newspaper circular from *Baby USA,* with some cribs, and other baby furniture circles in red felt tip ink. "Mom! Could you come in here for a second?"

"What is it?"

"Come over here," Bari Lynn insisted.

Caroline entered the living room.

"It's just like I thought," said Bari Lynn.

Caroline noticed the *Baby USA* ad on the coffee table. "Oh!" And what do you mean 'like I thought'?

"I'm not a baby anymore I've had sex education in school and I noticed she was acting strange. Maybe it was that she was expecting a baby, but it could have been something else."

"I didn't discuss it with anyone because she didn't feel comfortable talking about it right away with anyone."

"Why not?"

"She wasn't ready and I am sure if the incident hadn't happened that she would've in time announced to us. You have to respect what other people request. It's not about whether or not you are ready to handle things. "Uh oh!"

"What?"

"She had an appointment with her obstetrician last Wednesday and nobody bothered to call and cancel."

"We can still call and talk to the receptionist," Bari Lynn suggested.

Caroline went into the kitchen, over to refrigerator which fortunately had the baby doctor's magnet on it. She grabbed the phone receiver and tapped out the number of doctor's office on the keypad. The line was busy.

Bari Lynn walked into the bedroom and opened up the walk-in closet. Bari Lynn pulled out one suitcase and then she heard the door buzzer.

"I'll get the door," yelled Caroline, who had noticed the real-estate classified ads on the floor in the kitchen. She picked it up "Bari Lynn get the magazines out of the living room and hide them." Caroline took a look at some of the apartment ads circled in red felt tip ink and quickly hid them in the grocery closet under some canned goods. "I have a feeling …"

"What Mom?" as Bari Lynn grabbed the magazines and ran into the bedroom.

"Just talking to myself," Caroline opened the door.

It was Laura's parents. Sue Daniels said "The doorman told me that you were up here when we arrived. He is such a_____"

"Tell me about it," answered Caroline. The dishwasher was running. "The dishes had been sitting around for almost a week so I decided to run the dishwasher. I want to go to the trash room to see if there are any cardboard boxes that I can use to pack things up."

"I'd like to help," responded Mitch.

"I hope you don't mind," answered Caroline, "I just want to gather some boxes not play games."

Mitch and Caroline left the apartment and headed down the hall to the trash room. Sue Daniels headed for the bathroom. Bari Lynn had the suitcase opened up on the bed. She left it there and went into the bathroom. "Oh it's you Mrs. Daniels. Did you see my mom?"

"She went with my husband to get some packing boxes."

Sue Daniels noticed Laura's nightgown and bathrobe hanging up on a hook on the bathroom door. She took the nightgown and the bathrobe down and sniffed them. Bari Lynn was on the floor emptying out the hamper. "What are you doing? That looks disgusting."

Sue Daniels removed the nightgown and the bathrobe from the bathroom door. "I'm collecting some of Laura's clothes to give away to charity. I want to know if they need cleaning." She reached for the dirty clothes which were spread out on a heap on the floor. She treated the clothes as though they were gold. She started to pick through the clothing which could have belonged to Laura. She examined the clothes, even the underwear, soiled from sweat and body fluids.

"That looks sick," responded Bari Lynn. "She's dead. We already had the funeral. You don't need her clothes to help you remember her. We don't have any of my dad's clothes and we certainly wouldn't keep any of his clothes with body soil on it."

"I don't think you remember your father. Any way, I told you that I was giving these clothes to charity."

Bari Lynn rolled her eyes at that remark. "Maybe I don't, but Mom and Matt do. "**Enough!** You're killing me," replied Bari Lynn.

"Laura is my one and only and I'll do anything to hang on to her memory."

"Oh what's the use," Bari Lynn threw a bathroom towel across the bathroom.

There were joyful sounds of Caroline and Mitch coming back into the apartment. Mitch and Caroline came back with eight packing boxes in all. They put the boxes down on the living room floor when they entered. Caroline asked, "Bari Lynn did you pack the suitcases yet?"

"Not really," Bari Lynn answered fearfully.

"What do you mean not really?"

"I was helping Mrs. Daniels gather up the dirty clothes to pack away in bags and bring home to launder."

The dishwasher was off and washing the dishes were completed. Caroline went over to the dishwasher to open it up and remove the dishes, glasses and utensils. Caroline said to Laura's mother, "Why don't you help me separate these dishes and everything so that we know which are Laura's and which are Matt's."

Sue Daniels sat down at the kitchen table. "Does anyone have any idea what to call the baby?" After taking out a few bowls and stacking them up, Caroline stopped what she was doing. "That would be a nice way to spend the evening. I haven't done something like that in over sixteen years."

"Would you be offended if I didn't ask you for suggestions?"

"What's the matter with the name Bari Lynn?"

"Well …"

"You can name that baby anything you want to and it doesn't matter whether I like the name or not. So, don't run down my choice of names."

"Well I do like what you named your son and the baby is a boy."

"Well, you could name him Jacob."

"Biblical names, like you named Matt."

"No, we named Matt after a grandfather of my husband's."

"What other names are from the bible, Mark, Luke, Job …"

"Why don't you pick up a baby book in the hospital gift shop the next time you go to see the baby?"

"You think they will have one?"

"You could look it up on the internet. You do have a hook up to the internet?"

"High speed with AOL."

"You would have high speed and AOL for your service provider."

"It's only $21 a month."

"How could I forget? You are the interior decorator to the stars."

"Did I tell you that I'm working on Ivanna Trump's Florida vacation home?"

"Not Donald Trump's?"

"I don't know if he has a vacation home in Florida."

Caroline rolled her eyes for a second. "How about naming the baby Donald?"

"Donald Daniels, gee I don't know."

"There is something else that came up?"

"I also learned that Laura had an organ donor card on her in case anything happened to her."

"You mean that organization where people donate parts of their bodies like eyes, liver, kidneys so that someone who needs them can get transplants."

"What did you do about it? I was wondering why the closed casket at the funeral."

"The more I think about it, the madder I get. How many more secrets has she been keeping from me that I am about to find out? If she were here I swear I would yell at her."

"No you wouldn't."

"I wanted something of hers to live on. I don't just mean the baby. We checked it out and Mitch and I decided that most of her organs were contaminated and that is also probably why the baby is so sick. We had her eyes donated. I figure someone with eye problems could be helped. It would make me feel better. I also wanted Laura to achieve something great and maybe she will, anyway. Did you know she had an obstetrician appointment last Wednesday?"

"I just found that out today. There was something written down in the apartment as we were straightening up."

"The nurse gave me her purse and I looked over her appointment book in case she had any doctor's appointments like the dentist and things like that. I just called and cancelled every appointment in there. It wasn't easy. Oh I am so mad. I'm mad at the terrorists for taking away my only child and I'm at Laura for not confiding in me. I swear on the call I made to a doctor, I must have broken down and cried during the phone call. The receptionist told me that I wasn't the only one to break down on the phone."

Caroline shook her head and changed the subject. "You know, we ought to start looking through these cupboards and divvy up everything. Bari Lynn, I'm thinking of saving Matt's dishes, glasses and silverware for you when you go away to college in two years."

Bari Lynn was going through the boxes, checking out the room in them, "I don't want them," replied Bari Lynn sounding like she just had stuffed herself on dinner and is looking at dessert.

"You won't be going away to college for two years and maybe then you will change your mind."

"What am I getting? Everyone's hand me downs? I don't think I could use these dishes after the tragedy."

"Think about it." These probably would have gone to you anyway. I'm sure if Matt and Laura had married they would have gotten new ones".

Caroline turned to Sue and Mitch to discuss Matt. "His doctor wants to remove one-fourth of Matt's skull, on the right side of his brain tomorrow. He wants to relieve the cranial pressure. He also has some breathing problems which the doctor thinks is from the dust at Ground Zero."

All Sue could think of was "I really hope the baby survives. He's your grandchild, too you know."

"I know and I hope so."

"The doctor says the baby has poorly developed lungs and the residue from the bombing may have settled on his lungs."

"Suzanne! Why don't you let Caroline finish what she was talking about?" interrupted Mitch.

"That's O.K. I knew Laura was starting to put on some weight and I thought she was pregnant, but I wanted to respect her privacy."

"You knew and you didn't tell me."

"She was over twenty-one and asked me not to say anything to you. She probably didn't want to upset you. I don't know what I would do if Bari Lynn became pregnant out of wedlock."

Sue was silent, but her face was getting as red as a sunburn.

"Would you like to find out?" Bari Lynn added to the conversation.

Ignoring her, Caroline said, "I was thinking. You know about naming the baby. You could wait awhile. I mean the royal family waited for a few months before they named Prince William."

"William Daniels?" Isn't there a famous actor with that name? If he wanted to get into show business he would have to change his name to something else and I couldn't do that."

"Why do I even bother?" Caroline left the room.

"That reminds me of a joke I heard on *The Dick Van Dyke Show,*" mused. Mitch. "It was when they were looking for a name for Rob and Laura's new baby."

"Not the one where Ritchie wanted to know why his middle name was Rosebud?" asked Sue.

"No it was the Buddy Sorrel joke. He said 'why don't you name the kid Exit?' and Rob and Sally said 'why name the kid Exit?' And Buddy said 'so if the kid becomes an actor he will have his name in every theatre.'"

"Mitch, I'm serious. This is our grandson. This really should be the parents' responsibility, but since Matt isn't up to it and Laura isn't around anymore we have got to do it."

"Suzanne, cut it out."

Caroline, carrying the stack of magazines, "Bari Lynn and I found these when we arrived earlier.

Sue frowned as she looked at the magazines as though she had never seen such a thing in her life.

"I'm sorry she never told you, but maybe you could use these magazines and there is something here from *Baby USA* that might be of some help."

She saw the copies of *Parents Magazine.* "Do you really think I don't know how to raise a child that I need magazines on the subject?"

"I didn't buy these. Laura bought these because she wasn't sure that she would be able to be a good mother."

"Oh. I suppose I'm feeling sorry for myself."

CHAPTER 16

▼

THE ADJUSTMENT

I'm sitting here in my room looking over a newspaper scrapbook about Eastern cultural leaders like Osama bin Laden who Matt had put together before the accident. I'm trying to figure out why. Why do people who don't share the same beliefs as Osama bin Laden have to die or change their lives? What is all of this going to do for me? Bari Lynn wrote in her journal.

Matt sat at the dining room table in his wheelchair. He sat before a plate of cut up turkey, mashed, sweet potatoes and stuffing. He looked like he was intensely looking past everyone at the table (Bari Lynn, Mr. and Mrs. Daniels and Shauna) at something beyond them. He was in a different world. "Matt, Matt," Caroline tapped him on the shoulder trying to get his attention. He looked at her, in her eyes, yet still dazed. "Yeah?" he answered. When he spoke, the words seemed to come out by themselves without any thought. The least of the problems was the new haircut that Caroline chose for Matt to wear—a crew cut. Caroline had finished cutting up Matt's turkey into very small bite size pieces. She picked up his fork and started to feed him. Matt looked away from the table and stared into the living room. "Matt," Caroline tapped him on the shoulder, "Turn around I want to feed you. It's turkey."

"Why?" Matt asked.

"Why is this turkey or why should you be fed?" asked Caroline.

"What?" Matt asked.

"Come on open up and let me feed you." Caroline had some turkey on a fork and held it near his mouth. Matt took the turkey and held it in his mouth.

"Come on and chew the turkey."

Matt chewed his turkey for a couple of minutes and held it in his mouth. Caroline reminded him to swallow and he swallowed. Matt drank his iced tea through a child's plastic cup, a sippy cup with a thick plastic built in straw in the lid. Caroline held the cup up to Matt's mouth as he sipped the iced tea.

"I'm writing a report about what the attack on the World Trade Center means to me," announced Bari Lynn. "I believe it will help me to cope with all of these changes."

Matt seemed to go into a trance as he was taken back in time to February, 2001 when he stood in line waiting at the Windows of the World restaurant. There was that girl in her camel coat with the wide belt he saw earlier in the week. *There she is. You must make your move now, but how? Just clear your throat or something. "Excuse me Miss." The lady did not turn around. He tapped her on the shoulder. She turned around. It was her. "Excuse me Miss, do you always like to check out restaurants early in the day before opening time?"*

"What are you talking about?"

"Weren't you here early this week before it opened, peeking in?"

"What are you, the WTC spy or something?" she said annoyed. She quickly turned around and folded her arms.

"I was there. I was curious, too."

The woman put her arms down at her sides and slowly turned back to him. "You really ought to be careful what kind of lines you use."

"Do you mind my asking if you are meeting someone here?"

"No I'm not."

"I'd like to treat you to lunch to make up for my slight indiscretion."

"You are kind of cute. I never accept a date from a man I don't know."

"I'm Matthew Cobel from customer service."

"Where in customer service?"

"I'm sorry I wasn't clear. I work for Verizon."

"So do I. Laura Daniels. I am a receptionist on the 9th floor of the South building."

"I work on the 10th floor. How about that we both work for Verizon."

"How about that."

Someone tapped Matt on the shoulder. He turned around. "Yes? Do you work for Verizon, too?

It was another male employee of WTC. "No I don't. The line is moving ahead."

A hostess in a red uniform came up to Matt and Laura. "Are you two together?"

"Yes," said Laura.

She grabbed two menus from the check out and walked onto the dinning room floor.

"Do you have a table available by the window?" asked Laura.

"I'm afraid not," said the hostess who led them to a table for two in the center of the room. Laura picked up the small yellow menu. Matt said, "At least we found a table in the restaurant."

"It's a wine menu." She put it down and said, "This could be our first date."

"How long have you been working here?"

"About a month, and you?"

"Laura, I started here about a week ago." Maybe we could celebrate Valentines Day here if everything works out between us."

He suddenly went from February, 2001 to late November, 2001. It was Thanksgiving dinner with his family and Laura's parents, but there was no Laura.

Matt yelled out, "Laura Laura."

"Shhh," Caroline had her index finger to her lips, "Bari Lynn is talking. Matt had his head cocked to the right, "Huh."

"Bari Lynn is talking to Mrs. Daniels."

"Why?" asked Matt.

Mrs. Daniels replied to Bari Lynn, "Are you going to use the scrapbook which we found on the top of the coat closet shelf?"

"Yeah, in a way I suppose Matt will help me with his report. Of course I'll have to adjust to him not being able to help with this project other than the scrapbook. I don't know how I can get through this."

"We have a lot to get through, all of us," replied Mitch Daniels.

Caroline responded, "I'm sorry about Matt's behavior tonight."

"Don't be sorry," responded Sue Daniels, "this year I didn't think I had anything to be thankful for this year, but I do. Our little grandson is doing much better and he should be home for Christmas. We can put him in Laura's old room. We thank you for inviting us over here for Thanksgiving dinner. We made some new friends this year and I hope you feel the same way about us."

Caroline got up and started to clear the table.

Matt asked, "Why?"

Caroline ignored him, continuing to clear the table and carried the dirty dishes from the table into the kitchen. "Bari Lynn, would you keep an eye on Matt for me?"

"No" Bari Lynn propelled by anger, got up out of her seat and nearly slammed the chair into the table as she pushed it in. She joined Caroline and Shauna in the kitchen.

Shauna got up out of her seat and went into the kitchen. "Caroline, may I serve the pumpkin pie?"

Caroline was placing the dishes in the dishwasher. "Go ahead. Shauna as long as Matt is in the hospital I don't have to worry about Matt, but what will I do when he is released from the hospital?"

"We'll worry about that when it happens," replied Shauna who was stacking up small plates for the pie.

"Matt has come a long way since the accident. I almost expect him to get back to the way he was, but I think I am probably kidding myself."

"Mom," Bari Lynn said calmly as though trying to contain a wild tiger. "I need to speak to Shauna for a moment in private." Caroline closed the dishwasher door and went out into the dining room with the guests.

"What is it?"

"My future sister in law is dead and my brother is a mess. It's your all fault. You shouldn't have let it happen. I hate you and I never want to see you again." The wild tiger was about to snap from the leash and run for the jungle.

"Bari Lynn wait. Don't make me have to do this." Bari Lynn started to head for the dining room.

"Bari Lynn wait. Don't make me do this." Shauna flicked her right wrist and snapped her finger. Bari Lynn felt as though someone had glued her feet to the floor. There was the sound a thunder cracking as Shauna snapped her fingers. She looked up at the ceiling and said "Uh Oh." She looked back at Bari Lynn. "I don't want you to leave before I have had a chance to say something."

"Release me. I don't want to make a scene tonight."

"Not until I have had my say!"

"What is it!"

"It's not my fault what happened to Laura and Matt. It isn't up to me or the father to control what anyone does," she looked up at the ceiling for a second in fear. "The father frowns on that. The father created all of us to have a free mind to decide for ourselves. He didn't want to control people and make them do things. I'm here to help you cope, not to prevent things that happen. Do you understand?"

"Release me first."

Shauna raised her left wrist and snapped her fingers.

Calmer, she left the room. "I'll think it over." Bari Lynn walked through the dining room and the living room, then entered her bedroom and slammed the door behind her."

*   *   *   *

Friday November 23, 2001.

As the light of the new day started, Bari Lynn sat up in bed and thought to herself. *"I used to depend on Matt. The seven year difference in our ages was just beginning to not make a difference. Now the seven year age difference did a topsy turvy. I don't know if I can handle the new role as Matt's older sister."* Bari Lynn thought about when Matt first arrived home for the visit. He didn't even recognize the house as they pulled into the driveway in Matt's Volkswagen Jetta. They—Bari Lynn, Caroline, Matt and Shauna. Matt's wheelchair was in the trunk. Matt asked, "Where's Laura?"

Matt's mind transported him back to Laura's first week in customer service. She sat down with her chair slightly turned to the left. Matt went over to her and squatted over her lap. "What do you think you are doing?" She giggled.

"Can I sit on your lap?" he laughed.

"You're too heavy to sit on my lap!"

Matt stood up, turned around and quietly walked over to his cubicle.

Matt's mind was back in November, 2001. "Laura! "Laura! Laura!"

"Didn't you tell him?" asked Shauna.

"For the past month, over and over," responded Caroline, "Matt, Laura is dead."

"Yeah? Why?"

"We think it is because some people in the Middle East were mad at us Americans for some reason and they wanted to punish us," responded Caroline.

"How?"

"She died of her injuries from inhaling the smoke from the Twin Towers."

"I want to go back to work at the twin towers," responded Matt.

"I'm sorry Matt, but the twin towers no longer exist," responded Caroline.

Bari Lynn was brought back to the present by the noise of Caroline trying to get Matt out of his bed and into his wheelchair. It was so ironic. Laura was the stable one of the two and she was the one who was killed.

Bari Lynn looked out of her bedroom window. The family in the almost identical rancher house across the street had their big American flag on display, which in years past was always only put up for only Memorial Day or Independence Day. Now it was a daily ritual to have the flag up during the day and take it down when the sun set. Some of the cars and minivans which traveled down the street had either American flag bumper stickers or small flags taped to the car antennas. The red and blue on some of the car antenna flags looked like they were washed out from too much sun exposure. The world wasn't just changing in Bari Lynn's family, but so was the world around her. One of the neighboring North Jersey towns had to close down their post office because of an anthrax scare. Bari Lynn, at first, wasn't entirely sure what that was. There was a rock group called anthrax. *"I wonder if they will change their name."* Was it a substance that mimicked baking flour or table salt? Whatever it was, it caused anyone who came in contact with it to get a rash and have some breathing problems. There was usually a note defending the Allah and criticizing the Americans. When would all of this end? Bari Lynn previously looked forward to a fascinating new century and millennium. Washington, D.C. seemed to hear the cries of the Northeastern section of the United States. In Pennsylvania, Governor Tom Ridge handed over the remainder of his second term to his Lieutenant Governor, Mark Schweiker, in order to take the position of Homeland Security Secretary under President George W. Bush. Bari Lynn knew what that was all about since her own governor, Christine Todd Whitman left in the middle of her second term in office to become George W. Bush's Environment Secretary.

In Bari Lynn's room as she got up to get dressed, Secretary Tom Ridge was talking on the radio. Ridge talked about how everyone should stock up on large gallon bottles of water. "We should also use duct tape to secure plastic over our doors and windows in case of an attack. Have at least two flashlights and batteries handy, a radio with batteries and non perishable food handy in case of emergency." Tom Ridge was busy at work trying to compile those known terrorists who may have had something to do with the bombing of the World Trade Center Twin Towers. Bari Lynn thought to herself, "What will Matt get out of all this?"

Bari Lynn took out a black and white marble designed blue line ruled notebook. She wrote down her thoughts for a story about September 11, 2001, an English class assignment. *My brother, Matt, is probably one of the few people working at the World Trade Center to survive the plane which crashed into his tower. His tower was the second tower hit. His doctor is amazed he managed to survive because it is almost as though he knew the attack was coming. He saw the airplane hit the other tower first as he entered his building He suffers some brain damage like memory. He can't walk, but he can talk. He can't feed himself, but his doctors think it's possible.*

The question is who is to blame? During the first month Matt was in the hospital, my mother made an appointment to see a lawyer. As you know, I'm still in school and my mother has to work at the beauty salon, so if Matt comes home to live on a regular basis, who will be able to spend the day with him? How will we be able to pay for someone to come in to look after him and most of all how can we pay for his treatment? My mother and I read on the internet that rehabilitation starts when the victim is aware of what happened to him. He really doesn't seem to be aware, but his doctor thinks he will be able to remember what happened to him, in time. It was only two months ago since the accident. He needs time.

At the moment, Matt is home with us for just a few days. Sunday night he will return to rehab. We are going to work with him to help him understand what happened to him.

Since the time of the accident, my mother has taken a day off every now and then to go to see her lawyer. She has even attended a hearing concerning the president of the airline that crashed into Matt's tower building. It looks like we'll receive plenty of money by next year if we win the … There was a knock at Bari Lynn's door, "Bari Lynn, it is breakfast time. I really need you to help me with Matt's feeding."

"The other day, my American History teacher wanted to draw a comparison between the attack on the World Trade Center in New York City and the bombing of Pearl Harbor. I was surprised that I was able to listen to this story. Between the years 1920 and 1940 dictators came to power in Germany, Italy and Japan. Italy and Germany decided to become allies in 1939. They called themselves the Axis Powers. Japan joined the Axis Powers in 1940. The Japanese leader at the time was Emperor Hirohito. During World War II Japan became angry with the US for sending China war supplies because Japan was China's main war target. That was what brought about the bombing of Pearl Harbor. Plans for the December bombing were being made back in July, 1941. He told me that President Franklin Roosevelt made a speech the day after Pearl Harbor was bombed. Here is some of it:

"Yesterday, Dec. 7, 1941—a date which will live in infamy—the United States of America was suddenly and deliberately attacked by naval and air forces of the Empire of Japan …"

From Pearl Harbor Speech Franklin Delano Roosevelt Monday, December 8, 1941.

"Bari Lynn!" Caroline called out.

"O.K," Bari Lynn responded. She closed up her notebook and placed it beside her laptop that still had the desktop pictures of Justin Timberlake. Bari Lynn didn't have as much time for Justin, but she still liked him. She wouldn't completely give up her favorite group *NSYNC because of Matt's injuries. It wasn't *NSYNC's fault. In fact, maybe, if there were a way that someone could arrange a benefit either for Matt or for TBI (Tramatic Brain Injury) maybe *NSYNC would perform to raise money. Bari Lynn didn't have any connections and she would be too busy with school, and trying to help Matt to even have time to arrange for such a benefit. It is like that old saying, "Charity begins at home."

Caroline made a place at the kitchen table for Matt's wheelchair. Caroline placed her chair at an angle so that she could reach Matt. Caroline took a spoon and attempted to place the spoon in his fingers just as she had when he was a toddler. Matt looked over toward the kitchen counter, staring in a daze, as though something caught his attention. "Here, Matt. Hold the spoon like this," Caroline kept her hand over Matt's right hand. Matt turned his attention to his mother, and Caroline guided his hand up to his mouth. "Now let's try it with some oatmeal. It's cinnamon bun flavored, you'll like it." Matt looked over toward the kitchen counter again. Caroline tapped him on the shoulder and he turned toward her. Caroline guided his hand, clutching the spoon in his fingertips. "Now let's scoop up the oatmeal and up to your mouth."

"Why?" asked Matt.

Caroline put the spoon down in the bowl.

Because I want you to be able to feed yourself again," answered Caroline.

"Laura, Laura, Laura," uttered Matt. *He thought again about Laura's first week in the office when she walked up behind Matt who sat at his cubicle. The girlfriend began to massage his shoulders for a few seconds and then she returned to her seat.* "Matt, Laura is dead."

"Yeah?" asked Matt who returned to November, 2001.

Yeah," Caroline answered.

How?" asked Matt. "How did she die?"

"She died of her wounds from the bombing of the twin towers."

"I want to go back to work at the World Trade Center."

"Matt you can't go back there."

"Why not?"

"The twin towers were destroyed by two airplanes that crashed into them," Caroline said and started to sniffle.

"Why are you crying Mom?"

"Oh nothing. Please let's try this again."

Matt looked at Caroline inquisitively. Caroline picked up the spoon and placed it in his right hand again. She guided his hand up to his mouth and he ate the oatmeal off the spoon.

Bari Lynn and Shauna entered the kitchen and took their seats across from Caroline and Matt. "How's it going you two?" asked Shauna.

Caroline scooped up some more oatmeal with her hand over Matt's right hand. "Oh I don't know. You think it's time for him to try feeding himself?"

"I think you ought to give him more time," answered Shauna. "I know that it's difficult and exasperating, but in time he will be able to feed himself."

Bari Lynn got up from her seat as though she were being asked to go to the principal's office for failing a test.

While helping Matt to feed himself oatmeal, Caroline said, "Bari Lynn, you sit down and have some breakfast."

"I can't eat." She left the room.

CHAPTER 17

▼

CUSTOMER SERVICE.

There was a knock on the kitchen door. Caroline answered it. "Hello Mrs. Cobel," said Nicole.

"Well, hello."

"I heard that Matt was home for the holidays."

"He's right here." Caroline gestured towards Matt who was sitting there just looking down at his oatmeal. You know, I've been thinking. Do you have your cell phone on you?"

"All the time."

"I'd like to conduct an experiment. In a few minutes I would like you to call my LAN line."

"What's that?"

"I think that's my regular phone number. I think you have it etched in your mind." Caroline walked over to Matt. "I think we have had enough breakfast." She unlocked the brakes of Matt's wheelchair and pushed him out of the kitchen towards the bedroom area.

"What are we going to do?" asked Nicole.

"We're going to conduct a little experiment."

"Where are we going?"

"You're going to go into Matt's bedroom and he's going to come into mine." Once inside her bedroom, she wheeled Matt up near her night table by the telephone. "We are going to play customer service."

"I never heard of that game."

"I want you to go into Matt's room and sit at his desk. Then I want you to call our phone number on your cell phone."

"What for?"

"When Matt worked at the World Trade Center he was in Verizon's customer care department."

Matt and Nicole looked at Caroline as though she had green hair.

"Sit down on my bed for a few moments. I want you to call up my phone number and Matt will answer the phone. Matt you answer the phone 'Verizon, Matt speaking. May I help you?'"

Matt still stared at her as though she were making an odd request.

"I want you, Nicole, to order a new cell phone from Matt."

"I don't need a new cell phone."

"How about a new face plate for your phone?"

"I don't have a Verizon phone. I have a Nokia."

"Why do I feel like one of those sit-com mothers? I really would like your help. You've been a friend to this family since Bari Lynn started school. Before the accident Matt used to answer the phones at Verizon and take orders. I just want to know if he's gotten back any of those skills."

"Do you think he'll work in customer service again, perhaps at another Verizon?"

"I certainly hope so. If not at a Verizon, perhaps some place else. So let's think of something."

"I never called customer service for anything in my life. I don't know if I can do this."

"Why don't you order a cell phone for your mother for Christmas?"

"I have one question. Shouldn't we make it a little simple for the first time back?"

"We could. Maybe you can disguise your voice and play many customers."

"You're kidding."

"Go back Matt's bedroom."

Nicole entered Matt's bedroom, sat at his desk and pulled out her cell phone, she dialed the Cobel's phone number. The phone rang in Caroline's room. "O.K. Matt pick up the phone."

Matt just stared at it. His mind went back to when Laura started to work in the department.

"It's for you." She picked up the phone and smiled, "Caroline speaking. This is Verizon. May I help you?"

Nicole replied, "I thought Matt was supposed to answer the phone."

"Just give me your order," gritting her teeth.

"I would like a cell phone for my mother for Christmas. What kinds do you have?"

Trying to think of every cell phone sales pitch aimed at her, "We have a lovely flip phone model."

"Do you have one of those new ones that take pictures?"

"We have a lovely one that takes pictures."

"I'll take it. How much is it?"

"Thirty-four ninety-five." After thinking about it for a second, "Like I said, this is free."

"Let me think."

"You also get one of our phone plans. It's twenty dollars a month, free to talk after 7PM week nights and free on weekends. We have no roaming charges."

There was a pause on the line. Caroline gnarling her teeth "Take the phone and take the plan. This isn't working. Call me back as someone else and order a phone charger."

The phone rings again. "Matt I think this phone call is for you. Just pick up the receiver." Caroline pretends to pick up the receiver. "And you say 'this is Matt from Verizon. May I help you?"

"No!" Matt said with his hands folded in his lap. Matt just checked out and went back to when he was explaining the customer service job to Laura, who moved her chair beside his. *"When the customer agrees to the plan you have to read the confirmation verbatim. Understand?" He grabbed a hold of her hand.*

"I think so."

Not hearing Matt, Caroline picked up the phone, "Hello this is Caroline from Verizon may I help you?"

Nicole said, "This is Oprah Winfrey and I would like to order five hundred cell phone cases for my entire television studio audience. Can I get a good deal?"

"Nicole, this isn't working." The line is disconnected and Nicole soon entered Caroline's bedroom. "Mrs. Cobel, maybe this is too soon for Matt. That doesn't mean he won't be able to go back to customer service one day."

Caroline felt as though she had just returned from a five mile run as she sat thrown down on her bedspread. "Thank you so much for that." She turned to Matt, "Maybe we should try you out on a computer."

Matt just groaned.

"Maybe tomorrow."

Matt mentally returned from Easter time to Thanksgiving time, or had he? "If you cancel the plan before two years is up you have to play a penalty of $175.00."

"Is that part of customer service?"

"Yeah!"

"That's the nicest thing anyone has ever said to me all day."

CHAPTER 18

▼

THE COMPUTER.

Saturday November 24, 2001: The day didn't start out much differently from the day before with Caroline fixing breakfast. Matt seated at the table, looking at his oatmeal cool down and stiffen. Bari Lynn deliberately, looking the other way not to upset her stomach. Caroline brought over a plate of waffles with fresh strawberries and sauce spooned over. "Bari Lynn do you have any plans for today?"

"I don't know. I might go over to the library to get ready for mid-terms or I might go over Nicole's house if that's alright with you."

"I was going to ask you for a favor."

"Like the game you and Nicole played with Matt yesterday. That was funny."

"No it wasn't and I was thinking of doing something else with Matt, but I needed your help." Caroline sat down beside Bari Lynn.

"Do you really need me to be here today?"

"If I could use your computer that would be enough."

"What about Matt's computer?" Bari Lynn started to eat her waffles and strawberries.

"It's still boxed up from when we moved it here from his apartment." Caroline looked over at Matt, "Come on eat. I have something I wanted you to try when you're finished." She looked over at Bari Lynn. "I really appreciate it."

"Do you need help turning it on?"

"I think I'll be able to handle it."

"In case you forget, it's the little toggle switch on the right."

$$* \qquad * \qquad * \qquad *$$

Matt watched from the corridor as Caroline moved Bari Lynn's office chair away from her desk and over to the other side of the bedroom. The laptop was folded like a small briefcase. Caroline walked out in the hall and wheeled Matt into Bari Lynn's bedroom. "Remember the fun we had yesterday playing customer service?"

"No. What fun?"

Moving the latch and opening up the laptop, "Well, today I'm going to ask you to type something on the computer for me." As they spoke, she let the computer warm up a little and then pressed the MS Word 2000 icon using the mouse. The program came up revealing the icons and menus at the top and the bottom. The ruler and the white screen in middle.

"Why?"

"Because I want you to go back to work soon and I want to see what you can do." By the time everything came up, Caroline instructed Matt, "Place your fingers on the keyboard."

He looked at her as though she had asked him to milk a cow in their suburban home backyard. Caroline placed his hands on the key pad.

He typed a bunch of letters which didn't make up any words, tapped the enter key a few times and typed some more letters which didn't make any words. Matt pressed the space bar a little.

Caroline looked a Matt and started to cry "No this is not what I want."

Matt looked at her again with that 'you are strange' look on his face.

"Maybe when the snow comes I can get you to shovel some snow for me," she smiled trying to be hopeful.

CHAPTER 19

▼

LAWYER.

On Monday, November 29, 2001 Caroline drove to her lawyer's office in the Volkswagen Jetta with Matt sitting beside her and Shauna sitting in the backseat. The lawyer's office was located in an old early twentieth century white with black trim Victorian house which was converted into offices. It could pass for a house on the outside if not for the sign on the front lawn: Polk, Grisham and Harding Legal services. Polk was an injury lawyer. Grisham was a divorce lawyer, and Harding was a contract lawyer for big business. Parked in front of the house, Shauna got out of the car and removed Matt's wheelchair from the trunk. Caroline got out of the car and went over to Matt's side of the car. She opened Matt's car door. Caroline grabbed Matt by his sides and asked him to move his legs out to the right as though he were getting out of the car.

"Why?"

"Because I want to bring you in to see the lawyer."

"Laura Laura."

As though explaining for the very first time, "She's dead."

"Yeah? How?"

"She died of her injuries from the collapse of the twin towers."

"Yeah? I want to go back to work at the twin towers."

"You can't?"

"Why?"

"Because some airplanes crashed into them and destroyed them. There isn't anything left except a large hole and some rubble." Caroline carefully spoke the words, trying hard not to lose her temper.

"Yeah?"

"Yeah," she sighed, hoping it would be the last time that she has to explain the crash.

Shauna came around the front, rolling the wheelchair folded up like an accordion. "Caroline, I'll give you some help," called Shauna as she pushed the wheelchair up to the passenger front door. Shauna placed her hand on the folded up seat of the wheelchair and pressed down allowing the wheelchair to open up so Matt could sit down. Together Shauna and Caroline took Matt out of the car and placed him in his wheelchair. Like many Victorians there was a wooden porch with pillared columns and railings. The typical wooden steps on the side of the porch were replaced by a wooden ramp. Shauna and Caroline pushed Matt up the driveway and up the ramp until they got to the front door. The front door looked just like any Victorian home front door. It was as though the Victorian home itself were an undercover spy-ring for a law firm. The door was unlocked and Shauna opened it for Caroline to push Matt into what used to be the living room, but is now a waiting room for people with legal issues. What was once a dining room was now Gary Polk's office. Because many of his clients were having trouble climbing steps, he decided to have his office on the first floor.

Matt and Shauna waited in the waiting room while Caroline made her way to Gary Polk's office to announce she was there. Gary Polk's secretary, who was in the middle of some business with Mr. Polk, went over and asked Caroline to wait in the waiting room until she was called. Caroline left the room and took her place beside Shauna in the waiting room.

The secretary came out of Gary Polk's office. Like an administrative assistant at a doctor's office, she announced the lawyer was ready to see the Cobels. Even though Caroline was in the office once before, the large imposing maple desk made Caroline feel as though she were being kept after school to clean the blackboard erasers. Caroline released the brakes on both sides of Matt's wheelchair and wheeled him into the office. Caroline took a seat in a dark green leather chair and parked Matt beside her, locking his brakes. "I wanted you to meet Matt, my son," said Caroline.

"Hello, Matt," responded Gary Polk. Gary Polk was a muscular man in his early fifties. He still had brown hair on his head which was thinning and started to look like barbed wire over the top of his head.

Matt went into his trance again. He sat there with his eyes dilated and his mouth opened like a Ventriloquist dummy sitting on a chair waiting for the puppeteer to take him from the dressing room and onto the stage. He often looked like that these days. Matt was no dummy, he was in another world. *It was Valentines Day. Laura finally got that table by the window she wanted. The blinds were open. They could look out and see the skyscrapers and apartments. "Oh look at the view from here and the lights from the buildings and the street lamps. This is so romantic!" Laura took a sip of red wine. "This has to be the best Valentines Day dinner I ever had. Dinner at Windows of the World restaurant and violets, my favorite flower."*

"It's only the beginning. I have tickets to the opera."

"I've never been to an opera before." They got up from their chairs, held hands and left the restaurant. Matt came back to the present time

"Laura Laura," said Matt. He was back in the lawyer's office.

"Laura?" asked Gary Polk.

"She was his fiancée. They were going to be married this coming spring."

"Doesn't Matt know what happened?"

"I tried to and his sister has tried to make him understand, but it seems that we constantly have to go over this over and over. Frankly, I'm getting tired of it."

"Maybe you should ignore him. He may not be ready to listen to you yet."

"You think so? I 'm afraid he might think I am ignoring him or let him go on thinking … You don't know how bad it is sometimes. We can't even watch television anymore. I accidentally tuned into a cable network that was showing a rerun of *That Girl*. He pointed to Marlo Thomas, and shouted "Laura Laura Laura" until I changed the station."

"I'm used to this sort of thing. Just let him be and he'll work it out."

Matt kept calling out for Laura. Caroline and the lawyer tried to ignore him as though he were background music accompanying the words of a concerned mother and her lawyer.

"You know something; she really did look like *That Girl*. Usually it's just the long dark hair that gets Matt going."

"What a waste of human life!" He shook his head. "I've seen this kind of thing over and over with many of my clients. He has some kind of memory and retention problem. His short-term memory seems to be impaired."

"That's what his doctor said."

"If you really feel worried about ignoring him, just ask his doctor."

"I will. Well, about some of your clients with this memory problem, have any of them gotten over it?" asked Caroline. "I suppose I am starting to get like Matt."

"It's all right. This is new to you. Some have some haven't. It really depends on the individual."

"That's the same answer that the doctor gave, but that was back in September. It's been over two months now. I have quite a time. I have someone helping me out with Matt, but she has to leave soon."

"You mean he's home so soon after two months?"

"He's home for Thanksgiving. After our meeting we're taking him back to the hospital. We had quite a time with Matt, transporting him in the car and getting him in and out of the car."

Mr. Polk opened the top right side drawer and grabbed a yellow legal pad, He took a black refillable ballpoint pen, pushed the button at the bottom of the pen and released the point of the pen at the front. The lawyer started to take notes. "I'm thinking about making a list of things we can get with the money we win from the airline company."

"Oh?" asked Caroline.

"I think you can use one of those vans with a lift for Matt's wheelchair. You won't need it 'til he comes home on a regular basis."

"A van? Are you kidding?" asked Caroline.

"There are large vans and minivans. The minivans drive like a car."

"OOO, I don't know. However there's something else I wanted to ask you."

"What is it?"

"I'm driving Matt's car that he bought new a couple of years ago and now it doesn't look like he'll be driving anymore. How can I get the ownership rights transferred to me without Matt's consent?"

"Go to a license place and explain the problem. Show them the ownership papers of the car. Since you're now responsible for all decisions concerning Matt, and just get the ownership of the car transferred to your name."

"I see, but it makes me sad."

"Well, this isn't any consolation, Matt was one of the few people who survived the destruction of the World Trade Center. I'll help you do everything you can to get the best services for Matt."

"Am I doing the right thing taking the airline company to court?"

"It's like if I loaned you my car and then you injured someone very badly, I would probably be sued for the car since it's really my responsibility. However, we can't sue the terrorists because they're dead. The Federal Government is also working on capturing those people who are responsible for arranging the hijacking of the airlines that crashed into the twin towers and the pentagon."

"I suppose that I can sleep knowing that all I want the money for is to pay for Matt's medical and therapeutic bills."

"Matt has health insurance, I assume."

"Of course, but even though the insurance company will put up most of the cost." I'm not sure that I'll be able to pay what is left. I was thinking. He went to Territory Health Insurance which was located in the south tower."

"I'm sure they have other offices," the lawyer suggested.

"I suppose. He also had a bank account with a bank in one of the towers. Asbury Bank. I suppose they have other branches as well."

"I'm sure the bank and the health insurance are two of the few things that nobody is worrying about. You can look them up on the internet or in the phone directory."

"Don't worry so much."

"Mrs. Cobel, I would like you, Matt, and Matt's mother—in-law to come in next week for a deposition. What day would be good for you?"

"Monday is my best day. That's the day that they clean the beauty shop and it's closed that day. I don't know if the hospital will let him come with me."

"I've been through this before, Mrs. Cobel; the hospitals are usually very cooperative when it comes to things like this."

Caroline reached down and unlocked Matt's brakes and then she rose. Gary Polk went over to Caroline and shook her hand. "So I guess that I'll see you both next Monday. How about that, Matt?" Caroline got up and walked in back of Matt's wheelchair.

"What?" asked Matt as though he had too much to drink.

"Next Monday we are going to meet and you are going to be part of a deposition."

"Yeah?"

"Yeah. I am going to win you some money for your recovery."

"What?" Matt asked.

"Does he know what happened to him?"

Caroline placed her hands on each handlebar and pulled the chair back. "We keep trying to tell him, but he doesn't remember. We keep trying." She wheeled him out of the office.

*   *   *   *

Caroline wheeled Matt through the electronic door of the hospital. She and Matt went to the elevator, entering it and getting it out on the third floor. The door opened at the nurses' station where the nurses greeted Matt as though he were a football star making a hospital visit. "One of the nurses went over to Matt. "Hey Matt, it's great to have you back." She took the handles of the wheelchair and wheeled him back towards the end of the hall where his room was. The television sets were blasting the threats of the white powdered anthrax that were sent to some post offices, some television news announcers and to some politicians. The nurse lifted Matt out of the wheelchair by his arms and placed him to sit on his bed as though she lifting a six month old from his stroller into a high chair.

"How did you do that?"

"Oh, I'm used to that."

"I can't lift him up like that. Well, anyway, I have an appointment with my lawyer on Monday, December 3rd. I want to take Matt with me. Will there be any problem?"

"No. A few days before, I think you should talk to," she took a wire bound small tablet out of the front pocket of the nurse's uniform. She wrote down the name and number. "Here," she ripped off a page from the tablet. "I hope you can read my handwriting." She handed the piece of paper over to Caroline. "Call this man up at the number I gave you, this Friday and he will arrange for Matt to be dropped off at the lawyer. Give him the address and directions of where the law office is. What time is the appointment?"

"Ten O Clock."

"You get in touch with the person on the paper and Matt should be transported by the hospital lift van at ten sharp."

"What about when I take Matt home for good?"

"We have quite a few sources, like there's an ambulance company that's getting rid of some of their vans to the public for a reduced rate. You can look for ads in the daily newspaper, the classified sections. Sometimes someone is getting rid a van or there's a used car place that's selling secondhand vans. We'll work on that when the time comes. In the meantime, the hospital will be happy to cooperate in getting Matt to his legal appointments and you can rent a van when he goes home for visits. I guess he'll be coming home for Christmas."

"Yes he will." Caroline read the name and phone number on the piece of paper and opened her pocketbook, grabbed the wallet, and placed the folded piece of paper in her billfold.

"I have an idea, I think you may be strong enough to see your son now," suggested Caroline.

"A son?" he said in surprise.

"He was delivered early and he's been in the same hospital as you."

"I don't remember any son."

"We were so busy with you that we didn't have a chance to tell you that Laura had her baby."

Matt gave a blank stare.

"Do you remember Laura being pregnant?"

"No. I don't remember. What's his name?"

"We thought that maybe you might have some ideas."

"Jacob?" Matt asked with sudden brightness.

"The baby?" Caroline's mood inflated like a toy balloon.

Matt shrugged his shoulders, "I don't know. Who's Jacob?"

Caroline's mood also deflated like a toy balloon.

"I don't know, you mentioned him."

"Would you like us to wheel you in to see him, anyway?"

Matt shrugged his shoulders again.

"It's been awhile and I think we should visit him."

Bari Lynn asked, "Are we going to have to pay for the baby's insurance as well?"

"Mitch and Sue said they would handle that for him." Bari Lynn and Caroline wheeled Matt to the hospital wing and floor where the newborn was.

When they reached the ward, they were ushered to the area where Jacob was, Bari Lynn noticed the infant's face seemed to have a pale blue tone to him. "Maybe we should inform the doctor or the nurses."

"I'm sure that they all know about it and are trying to help him, although I do need to tell them something."

CHAPTER 20

▼

FOCUSING ON MATT.

Three uniformed cheerleaders entered the kitchen doorway part of Home Economics as though they were part of a street gang. Bari Lynn sat on a hard plastic chair at the large round table. She had a plastic bag with the logo of a sewing place on it. The cheerleaders entered the classroom as though they were parts of the same body. They were like conjoined triplets—two joined at the thigh and one at the stomach and back. Bari Lynn took the plastic bag off the table, placing it on the floor between her feet. The cheerleaders separated from each others' bodies and found three seats beside each other at the table. The girls wore pantyhose on their legs because it was still wintertime. The cheerleaders wore white ankle socks with thin maroon borders at the top of the ankle socks. On the top of the white cheerleader shoes near the laces were maroon and white pom poms made from yarn. The cheerleaders took a seat near Bari Lynn. The middle girl stretched out her leg, trying to touch Bari Lynn under the table and remain composed at the same time. The other girls sat on each side of Bari Lynn turned and gave her a small sinister smile as though they were planning something mean. When the teacher turned to the cheerleaders to ask if anyone had an idea for their sewing project, the pom pom girl pulled back her leg. "I have material for a pillow that I want to make for my brother's wheelchair," answered Bari Lynn.

"Oh yes, how is he doing?" asked the teacher.

"He can feed himself and the last time I was visiting him we played catch with a Nerf ball."

The cheerleaders softly snickered.

"And what about the three of you?" asked the teacher.

The middle girl spoke, "We're considering making gowns for the Junior Prom next month."

The cheerleader to the right mouthed to Bari Lynn, "Traitor." The girl on the left spoke softly to Bari Lynn, "I did a lot of favors just to get you the head cheerleader position." The three cheerleaders gave Bari Lynn sneering smiles which said for her to beware.

Bari Lynn trudged in the front door of her house. "What's wrong?" asked Shauna.

Bari Lynn sat down on the sofa, removed her backpack and placed it beside her. "I need a sewing machine right away."

"The cheerleaders tried to scare you?"

"I told the teacher I felt uncomfortable doing the sewing project at school and she let me do it at home, but she wants to see the pillow before I bring it to Matt. I wonder if Mom will let me borrow her sewing machine. What should I do about the cheerleaders?"

"Don't do anything unless they start something."

"You would think that I did something terrible to them by quitting cheerleading. I have Home Economics with three cheerleaders and one of them said that she did a lot of favors in order to get me the head cheerleading spot. I didn't do anything. It wasn't my fault that Matt got injured. Things changed after the incident."

❊   ❊   ❊   ❊

Bari Lynn should beware.

One week later Bari Lynn strolled down the familiar section of the hospital towards Matt's room. Bari Lynn heard the sound of television sets announcing tainted anthrax letters found in post offices and government buildings, from the hospital rooms. One television set from a hospital room announced that there was a bomb found in a briefcase beside a local mailbox. It seemed hard for Bari Lynn to feel secure enough to leave security up to the Bush Administration when there are tainted letters and bombs found by mailboxes.

Bari Lynn entered Matt's hospital room. It was empty. His sheets were rumpled, his pillow was wrinkled. The sides of his bed were down. The machines which monitored his heart and brain waves were gone. The door of the adjacent bathroom was closed. Bari Lynn could hear the nurse talking to someone on the other side of the door to hold the urinal still. Bari Lynn knocked on the door. "Just a minute. Who is it?" asked the feminine voice behind the door.

"I'm Matt's sister. Can I stay and wait here for him?"

"We'll be out in a few minutes. Just sit down in the chair by the bed."

Bari Lynn sat down.

The nurse left the bathroom, wheeling Matt into the hospital room. She parked him near the dresser. "Do you two want the television set on?"

Bari Lynn waved her left hand as though it were a windshield wiper brushing against a wet windshield. "Oh please don't." The nurse left Bari Lynn and Matt alone.

"Happy Birthday, Matt," said Bari Lynn.

Matt nodded his head and Bari Lynn opened up her sewing supply store plastic bag. She pulled out a pillow with the poem *Footprints*. She showed him the pillow. "There's something on the pillow. Want me to read it to you?"

Matt nodded. He looked at Bari Lynn yet through her.

"Don't you speak anymore, Matt?"

"Uhhuh."

"Here," After she read the poem on the pillow, Bari Lynn placed the beige pillow on the right side of Matt's body between the right frame of Matt's wheelchair and the right side of his body. "How's that?"

"Uh huh," he smiled. He looked toward his bed. Bari Lynn reached out and touched his chin, getting him to turn towards her again.

"Matt, how old are you on this birthday?"

"Twenty-three." He looked away. Bari Lynn tapped him on the shoulder and he turned around to her.

"How old were you on your last birthday?"

"Twenty-two." He looked away. Bari Lynn tapped him on the shoulder again.

"What year do you think this is?"

"2001."

"Where is Laura?"

Matt sniffled and a tear came down from his left eye. "She's in Heaven."

"I'm sorry, Matt," Bari Lynn went over to the night table and took a tissue out of the small gray cardboard box the hospital supplied. "Here," she wiped his cheek and lower eye lid. Matt took the tissue out of Bari Lynn's hand. He wiped his cheek and his under eyelid. "Look at you. You've come so far."

"Uh huh."

"How old am I Matt?" asked Bari Lynn.

"Huh?"

"Who am I? Do you know who I am?"

"My sister," he responded

"How old am I?"

"Fifteen."

Caroline walked into the hospital room.

Bari Lynn looked up and then looked at Matt. "Look at the doorway."

"Where?"

Bari Lynn guided Matt's head to the left. "Do you know who that woman is standing there?"

"Why?"

"Because I want to know if you know who that woman is standing in the doorway."

"That's Mom."

Caroline entered the room. "Bari Lynn, Matt I've been talking with the doctor and he thinks that it's time for Matt to move out of this hospital and into a Rehab center near our home."

"Why?" asked Matt looking at his mother and yet through her.

Caroline pulled up a second chair in the room and placed it next to Matt. "Because you're doing very well. They think that you don't need medical attention."

"Huh?" asked Matt.

"Here's the best part. The doctor knows a rehab center which isn't far from home. It's located in North Jersey and we don't have to travel so far to see you. Isn't that nice?" asked Caroline.

"I like it here," demanded Matt.

"Well you see they don't think you need medical treatment anymore. They need your bed for someone who does need it," said Caroline.

"It's my bed. It's my room," Matt started to cry again.

Caroline started to get out of her chair when Matt wiped his cheek and his under eyelid with his crumpled tissue.

"Isn't that just fantastic Mom?"

"Yeah," answered Caroline.

"What?" asked Matt.

"You are that's what, Matt," said Bari Lynn. "Mom is he coming home or is he going to live at the Rehab center?"

"He is going to live at the rehab center."

"I don't want to go. I want to stay here," Matt replied.

"Matt, your room at the rehab place is not going to be any different than this room. You'll be closer to home. We'll be able to visit with you longer. Maybe we'll be able to bring you home on the weekends." Caroline's head hung down and she slowly got up from the chair.

Bari Lynn said, "Don't feel bad because Matt has to go to rehab center. He'll eventually come home."

"That isn't it. I need to see you out in the hallway." The two young women left the room. "Keep your voice down," Caroline said just above a whisper.

Bari Lynn asked, "How did the Daniels feel about us naming the baby, Jacob?"

"Well, I told them that when I mentioned the name Jacob to Matt, he had a twinge of memory that I hadn't seen in a long time. They bought that and accepted the baby's name. What I didn't tell them was that Matt doesn't seem to link Jacob to the baby." Caroline started to frown.

"What's wrong, Mom?"

"It's Jacob. He didn't make it. The mood that Matt's in about going to the rehab center tells me that telling him won't be a good idea."

"He never asks about Jacob, anyway. I heard he was doing better and he would come home to Sue and Mitch over Christmas."

"Isn't that the way it usually is? He was premature. He was born six months too soon and I don't know what they were thinking about expecting him to spend Christmas with them. At least he spent the yuletide with them."

"You think it was because he left the hospital too soon?"

Caroline shook her head, "No, he was born with respiratory problems due to the debris Laura breathed in. I guessed the medical staff figured it didn't make any difference at that point. Give him at least one trip in his life to see something beside the inside of a hospital."

"I'm almost afraid to accept any good news about Matt."

"Don't be like that."

"Will there be a funeral? I mean he was so young and he hardly had a chance to really live."

"This weekend."

".He will probably be buried in Laura's casket."

"Will there be room for both of them."

"He's very small and they might wrap him up in a blanket and place him in her arms."

"That sounds so gross."

"It will probably be a graveside service. They're thinking about reburying her before the service."

"I should hope so. I never saw an exhumed body and I never want to."

CHAPTER 21

▼

RE-ABILITY

One of the therapy assistants gave Caroline, Bari Lynn and Matt the grand tour of the department at the rehab center. A man about the same age as Matt was wheeled into the physical therapy room. He stood up with the help of a therapist. She stood in front of him and walked backward, guiding him towards a walkway lined with rails on both sides. The young man dropped each hand from the therapist's hand and grabbed onto each rail, applying his weight on the rails. Little by little he put one foot in front of the other, right foot out and then followed by the left and so forth.

The tour guide said, "This is James. He's been with us for about a year."

"What happened to him?" asked Caroline.

"He was a senior in college, on the way home during a winter storm last year. His car skidded on the interstate and he crashed into a rail. He's been with us for almost a year, confined to a wheelchair. We are going to try to get him ready to use a walker. Many people doubted that he would ever be able to walk again."

"Does he have a head injury?" asked Caroline.

"Fortunately he was wearing his seatbelt, but the impact of the railing took a toll on his lower spine. Come with me and I'll show you our hand therapy department." The threesome headed for it. A therapist and a girl about Bari Lynn's age came around the corner. The girl had only two thighs covered with socks placed in plastic suction cups. Beneath the cups were two metal poles with blond wood mimicking toeless feet at the end of the poles. She hung on to a walker, bringing it forward and sliding her pole-like legs afterwards. She and the therapist walked inside the physical therapy room.

Bari Lynn cringed, "My goodness, what happened to her?"

"Car accident. Probably one of those all night teen parties," said the therapist.

Caroline turned to Bari Lynn, "I hope you realize that when you go to a teen party not to accept a ride from someone who has had too much to drink."

Matt uttered, "I want to go back to the hospital." Matt was ignored by the group.

"Don't lecture me," complained Bari Lynn, "I didn't do anything. She did. I'm beginning to feel sick. Is she going to have to go around like that permanently?"

"In time she will be fitted for a pair of prostheses."

"Prostheses?"

"That means two false legs."

"I feel like I'm in a spook house or something. I thought about going into something like this, volunteer work or something. Now I don't know."

"Bari Lynn, it takes time to get used to things. If you haven't grown-up with the disabled, then it can be a shock. Maybe we shouldn't go to the hand therapy department if you think you can't take it."

"I'm afraid to ask. What's there?"

"We have people there who are getting used to using their hands again. Some of them lost some fingers or even a hand or two. They're learning to cope." The trio reached the hand therapy department and stood outside talking. "What do you think?"

"You mean I am going to have to see a false hand?"

"They look better than they did in my day."

"I'd hate to ask."

"It was a plastic arm the same color as their skin-tone, with a rod and the two metal claws for hands."

"Spooky."

"Today we are trying out mechanical hands that look just like the real thing if you don't look too close. You know it really isn't that bad to look at."

"Why not?"

"You like to go shopping in department stores?"

"Of course."

"Bari Lynn is a real shop-a-holic," mentioned Caroline.

"Oh Mom," moaned Bari Lynn.

"I want to go back to the hospital," complained Matt again.

"Well, looking at the prosthetic hands isn't any different than looking at the hands of one of those store mannequins."

"What about those hand claws you were talking about?"

"There are still some out there for children who lose a hand or an arm and for people who can't afford the new mechanical arms and hands. I think in time the only way you'll be able to see the clawed hand is in some type of museum."

"Not me. It sounds spooky."

"What do you think? Would you like to go in and see?"

"Well I can handle looking at the hands of mannequins in department stores so I guess I can see this."

Matt uttered again, "I want to go back to the hospital."

"We also have speech therapy, but I don't think you, Matt, need it," said the therapist guide. "I'm sorry that you don't like it here."

Matt silently looked down at his sneakers planted on the pedals of the wheelchair.

"Matt, look up at me."

Matt looked up at the therapist.

"Would you like to get back to the person you were before the accident?"

"Yes. Can I have Laura, too?"

"Who is Laura?" asked the therapist guide.

"She was his fiancée. We lost her in the accident," answered Caroline.

"Accident?"

"The World Trade Center."

"Well Matt I can't get Laura back, but I can get you in touch with support groups and activist groups for people who lost loved ones in the World Trade Center. I want you to know that there are many many people who feel the way you do."

"Jacob!" Matt uttered in recognition. "Who's Jacob?"

Bari Lynn added, "He doesn't remember things very well."

"Matt, before you leave here we are going to get you involved in one of those support groups for people who lost loved ones at the World Trade Center. Shall we go in?"

"O.K," responded Caroline and Bari Lynn.

"I want to go back to the hospital," moaned Matt.

As soon as the threesome walked into hand therapy there was a woman sitting at a table. It was reminiscent of the manicure sessions which went on in Caroline's beauty parlor, except the woman wasn't getting a manicure. She was trying to hold on to a Styrofoam cup of coffee with her right prosthetic hand. The therapist guide went over to the woman. "These people are touring here in hopes that this young man will join the rehab. May we ask you what you are doing?"

The woman's name was Maxine and she was about the same age as Caroline. "I was moving my son's motorcycle. It was in the driveway. I always parked my car in the garage and there his motorcycle was. I tried to move it and it fell on my arm right below my elbow. I was lying there for about an hour before my son came home. At least it seemed like an hour."

"I don't understand. If he had a motorcycle what was doing away from home without it?" asked Caroline.

"He said that he was having trouble with it and he needed a part for it to fix it. A friend of his drove him to an auto parts place. He picked up the motorcycle, but my arm was turning green and black. He picked me up and helped me into the house. My son did everything for me. My boy even applied ice to my arm. He called the paramedics. They came to take me to the hospital, but it was too late. Gangrene had set in and I had to have my arm amputated." Her arm at the elbow looked like it was covered with an ace bandage. Below her elbow she looked like a mannequin from her forearm, her hand and her fingers.

"Oooo," Bari Lynn reacted. Caroline elbowed Bari Lynn on the side and although Matt said nothing, the expression on his face matched with Bari Lynn's verbal remark.

The woman had a lot to deal with in the past year and a half since her accident. People who lose their limbs have what's called a phantom limb. Sometimes she felt as though her arm was still underneath the motorcycle. The woman felt she was becoming addicted to the medication she had been on for the past eighteen months to ease the phantom pain.

The therapy she was undergoing with her prosthesis was very new to technology. It was only around for the last five or ten years. Caroline and Bari Lynn looked on as the woman tried to lift up an empty Styrofoam cup in front of another therapist who sat opposite of her. The woman picked up the cup and crushed it into large pieces. She cringed. Her therapist said, "Now think about what could have happened if you still had coffee in it."

"I know," she cried in laughter. The guide took Caroline, Matt, and Bari Lynn to the side. She explained the hand was wired to feel cold, hot, warm, and even heavy and light. It was a long road of trial and error to know how much pressure to put on hot, warm and cold drinks without crushing the container as though she were an android.

She took them to the inpatient hospital rooms. There they saw the teenage girl seen earlier when she was using her walker. This time she was being pushed in a wheelchair back to her hospital room. In front of the seat of the wheelchair was a board as wide as the seat of the wheelchair. The board was covered with linen-like material. The girl's legs were resting on top of the board. It was hard to see how the board was secured, even when the nurse wheeled her by Caroline, Bari Lynn and their tour guide.

Matt said, "My room is at the end of the hall."

"Matt, where are we?" asked the therapist tour guide.

"Back at the hospital."

Matt moved into the rehabilitation place and stayed there for the rest of 2002 or at least until the spring.

✳   ✳   ✳   ✳

The lift van was located two blocks from the rehab center. As Caroline, Matt and Bari Lynn reached the van, they saw Bari Lynn's friend Nicole holding a shopping bag, running across the street. Bari Lynn hadn't seen Nicole since Thanksgiving weekend. "Bari Lynn!" cried Nicole as she raced across the street. When she looked at Matt in the wheelchair by the side of the van, as Caroline was sliding the door across in order to reach the lift, her mood dropped. "What happened?" Nicole cried. "Oh Bari Lynn I thought you were mad at me, because we never got together."

"No. Matt was busy with therapy and we were looking at some rehab centers," answered Bari Lynn. During the reunion between Bari Lynn and Nicole, Caroline wheeled Matt onto the lift, ran the lift, and then placed him near the left side of the van. "Nick, why don't you join us? Mom?" asked Bari Lynn.

"I'll be with you in a second, Bar. I'm belting Matt in place." Caroline straightened up and looked out through the opened sliding door. "How about if I lower the lift and give you two a ride up into the van?" asked Caroline.

"Would you?" asked Nicole.

"Get on."

Caroline lowered the lift and the girls stepped onto it.

"Hold on to the sides girls," Caroline warned as she pushed the button and the lift went up. When it came up and the girls got off, Nicole asked, "Where should I sit?" Bari Lynn led her to a long seat behind Matt who was facing forward. Caroline slid the door in place and locked it. She walked bent over to the driver's seat of the van. As she drove off, Caroline asked, "How do you like my new van, Nick?"

"I like it. I have a confession to make to Bari Lynn."

"What is it?"

"I was kind of mad at you a little for becoming head cheerleader because when I tried out in August, I was cut from the squad."

"I quit the whole cheerleading squad and now I guess you know why?"

"I feel ashamed now. Who needs them? They didn't even want me for pom-pom girl. I can always do something else", vented Nicole.

"Good attitude," replied Caroline. "We have to drive Matt back to the hospital for some tests and then take him back to the rehab."

"How long was he there at the hospital?"

"Six months, but now we just moved Matt into a rehab near us."

"Oh. Do you think he'll ever be normal again?"

"I don't know, but he has come a long way in the past five months."

"You mean all those games we played with him. Can he use a computer and answer the phone?"

"No, but in other ways."

"Where's the hospital?"

"It's in New York City. Do you mind?"

"I guess not. I haven't been to New York City since 9/11. Are we going to drive by Ground Zero?"

"Absolutely not," answered Caroline from the driver's seat. "I will however, take you girls to lunch at a classy New York City restaurant. That is if you haven't eaten yet, Nick."

"I want to go, too," groaned Matt.

Nicole cringed at the sound of Matt's monotone voice. She still couldn't get used to his voice.

"Is something wrong, Nick?" asked Caroline.

"No. I suppose the lunch at the New York restaurant will be fine. Thank you Mrs. Cobel."

Matt repeated, "I want to go to the restaurant, too."

"Oh No. I have to take you back to the hospital, Matt. Maybe later on when I bring you back, I can treat you to dinner." They're expecting you at the hospital."

"I want to go to the restaurant." Matt repeated. When Matt got like this Caroline and Bari Lynn learned to ignore Matt.

*   *   *   *

Caroline, Bari Lynn and Nicole were in the middle of their large supreme pizza when the Daniels walked over to the table. "I thought that was you, but I wasn't sure," said Sue Daniels.

"It's good to see both you. I haven't seen you since the trial," responded Caroline.

The couple remained standing at the end of the table. "Mitch and I just got back from an appointment with a marriage counselor."

"A marriage counselor?" asked Caroline. Bari Lynn and Nicole looked on silently munching on their pizza and watching as though they were at a dinner theatre.

"You know that Mitch and I have been having marital problems."

"He thinks that maybe we should try a trial separation period and then see what happens," added Mitch.

"We discussed my possibly cutting back on my interior decorating. Ever since Laura I haven't been interested in the celebrity interior decorating business. I've been rethinking my life a lot since Laura and the baby died."

"What do you think you will do now?" asked Caroline.

"I think I'll tone down my business just for the middle class and forget about celebrities."

Mitch added, "We discussed moving to a smaller house."

"Possibly a small cottage like yours, maybe even in your area. Are there any homes for sale in your neighborhood?" asked Sue Daniels.

"Well, I don't know," answered Caroline.

"We must be going," Mitch said, nudging Sue on the shoulder. The couple left in the happiest mood Caroline had ever seen them in since she first met them. Caroline was about to get her second slice of pizza and noticed the entire pie was gone. "What happened to the pizza?" asked Caroline. Bari Lynn and Nicole held up their half-eaten slices of pizza.

"Does anyone want dessert? asked Caroline.

"Are you kidding?" asked Bari Lynn

"I'm stuffed," replied Nicole. "Thanks for the pizza lunch Mrs. Cobel."

After a sip on her iced tea, Caroline replied, "You're welcome." The waitress came over and asked if anyone wanted desert. Caroline told the waitress she just wanted the check. The waitress handed her the check. Caroline handed her a credit card to pay for the lunch.

"I'll be back in a moment," the waitress said leaving.

"I hope we get to ride on the lift again," said Nicole.

"I'll think about it," said Caroline as she looked at her receipt for the lunch.

CHAPTER 22

▼

RE-ABILITY II

Sue Daniels drove her silver Mercedes Benz down a small paved road between two sections of the cemetery. She stopped her car, got out, put her alarm system in gear and shut the door. The mother sat on a granite bench with the name *Daniels,* which was located along side the road and in front of Laura's plaque which said on it *Laura Lee Theresa Daniels.* The dates were sandwiched in with a crucifix at each end. *March 15, 1979-September 11, 2001.* Beside that was Laura's *son, September 11, 2001–January 18, 2002. Mother and Son* *Forever in our hearts.* Sue Daniels, sitting on the bench, spoke to Laura as she used to speak to her on the telephone. She placed a bouquet of violets above the plaque. "Your father and I decided to see a marriage counselor. He suggested that we have a trial separation. Before we went to see the marriage counselor I couldn't wait to leave your father, but now I don't know what I want from the marriage. I don't know if I want to have a trial separation, a divorce, or just to stay married. We're thinking of moving to New Jersey into a smaller house. I really do miss you both. I loved having the baby visit us during the holidays, but now what am I going to do about all the baby furniture that I bought for him? He seemed fine the whole time he was with us, but it seemed like right after we brought him home without all that hardware, he started to go down hill. We had to bring him back to the hospital on Christmas Day. We named him Jacob because Caroline said Matt responded well to the name. I hope you don't mind." A mourner lady walked by and saw Sue having a conversation with her daughter; she squinted and wrinkled her nose as though it were crazy to talk with the dead at graveside. Sue never saw her and just continued the conversation as she had many times while her daughter was alive. "For a change I don't have you interrupting me. That used to annoy me, but now I wish you would interrupt me. I'm sorry for whatever I did when you were pregnant and I wish you could have confided in me. Is it a grandparent's place to name their grandchild? Matt doesn't know what is what anymore and I don't know if he ever will. He isn't even the harebrain he was when you were here. He doesn't even know his son or remember anything." She had gotten off the bench and got down on her knees. The mother kissed the grave plaque, rose and headed to her car. Mrs. Daniels turned back and looked at the plaque. "I am also thinking about going to see one of those mediums. I want to talk to you and know what you're thinking." Sue Daniels headed towards her car, got into the car and belted up. The tears flowed. "You invest twenty-two years into a daughter and then this. One day you are planning an engagement party and the next day you are planning a funeral. We never saw eye to eye on a lot of things, but at least you wanted the wedding at St. Patrick's Cathedral. A sacred heart ceremony. That was the place where your father and I were married. You were baptized there when you were only a month old. Your First Communion was there at age seven and the Sacraments of confession when you were twelve. I thought of all of them when I drove past the St. Patrick's Church." The tears blurred her vision just like a heavy rain on the windshield. She took a tissue from a box which sat on the floor of the front passenger's side. Laura's mother wiped her eyes, taking off her eye makeup along with her tears. Sue drove from New York City towards North Jersey and the rehab to see Matt. *I don't even mind that Matt is a protestant in a computer job. I forgive you for having a baby out of wedlock. He was beautiful. I wonder if you knew you had a son.*

Matt was in the middle of his first week at the rehab. Shauna was his therapist and helped him learn how to use some sort of bike machine which connected to his wheelchair. It was similar to the one Christopher Reeve used to get him ready for walking. Shauna had to keep getting Matt's attention. He would only look at his feet strapped down to pedals which were similar to what one would find on a standard bicycle. Matt would look down for seconds and then look away. After Shauna demonstrated by guiding his legs up and down as though they were pedaling a bicycle, Shauna said, "Matt, now I want you to try it." Shauna let go of his legs.

"No. I don't want to," Matt said authoritatively.

Shauna took a hold of his legs again and continued on with the pedaling motion. As they were in the process of the peddling therapy, Sue Daniels showed up in the doorway.

She stood there looking, for a moment, and then she strolled in. "You look familiar. Don't I know you?" she asked Shauna.

"I know you, too," responded Shauna.

"If I remember correctly you were helping the Cobels out with Bari Lynn's Sweet 16 party."

"I'm very talented. I can dabble in plenty of things," Shauna answered, still peddling Matt's legs.

"Even therapy?"

"I'm not a therapist. I'm a therapy assistant."

"I'm tired," uttered Matt.

Shauna let go of Matt's legs. "I think I'll give you a break."

Matt nodded his head.

"What do you want?" asked Shauna.

"I really came here to visit Matt."

"Why?"

"Because my husband and I have become good friends of the Cobels that's why."

"I heard you are looking to move to a smaller place in this area."

"How do you know that?"

"Let's just say that Caroline Cobel informed me."

"You also excel in real-estate?" asked Sue Daniels with a tinge of jealousy.

"What kind of a place are you looking for? An apartment? A smaller house than you have already?" asked Shauna

"Oh I don't know. Are there any small homes available?"

"You mean with one bedroom off the first floor with maybe a loft on the second floor?"

"That sounds nice. We don't need anything too big. It's not as if we'll be having any in-laws or grandchildren stay over." Sue started to sniffle. "It must be a cold coming on."

"But you do have other relatives that might come and stay with you sometimes, don't you, Mrs. Daniels? I'll get back with you when I find some places that might interest you."

"I would really like to visit with Matt, but I do have one more question for you."

"What is it?" asked Shauna.

"What do you think of using mediums to help you contact the dead?"

"I think The Father would be very disappointed in you. That's toiling with the devil."

Before Sue could respond to what Shauna said, Shauna continued.

"Look, he will be finished with his therapy in a little while and then you can visit with him. Perhaps over lunch?"

"I have one more question. What kind of therapy are you giving him?"

"It's kind of a pedaling therapy, like the kind that Christopher Reeve is getting."

"Do you expect Matt to ever walk again?"

"We most certainly do, but not right away."

On the way down the hall to Matt's room, Sue Daniels stopped at the nurses' desk. She thought about what happened at the support group with Maureen and decided maybe some volunteer work might be a good idea.

"May I help you?" asked one of the nurses."

"I was thinking."

"About what?"

"Volunteer work."

"Well, I suppose you could. You'll have to go to the lobby where the offices are. Can you find the lobby from here?"

"I think so." Sue Daniels thought to herself that maybe she could stop off in the administrative section of the lobby and pick up a form about volunteer work. She pondered about whether or not she should go to Matt's room first or go to get the information about the volunteering, first. On her way to the administrative section of the rehab center, Sue Daniels felt a bitter taste in her mouth the more she thought about doing volunteer work in the rehab center. It was as though someone else were forcing her to do volunteer work. She never had any schooling in the medical field or in therapy. Clerical work bored her to tears. It would have been bad enough to handle if she did clerical work for a salary, but for free? Sue soon found herself sitting in front of the desk of the woman in charge of volunteer work.

"Yes, may I help you?" asked the woman in charge of volunteer work.

"I'm Mrs. Daniels and I am interested in doing some volunteer work at the rehab."

"What kind of experience have you had?"

"I've been working as an interior decorator."

The woman handed Sue Daniels a typed up list of volunteer jobs available at the rehab. Sue Daniels looked over the list as though she were a student looking over a failed test paper. "Can I keep this?" she asked.

"You sure can," said the woman. They stood up, and shook hands. Sue Daniels reached down the side of her chair, picked her purse and the shopping bag which she brought in with her. The woman in charge of volunteer work noticed the shopping bag, but just smiled. "It was nice meeting you Mrs. Daniels. I hope that you decide to volunteer with us."

Sue Daniels started to taste bitterness in her mouth again, "I'll get back to you," she said without enthusiasm, and left. She strolled out to the lobby feeling queasy, even though she hadn't eaten anything which didn't agree with her. She knew it was all in her mind. She headed for the inpatient rooms of the hospital and strolled down to the middle of the hallway of hospital-like rooms. Sue bumped into Maureen from the support group. She removed the head phone, letting it dangle around her neck, and turned off her tape player. "You remember me. My daughter was killed on that airplane that was headed for Washington DC from JFK terminal. It crashed into Potomac River."

Sue gave her a blank stare and shook her head, but the lady continued.

"There were no survivors. She was going on an eighth grade class trip to see the Whitehouse and meet President Bush. The last time I saw her was in the waiting area to see her off. The last thing I said to my blonde pigtailed, blue-eyed daughter was 'If you meet President Bush don't tell him that we voted for Al Gore in the last election.'" Maureen could still see that smiling face with the mouth full of metal braces. She had a molar missing on the left side of her mouth. It was the last of the baby teeth. For Becky it was not just the end of the baby teeth, but the end of the world.

"I have to go visit someone," Sue hinted as she started to walk. Maureen joined her. Laura's mother muttered, "You think you're the only one who lost any children." Maureen didn't hear her, she placed the headset back on her head as though she were placing a hair band on her head. She turned on the tape deck.

Sue noticed Maureen still carried that Walkman with the C-30 cassette tape inside. "I see that you didn't take our advice and get rid of that cassette tape with Rebecca's farewell phone call." Sue stopped what she was saying and looked up at the ceiling.

"What's wrong?" asked Maureen, as she stopped the player.

"I thought I heard someone say something to me."

"That was me," said Maureen.

"No, I don't mean that," Sue said recalling her conversation several months ago with Bari Lynn about holding on to Laura's old clothes for memory. "I'm embarrassed to tell you this, but maybe we can make a deal."

"What kind of a deal?"

"Well, I still have my daughter's clothes from her apartment hamper. I've been holding on to them for the same reason that you hang on to this tape." Sue couldn't understand Maureen wrinkling up her nose at Sue's confession. "I don't understand it, you should understand."

"This is a tape, not dirty clothes that smell."

"Would you listen to my offer? If you get rid of that tape, I'll get rid of those clothes. Is it a deal?"

"How do I know you will make good on your deal?"

"Maybe at our next meeting in front of everyone. We can bring the clothes and the tape and get rid of them together as a ritual of some sort."

"I'll think about it."

"Now can I get going?" Sue walked away and Maureen turned around and headed for the lobby. They both had smiles on their faces.

Sue made a turn to the left into Matt's room. Matt was sitting in his wheelchair. He had a three shallow wall sided tray attached to his wheelchair. He was having a lunch of tomato soup, a small tuna sandwich and sippy cup of apple juice with a built in thick straw. Sue Daniels walked in and sat down on a low plastic chair with metal legs. It was a backache waiting to happen. Matt put his tuna sandwich back on his plate. "Go away," he groaned.

"I'm thinking about doing some volunteer work here sometime. Isn't that nice?"

Matt looked like a statue holding on to a partially eaten tuna sandwich. "What?" he responded.

"I said wouldn't be nice if I volunteered here sometime?"

"No!" he said emphatically.

"Why?"

"Because."

"Because what?"

"Why is it a bad idea for me to do volunteer work here?"

"Because I don't know."

"Is it because of Laura?"

"Yes," answered. Matt.

"You really should finish your lunch."

"Why?" Matt sat there posing with his partially eaten sandwich in hand and his hot soup gradually cooling down to room temperature.

"Because it will make you strong when you go to therapy."

Matt looked at the bag, "What did you get me?"

Sue Daniels opened the bag and pulled out what looked like a large black book bag. "What do you say when someone gives you a present?"

"I want it!" he announced. Matt looked as Sue Daniels held up the bag.

"It's for your wheelchair, to keep things in."

A nurse came in to see how Matt was doing. "Come on Matt finish your sandwich. Matt took a bite out of his sandwich. The nurse looked at the particularly consumed bowl of soup. "Your soup is getting cold."

"Why?"

"Because you are not eating it."

Matt finished his sandwich and began to continue eating his soup.

"I think I better go now," said Sue Daniels, "Goodbye Matt. She walked to the back of the wheelchair and slipped the handles of the bag onto the handlebars of the wheelchair. She left the room.

*   *   *   *

It was springtime before long.

Bari Lynn and her friend best friend Nicole stopped in at the local AAA after school. Bari Lynn felt guilty not heading for the rehab after school like she usually did. Weighing everything, she decided t this was the best thing to do. Nicole was attracted to the pamphlets that were placed on the wire display tree. There were also some accessories for cars like those sun visors for the windshield and anti-theft clubs in assorted colors. The AAA even sold some inflatable rafts and had a yellow one on display, "Would you look at that, Bari Lynn!" Nicole exclaimed when she saw the display raft in the corner.

"Come on, Nicole," nudged Bari Lynn. The two girls walked over to the counter into a short line. When it was their turn the clerk, a tall dark haired balding man asked, "May I help you?"

"My friend and I would like to know if you have any books about driving."

"Are you seventeen?"

"My friend will be seventeen in couple of months and I won't be seventeen until September."

"I'll check." In a moment the clerk came back with two thin New Jersey driving manuals. "Here you are." The clerk placed them on the counter. Bari Lynn opened up the book to the page with the slogan *New Jersey and you perfect together*. Under that it said *Christine Todd Whitman, Governor*. Bari Lynn looked at the page and frowned. "Don't you have a more recent manual? Mrs. Whitman isn't the governor anymore."

"I assure you that the rules in this book are up-to-date and you have nothing to worry about."

"I'd like to ask you something else. Do have any pamphlets for driving mini-vans?"

The man in line behind Nicole and Bari Lynn chuckled a little and said, "My aren't we in a hurry to grow up."

"Look," said the clerk, "there are other people in line and I don't have time. When you take drivers Ed, I would suggest that you ask that question of your teacher. NEXT!" yelled the clerk. The two girls with manuals in hand left the AAA building. "Really!" fumed Bari Lynn, "All I want to do is share the responsibility of taking care of Matt when he comes home from the rehab center. Is there anything wrong with that?"

"No, I suppose not," replied Nicole as the two headed for their bicycles which were chained up at the bicycle rack. Bari Lynn undid her chain and placed it in her jacket pocket. Nicole was unchaining her bicycle. "Look, maybe he was right."

"Who?" Bari Lynn responded.

"The clerk of course. Look, he's only a clerk, not the teacher. They have Drivers Ed at school. You could drop by and ask."

"Once in awhile you do come up with a good idea, Nicole."

The two headed to Bari Lynn's house excited about looking over the driving manuals. The conversation was overtaken by the loud sound of an airplane engine. Bari Lynn ran and ducked behind some bushes. "I don't understand, Bari Lynn, you love airplanes. In fact, you had an airplane sky write *Happy Birthday* when you came home from your Sweet 16 last year."

'That was last year. I hate airplanes and I'll never ride on one ever again. "After the aircraft disappeared, Bari Lynn walked out from the bushes, clinging on to her driver's manual for dear life. "I think I'll attend a college that I can drive to or at least take a train or a bus to."

*   *   *   *

Matt sat on the edge of a room-size pool three-foot deep made entirely of aluminum. It looked something like a huge kitchen sink without the drain or the faucets. The young man sat in a plastic chair, strapped into it so he didn't fall. He sat with his bare legs over the edge of the pool. There were light weights attached to his ankles. Shauna, wearing a simple one-piece bathing suit ,stood in the pool. The water went up to her lower back. She got down on her knees in the luke warm water and lifted Matt's legs up straight out and then put them back down. Caroline and Bari Lynn walked to the doorway of the therapy swimming pool-room. The room smelled of strong chlorine. Shauna noticed the Cobels, and said for them to come in and sit on the bleacher over on the wall directly across from the pool and in vision of Matt's therapy. "Look who's here to see you, Matt," announced Shauna.

"Who?"

"Your mother and sister."

"What?"

Matt looked up and saw Caroline and Bari Lynn waving at him.

Matt nodded to them. They smiled. Bari Lynn said to Caroline, "So can I please learn how to drive the van, Mom?"

"Why?"

"You know that I want to help drive Matt around."

"I also know that you don't have any experience driving yet. Besides that you are six months away from being old enough to get your drivers license."

"The salesman said that the minivan drove just like a car."

"Bari Lynn, please. Not here."

*   *   *   *

Bari Lynn and Caroline stood in line at the rehab cafeteria awaiting their turn with the cashier. Bari Lynn started up again about wanting to take Drivers' Ed with the minivan. There was a woman, about Caroline's age, behind Caroline who couldn't help overhearing. "Let her learn how to drive the minivan." Caroline turned around with 'a who asked you look' on her face. The woman continued, "You probably have a relative who is confined to a wheelchair. You know, I hate all of the false hope that goes on these days." Caroline started to look at the woman with interest, looking away only to move her tray along the metal track towards the checkout.

"Ten years ago my husband was in a car accident. He was confined to a wheelchair. I used to believe in all of those exercises and all of that crap promised to get my husband to learn how to walk. You know what I can't stand?"

"What?"

"It's all that stuff about Christopher Reeve. He keeps talking about how he expects to walk by his fiftieth birthday. It ain't gonna happen."

"I once thought he was courting false hope, but now I think I know what his family must feel," said Caroline.

"That Christopher Reeve is going to remain paralyzed and wheelchair confined for the rest of his life. Sooner or later he is going to face the facts. I had to and now we live life."

Thinking Reeve was able to move his left pinky finger, Caroline decided not to talk about that." Then what are you doing at the rehab?"

"I don't know. I guess I want to see if they have any new equipment for my husband," said the lady.

Caroline turned away and moved up. She placed her salad on a scale. The cashier gave her a price and asked her about her Styrofoam cup. "This is diet Sprite." Caroline and Bari Lynn found a table alone until the woman who stood in back of Caroline found a seat near them at the same table. Caroline said to Bari Lynn, "I'll get everything and you just stay here with our lunch."

Bari Lynn sat down and started on her pizza fries. Bari Lynn silently looked at the woman as though she had held up the cashier. The woman sat on the other side of Bari Lynn, about two chairs down the right. Caroline came over with a couple of straws, some utensils and some napkins. As she sat down across from Bari Lynn, she looked at her daughter's face. "What's the matter?"

"Can we move to another table, please?" Bari Lynn nodded her head to the right. Caroline looked over and found the woman who was behind her in the line, now sat two seats away from Caroline. "Bari Lynn, what are you going to do? Are you going to check out everyone you sit near to see if they agree with you?"

"I get too many people telling me that Matt will never get better … I mean improve."

"He's not going to be as good as new, but he will be able to function. Maybe he will be well enough to go back to work, even," said Caroline.

The woman turned to Caroline and said, "Don't get your hopes up because ten years later, the only work my husband does is open up the envelope of his disability check every month."

Bari Lynn yelled, "Well every month since the terrorist attack my brother improved more and more."

"Shush! Called Caroline.

"I won't shush, I can't stand all this negative talk. I don't know what's wrong with your husband, but my brother has had some trauma to his brain and he is getting better all the time. Maybe your husband has a spinal cord injury."

Ignoring Bari Lynn, Caroline said, "Well, lady, his injury was ten years ago. I'm sure that the medical profession has made some advances since your husband's accident."

"I thought that same way ten years ago. 'Well, it's 1992. I'm sure that the medical profession has improved a lot since 1982.' Well now it's 2002."

"There is some talk about stem cell research."

"Every ten years there is some talk about some miracle operation."

"Mom, I can't eat anymore of this."

"Maybe it's that junk you are eating," suggested the woman.

"I think it is you, lady. I really don't want to hear all of your negativity. It's really bringing me down."

"Bari Lynn!" exclaimed Caroline.

"I just can't listen to any of this." Bari Lynn scanned the tables to find an empty spot, but she couldn't find one.

"O.K. I get the message. I'll keep quiet from now on and let you to your own fantasies."

"Mom did you really think Christopher Reeve was never going to improve?"

"Yes I did."

"Was it Matt who made you change your mind?" asked Bari Lynn.

"I would really like to have him back the way he was before the accident. When I see him in his therapy sessions, I sometimes feel as though I might get him back. I have to remember there's only so much recovery he's going to make and then we'll just have to face reality."

Bari Lynn, tears in her eyes, looked at her mother.

"Bari Lynn, you see Christopher Reeve has a spinal cord injury and Matt has a head injury."

The woman looked over to her right with a look on her face as though she were about to say something, but then she turned back to her partially eaten turkey sandwich on a roll and took another bite out of it. "Christopher Reeve only has to regain the use of his legs and his respiratory system. We have to deal with a brain injury and we don't really know how much Matt can improve."

*   *   *   *

Sue Daniels drove her 1996 brown four door Mercedes down the same block where Matt's lawyer was located. At the end of the block, the opposite end of where the law firm was located, she made a right turn. She drove an additional one block until she saw a single red brick home which might have been built in the early 1950s. There was no sign of a second floor except for the two white aluminum sided dormer windows located on the down sloping part of the roof. She shut off the motor of the car and stepped out. She noticed the brownish green lawn and a bare tree near the service porch. On the service porch a clothesline hung with some button-down shirts hanging from the line.

On the lawn on the right side of the house was a sign which advertised tarot card readings, palm reading, contact the dead. The front door was opened at the end of the concrete walkway. Although the house appeared to be a normal modern house, Sue Daniels slowly walked down the walkway as though she were heading for an old broken down nineteenth century haunted house. She walked up the two steps in front of the door. Mrs. Daniels walked up to the grayish aluminum storm/screen door which was probably the original storm/screen door from when the house was new. Sue lightly tapped on the glass door, looking into what looked like a lived-in average ordinary living room. It had a large dark print area rug over the bare hardwood floor. In the corner on the floor near the staircase, against the wall was a small stack of paperback books which seemed to be waiting to be carried to a bookcase somewhere, upstairs maybe? A blonde woman, who looked like she might have been a top fashion model in the recent past, walked up to the door. "Yes? Are you looking for something?"

"I'm Sue Daniels and I noticed a sign outside that said psychic readings here."

"Yes, that's me." The lady opened the storm/screen door. "Come in," she smiled like an Avon lady. "Right this way into the dining room. I'm Madame Francesca. Please excuse the living room."

Sue Daniels was too intrigued to think about criticizing the housekeeping. The dining room was filled with dark mahogany fine old furniture which may have been handed down to this woman from an ancestor. There was an old fashioned off-white lace table cloth on top of the oval-shaped dining room table. They sat down at the middle of the table, across from one another. "What type of services are you interested in?" she asked.

"I'd like to contact a dead relative."

She sighed heavily and then she said. "O.K." closing her eyes. "I'm trying to contact those who have crossed over," she spoke as though she were in a trance. Sounding as though she were coming back to the land of the living, "I can't seem to be contacting anyone at the moment, but just give me a few seconds. I'm getting something. A young woman is tapping me on the shoulder right now. Do you know anyone named Matthew?"

Sue Daniels nodded.

"He's still with us and he seems very close to the young woman. She wants you to tell him that she's happy and alright now."

"Does she say anything to me?"

"Let me see. Oh yes. She wants you to know that she forgives you for sending her away to school in France. She also wants you and your husband to know that she is alright and that you need to thin out your life."

"Thin out my life? She never spoke like that."

"I'm paraphrasing"

"She thinks you're living too extravagantly and she fears that if you don't change your ways then you'll continue to be unhappy."

Sue Daniels got up from her seat defensively. "Really!"

"I didn't say anything to insult you. That was Laura. I'm a medium between you and Laura. She wanted to thank you for taking care of her baby until she was able to care for him herself. She appreciated the name Jacob. That was what she wanted to name him, anyway. That will be twenty dollars for the reading."

"I refuse to pay after getting a reading like that."

"Well, perhaps you can tell your friends to come."

"**Absolutely not!**" She headed for the front door and walked out, down the two steps, down the walk and out to her car.

Madame Francesca walked into her kitchen to help her glamorous daughter with the dishes.

▼

CHAPTER 23

SUPPORT GROUP

Sue found herself in bed alone. Mitch had gotten up before sunrise to go down to the car dealership. The sun had just come up and was shining through the white blinds in her bedroom. She had to get up in order to go to the hospital for her weekly meeting. Mrs. Daniels yanked open her closet door and grabbed her robe. She headed for Laura's old bedroom which had been made into a nursery, complete with all the modern border trim on the walls. Sue went over to the crib and brushed her hand against the mobile of birds which hung above. She liked to pretend the baby loved the mobile and used to laugh and grab for it, but really he used to silently lay there and look at it because he was so sick. The crib remained with its pad and sheets on the baby bed as they left it when they took him back to the hospital on Christmas Day. It was a miracle he hung on those three more weeks. Sue left the room and headed into the extra bathroom where the plastic garbage bag of Laura's clothes laid The grieving mother sometimes would open the bag and spray a little Febreeze on it so it wouldn't overpower anyone who came near the bathroom. Sue opened the lid of the hamper and pulled out the large garbage bag, dragging it downstairs and into the foyer. She ran back up because she remembered she had to get dressed. She was hoping Maureen would remember to bring that cassette tape. *How will we test the tape to make sure it's the right tape? There must be a tape recorder or player somewhere, and besides Maureen always brings her Walkman. There's another thing. There's a way to duplicate audio tape.*

It was an hour later when Brielle, a gradate student in Psychology, was standing before her group of two men and two women at the 9/11 support group. The African-American brushed her dreadlocks out of her face and said, "I heard that today's going to be a big moment for our women. Maureen has agreed to throw out that audio tape with her daughter's phone call on it. I have the piece of paper that she signed the last time we met."

Sue thought to herself, *Oh I forgot about that, but what if she was lying?*

"Sue promised to bring in her daughter's laundry."

The men and Maureen wrinkled up their noses as Sue grabbed the large garbage bag by the handles from under the table. "Don't worry; I sprayed it with Febreeze so it wouldn't offend anybody."

Maureen thought to herself *How do I know that's all of the laundry?*

Brielle took another note from her folder. "Sue signed a note for me too, stating this is all of the laundry that was in the apartment."

Maureen brought along her Walkman cassette player as usual. Brielle took it from her and opened up the compartment. "O.K." this looks like one of those tapes that you buy to put in a telephone answering machine." She put the earphones on and then pressed a button to rewind the tape. The therapist listened to it. It reminded her of what she had seen on the news for the past year, goodbye calls from passengers of several airplanes that had been hijacked. This one nearly made her cry. Thirteen is not an age in which a girl should be saying goodbye to her family.

"I have a question."

"Yes Sue."

"What if she has other copies of that final call?"

"Her husband told us that he made sure she didn't have any other copies."

Maureen piped up, "Well what if she hasn't brought us all the clothes from the apartment?"

"Just a minute," Sue retaliated.

"That's enough. We're here to support each other and get over this crisis," Brielle said, holding her hands out like a crossing guard stopping traffic. She got up and walked toward the door where a large plastic trashcan was standing. "Who wants to be the first one to do the discarding?"

"I will!" insisted Maureen. She walked up to the trashcan, removed the lid and tossed it on the floor. The bereaved mother opened up her Walkman and removed the cassette, showing, holding it, displaying it as though it were "show and tell" in grade school again. "Would anyone like to examine the tape?"

"I played the tape," Brielle spoke up, "It definitely has the phone call on it."

"But maybe there are some people who think I made a copy of this tape."

"I think we went through that already. Just get rid of the tape," Brielle replied.

Maureen started yanking the tape out of its casing until most of it lay on the floor.

"Wouldn't it have been easier for you to just throw the cassette out into the trash?" suggested Brielle.

"Some people might think I would come sneaking back in to retrieve the tape," leering at Sue.

"Nobody would think that."

She pulled the rest of the tape off the capstans and reels, then threw the empty container into the trashcan. Before Brielle could say anything, Maureen got down on both knees and scooped up the wad of magnetic tape, stretching a section of it out until it broke; little by little she took each broken piece and dumped it into the trashcan.

One man started to complain, "This looks like it's gonna to take a long time. I have to meet my wife for lunch soon."

"No it won't," said Brielle, "We have a forty-five minute session and we only began it fifteen minutes ago."

"I'm finished," Maureen said calmly as she returned to her seat. "Would you like a pair of sharp scissors, Sue?"

"No Thank you," Sue said abruptly.

"What's with you two?"

Sue and Maureen were silent as Sue got up and grabbed the large garbage bag. She held the bag in high in the air with both hands. "Would anyone like to inspect the clothes?"

Everyone shook their heads. Another man answered, "How can we tell these were the clothes that were in the apartment and not some clothes that she left behind?"

"She cleaned out her entire closet when she moved."

"But how do we know that?" the second man replied. "How do we know that these aren't some of your old clothes that you want to get rid of?"

"These clothes are too tight on me."

"You tried them on?" asked Maureen.

"No, I happen to know that my daughter wears a smaller size than I do. Make that wore a smaller size than I do."

The first man added, "Why didn't you wash them and give them away to charity?"

"I never thought of that and they were sitting in the hamper for a week before we got to them. You see, Laura didn't think she would die before she had the chance to do her laundry. We were so busy with things that we didn't get back to the apartment for a week after the incident." Sue picked up the bag and gently placed it in the trashcan.

"Then you should have thrown them out in the trash," the second man responded.

Brielle said, "I'd like to spend the next half an hour understanding why you are at each other's throats," directing her attention to the women.

"I resent people getting into my private business. What's it to her that I kept my daughter's last phone call?"

Sue spoke, "I lost a daughter, too. In fact, I just lost my grandson. He never had a chance. He was hooked up to a respirator ever since he was born. He finally died of a heart attack. Can you imagine a four month old dying from a heart attack? I never even got to say goodbye them. You got to at least say goodbye to your daughter. I know she didn't live as long as mine, but at least you got to say goodbye to your daughter."

*   *   *   *

Twenty Minutes Later.
Sue was the only one left in the room with Brielle.

"That was quite a show you and Maureen put on today," Brielle moved the trashcan further to the door. Sue closed it.

"I think I made an enemy."

"Oh she'll get over. Losing that cassette was like losing her daughter all over again."

"I hope so. I really didn't do anything wrong."

"Well, I want to take this trashcan out to the dumpster and then return it to the cafeteria where I borrowed it. After that I have another group meeting right before lunch."

"I was embarrassed to mention this during group, but last night I had a dream."

Brielle lifted her eyes from the trashcan and looked into her patient's eyes. "OH?"

"I went to see a fortune teller. I remembered that Pete mentioned in the group last week he was thinking of going."

"I guess your knowing that you would be coming again today made you think of that moment."

"We talked about Laura and how she felt about my relationship with Mitch and the naming of the baby. Especially the baby. I'm still annoyed that Laura never discussed being pregnant when she was alive."

"How did your dream about what Laura told you make you feel?"

"Good because she's glad that I'm working on making my life simpler by cutting back on my work. Maybe that will help. When Laura was pregnant, she not only didn't tell me she was expecting she didn't even discuss with me or her father what she wanted to name the baby. You think that Caroline was telling me the truth about what Laura wanted to name the baby."

"I don't see why she would lie to you."

"Aren't daughters supposed to discuss everything with their mothers and not their future mother in laws?"

"Well, not necessarily, but it is something to think about."

"Do you mind telling me how old you are and what your credentials are?"

"I'll be twenty-four. I'm a Psychology major going for my Masters Degree and I expect to complete it this May. I'm planning to start work on my PhD this fall."

"My would have been son-in-law just turned twenty-four. Because of his injury from incident he couldn't help us name the baby. Laura would have been twenty-three in March." I've been thinking about that dream ever since I got up this morning."

"In dreams people see the dream version of the person, and Laura probably would have wanted the two of you to resolve your differences and be happy together."

"Then you don't believe the dead can speak to you in your dreams?"

"I don't personally believe such things," when Brielle shook her head you could hear the clanging of the wooden beads strung on her dreadlocks. "Some people do and if it helps them and it if it helps you." She shrugged her shoulders, helplessly.

"Sometimes I go visit Laura, just to talk. I was thinking about packing a picnic lunch and spreading it out near her grave."

Brielle laughed. "You better check with the office about that. I never heard of such a thing, but it sounds like a good idea. Would you do me a favor and help me take this trashcan down to the dumpster?" Sue opened the door as Brielle dragged the trashcan into the hallway. The two held the handles on each side of the can and carried it to the elevator.

CHAPTER 24

▼

THE SECOND YEAR.

"**No you can't see it!**" Bari Lynn cried out. "**It's so ugly that I wish I could throw it away. I am going to place it in my wallet behind my student identi-fication card and only bring it out when absolutely necessary!**"

"I showed you mine when I got it three months ago," replied Nicole.

Caroline walked out of the kitchen and into the living room, dressed in a short-sleeved blouse and shorts that went down to her knee caps.

"Cut it out you two. I'm going to bring Matt home today and I want you," she looked directly at Bari Lynn, "to dust and vacuum his bedroom and get it ready for him while I'm gone." Caroline scanned the room, looking for her purse. She spotted it on a chair near the sofa where Bari Lynn and Nicole were sitting. Caroline walked out of the front door and headed for the minivan. Just as Caroline started the motor, Nicole turned to Bari Lynn, "Would you like to go over the college catalogs I brought over for you to see?"

Bari Lynn got up from the sofa, "I don't know why? I can't go away to a nice four-year college like I want to. Wow, one year ago, I wouldn't have hesitated."

"Is it because of Matt?"

"Yes, but you know something. I just thought of something."

"What?"

"I suppose I wouldn't have been able to go to a four-year college a year ago because my mom would have told me that it was too expensive."

The girls headed for Matt's bedroom.

"Didn't Matt go to a four-year college?"

"He went to a two-year college, got an associates degree and then he went to some kind of other two-year college that had other courses that he needed to get his bachelors."

"Oh that's a waste. Bari Lynn, if I get accepted at one of those residential four-year colleges I'm gonna miss you."

"I'll miss you, too. We still have until June before we graduate. Niki, do you have any idea what you would like to major in when you get to college?"

The two girls sat down on Matt's bed and talked.

"I thought about art or something like that, but if I did my parents would kill me," said Nicole.

"Really?"

"They want me to major in something that will give me skills to earn a decent living when I get out of college. The trouble is that I don't know what I want to do."

"I was like that last year. All I cared about was cheerleading."

"You really know what you want to study in college? You're probably the only friend I've got who knows what she wants to study in college."

"I want to become some kind of therapist, either in a hospital or in a rehab center. I want to help people like Matt to get better."

"You mean a physical therapist?"

"I don't know what they call it, but they work in rehabs and teach people skills they can get jobs in."

"An occupational therapist?"

"Something like that, but not someone that teaches people to make wicker baskets. I'll find out what the name of it is."

"That's really noble of you, Bari Lynn."

"Let's hope I can get accepted in a college. I think I became inspired a little bit too late."

"Why is it too late?"

"I went to see my guidance counselor about my plans for college and she said that a C average in the sciences is not exactly what a good medical college is looking for."

"OOO," Nicole responded as though she had seen a bird electrocute itself on the telephone wire. "What are you gonna do?"

"I asked her, if I really study hard and get a good grade on my SAT test maybe that will make up for all these years that I didn't do well in science."

"What about that C—you got two years ago in biology? You know, the grade your mother calls the mercy grade."

"I asked my guidance counselor and she told me that I would have to find a teacher who's teaching biology that wouldn't mind if I re-took the subject in his class."

Nicole looked around the room at the black and white pictures on the wall of Matt's high school days. "I didn't know Matt was a football player in high school?"

"Quarterback," Bari Lynn said as she got up from the slightly wrinkled bed, went to the pictures on the wall and started dusting them off with one of Matt's old T shirts. "When I think about how he is now, I get sick."

"Don't look at it like that. He has gotten much better."

"My mom tells me that he's going to get better all the time, but we shouldn't expect him to get completely better."

"I've been listening to this for an entire year and I'm really getting tired of hearing it. I think it's great that you want to be a therapist some day."

"You're right. Now that I think about it I'm getting tired of hearing myself talk about it."

"Here's something to think about. Your mom is coming home with your brother soon and if you don't finish the dusting and vacuuming, she is going to kill you."

"How do you know she is going to kill me?"

"In my experience, Bari Lynn, mothers like to go at their children when they don't do what they are told to do."

"How many mothers have you researched?" asked Bari Lynn, picking up men's' toiletries from the top of Matt's dresser and placing them on the bed.

"Just one and one is enough for me," replied Nicole. Nicole moved over a little to make room for the toiletries that started to slide down into the temporary crater that Nicole made sitting on the bed. "These things are sliding into my thigh," Nicole said as she scooped them up in her hands.

"Hold on to them for me and you can hand them back to me when I am ready."

"I'll do that," she said examining the toiletries. Nicole looked over the toiletries and commented on them, "Matt uses *Old Spice*. You're kidding, my dad uses this stuff," she laughed. Bari Lynn stopped dusting the dresser, turned around, tilted her head to the right and placed her hands on her hips. Ignoring the body language, Nicole continued, "I didn't know that Matt used *Brut* cologne, but wouldn't that clash with the *Old Spice*?"

"Come on, Niki, hand it over," insisted Bari Lynn.

Nicole was about to toss the *Old Spice* and the *Brut.*"

"Just hand them to me one by one. If you toss them, they may break and get all over the floor and then we'llhave a mess." Nicole got up off Matt's bed and one by one handed Bari Lynn the aftershave and the cologne to place back on the top of the dresser. "Are you planning to clean up his underwear drawer?" asked Nicole.

"No, that's my mom's area. Whatever do you want to check out the underwear drawer for?"

"You really do need to take biology again. I want to know if Matt is a boxer or brief man."

"I'll tell you one thing," said Bari Lynn.

Nicole was like a dog eyeing a strip of bacon.

"If we don't get this room dusted and vacuumed by the time my mom gets home I am going to put the blame on you for distracting me."

Nicole looked about as down as an audience participant whose raffle ticket lost her the prize by one digit. "You really know how to let people down, don't you?"

"The vacuum is out in the hall closet, Nik. Go get it for me, please."

Reluctantly, Nicole left Matt's bedroom and went over to the hall closet and got out a vacuum cleaner with the bag in the front. She dragged the vacuum cleaner out of the closet as though she were a plow horse trying to get a farm field ready to planting. "This thing is heavy," Nicole complained to Bari Lynn. Bari Lynn remained standing at by the dresser, watching Nicole. Nicole dragged the vacuum cleaner into the bedroom; she unwrapped the cord from the cord holder and then plugged the vacuum into the wall. The friend turned on the switch of vacuum cleaner and nothing happened. "Great! All of this trouble lugging this thing in here and now it doesn't even work," grumbled Nicole. Bari Lynn walked over to the Nicole and flicked the switch on the wall beside the entryway. The motor roared. "Now what else do I do?" asked Nicole.

"Press this lever down with your foot and it will make the vacuum cleaner easy to operate."

Nicole was able to move the vacuum cleaner around in the room.

"Did you check to see if there is a bag in the vaccum cleaner?" asked Bari Lynn.

"Uh Oh!" panicked Nicole as she stopped the vaccum right in front of Matt's bed. She went around the front of the vacuum cleaner and opened up the lid that hid the vacuum cleaner bag. She breathed a sigh of relief when she realized that there was a bag in the vacuum cleaner. After examining it for a few minutes, she realized that it was half full. "Should I change the bag?" asked Nicole.

"You can change vacuum cleaner bags and you can't run a vacuum cleaner?" asked Bari Lynn.

"Well it does look easier than the one my mom has. She has the kind with the bag in the back of the machine. You know the kind with another plastic bag that snaps up the front of the bag to hold in the paper vacuum bag in place."

"We had that kind. It used to expand like a balloon when the bag got fuller. I used to think it would explode, but it never did," answered Bari Lynn. "Look, I'll go to the coat closet and get a fresh bag." Bari Lynn left the room. Nicole got up and quickly sneaked a peak inside Matt's dresser and quickly closed it up. She smiled like an imp.

"Speaking of explosion," Nicole asked, "Do you ever fear for the future?"

Bari Lynn came back in the room carrying a new vacuum cleaner bag. She got down on her knees, undid the lid of the bag container on the vacuum cleaner. She noticed the nearly hysterical look on Nicole's face. "I don't think I want to talk about that," said Bari Lynn.

"Why not? I think about it," answered Nicole fearfully.

"Well, the president has the new team, the homeland security. I think Tom Ridge sounds like he knows what he's doing."

"Don't you ever wonder about the future? Don't you ever wonder if you will ever be able even finish that first year of college?"

"I'm working on my grades and if I have any problem. I can also get a tutor."

"That's not what I mean. I mean the plane crash."

"Are you scared?"

"Yeah."

"The government is working to try to do something about it. They are stepping up security and they even have all kinds of equipment to scan with so that they can tell if someone is carrying a concealed weapon. I heard that if someone is taking a trip on an airline that they can't even come up to the waiting area and wait with you there anymore. It's not like the entire attack is being ignored. I see things on the news all the time about people being arrested because our government thinks they may be behind the incident."

"Do you really believe that?"

"O.K." said Bari Lynn, snapping on the cover and then getting into a standing position. "I just replaced the bag and we are ready to start vacuuming again. Nicole, lift up the ends of the bedspread so that they don't get caught in the vacuum cleaner." Nicole lifted up the ends of the bedspread and flipped them slightly over for Bari Lynn. "If I wanted to do housework, I would have stayed home and clean my room."

"Bari Lynn, I asked if you really believed that?" The answer was never given as the girls heard a vehicle pull up to the house.

✳   ✳   ✳   ✳

Caroline pulled up into the driveway in the minivan. She parked it right behind the Volkswagen Jetta which was parked behind the Geo Metro. After finishing the vacuuming in Matt's room, Bari Lynn no sooner unplugged the cord when she heard Caroline wheeling Matt into the house. Bari Lynn and Nicole left Matt's bedroom, walked down the hall and entered the living room. One at a time putting the brakes on Matt's wheelchair, Caroline was smiling from ear to ear. "I have to go out to the car; I mean the van for something. Matt and I have a surprise for you." Caroline left the house again. Bari Lynn and Nicole looked at each other with that *what's up with her* look on their faces. The two shrugged together. "O.K. Matt!" exclaimed Bari Lynn. Matt looked at Bari Lynn and said, "What!"

"What is the surprise?"

CHAPTER 25

▼

MATT'S SURPRISE.

"I don't know," Matt responded.

"But you were in the van with the surprise?" pleaded Bari Lynn

"I was?"

Caroline opened the screen door with only one hand, while the other hands held what looked like a folded tray without the tray. Matt looked as surprised as Bari Lynn and Nicole.

Caroline couldn't have been more delighted if she were about to model a mink fur coat. She set the folded piece of metal down on the rug and pulled the contraption apart with both hands pulling in opposite directions. "What is it?" asked Nicole. Matt had a look on his face that read the same question that Nicole just asked.

"Matt you know what it is," answered Caroline. The metal contraption had wheels on the back end, much like the small front wheels of Matt's wheelchair.

The front of the metal contraption had white rubber tips on the bottom which one would find on canes and crutches. "Come on Matt. I want you to get up and show Bari Lynn and Nicole how you use your new walker."

Bari Lynn started to think maybe she would lose her chance to drive Matt around in the van. Since he will be walking, maybe Caroline might sell the van. Bari Lynn felt like asking her mother, but decided to fight back the urge.

"No! I don't want to," Matt protested to using the walker.

"Why not?" asked Caroline.

"Because I don't feel like it."

"You don't want to be in a wheelchair all your life? Do you?" asked Caroline.

"Yes," Matt nodded.

"Girls, you should have seen Matt walking along the hall at the rehab center. You'd be so proud of him."

Nicole spoke up, "Matt, Christopher Reeve would love the chance to use a walker like yours."

"Then give him my walker," answered Matt.

"I didn't mean it the way it sounded," applogized Nicole.

"Matt, I realize that you are used to your wheelchair, but you see this walker is an improvement. You're getting better. Very soon you will be ready to be retrained for a new job," said Caroline.

"No."

*   *   *   *

Matt sat up in bed and called out to his mother. Caroline entered. She brought his walker close to the side of his bed, positioning it so he could stand up and use the walker. As Matt stood up on his two legs and hung on to the walker, Caroline stood up in front of him like a traffic cop and began to direct Matt from his bedroom into the bathroom. He started banging into walls and furniture with his walker. Caroline knew her son was only used to using his walker down a long stretch of hallway and not inside a bedroom. Caroline learned from the entire year's experience it'll take the young man some time to get used to the walker, just like it took some time for him to learn how to feed himself again. Matt entered the bathroom and attempted to empty his bladder without shutting the bathroom door. Caroline covered her eyes with the palm of her right hand, closing the door with her left hand. She thought to herself Matt had never been like that since he was a preschooler. In a few seconds, Matt exited the bathroom. Caroline went over to Matt and felt his hands that were bone dry. She asked Matt if he washed his hands. He told her he didn't remember. As she guided him back into the bathroom, guiding his hand to flush the toilet and then leading him to wash and dry his hands, Caroline started to think she was reliving Matt's preschool years with him. How long would he behave like a preschool age child— forever? Caroline, as she handed Matt a towel to dry his hands, knew Matt could only heal so much and then Caroline had to accept him with his permanent disabilities. Matt held the towel in his hands, looking at it as though it was the first time in his life he had ever seen a towel. "Wipe your hands with it. It is for drying your hands with," said Caroline.

"Yeah?" asked Matt as though he had just discovered something new and revolutionary. He continued to stare at his hands holding the towel. Caroline had to demonstrate for him as she wiped his hands with the towel. Caroline had to keep calling Matt's name as he continued to look at what Caroline was doing and then looking away. "I want to leave the bathroom," Matt moaned.

"Not until you turn off the water," said the mother.

"I don't want to," said Matt. She took his hands and placed them on the spigots. Matt turned the spigots off one at a time. "That's great!" said Caroline.

Mrs. Cobel gave instructions to help Matt move his walker safely out of the bathroom with as few bang ups as possible. "Keep it straight. Line it up in the center. That's it." It worked for about a few seconds. They headed for his bedroom to get dressed casually in jeans, sneakers and a sweatshirt for the day.

Walking in front of Matt, with her back to the walker, Caroline guided him through the hallway, through the living room and into the kitchen. Caroline pulled out a chair, turned to him and motioned for Matt to sit down. Then she pointed for him to stand up so she could move the chair closer to the table." Make up your mind!" her son insisted. Matt sat about a half an inch or so away from the table as Caroline went over to the stove and started to make scrambled eggs for him.

In about five minutes Caroline took the frying pan off the cooling down burner and dumped the scrambled eggs out onto a plate. Caroline took out a fork from the drawer and carried the plate and fork over to Matt. She placed them both down. Her son picked up the fork and started to pick up the entire scrambled eggs on the fork. "No," Caroline said. "Scoop up a little on the fork at a time and eat it." Matt scooped up a little on his fork and placed the fork in his mouth. He placed the fork down on his plate, chewing his food with his mouth opened so anyone could see him mush up his food. "Matt close your mouth when you eat," Caroline said gently. She went over to the refrigerator and took out some milk, pouring it into his Sippy cup with the thick plastic built—in straw. She brought it over to the table. In between Matt eating his eggs, Matt sipped his milk.

After the meal, Caroline got Matt his light jacket and got him ready for his first walking session outside. She guided him out the kitchen door, down the walk and out to the sidewalk. Matt had no trouble walking down the sidewalk. The walker was gently lifted up and placed a few feet in front of his legs."You don't have to lift it up. It's a rolling walker. All you have to do is just glide it." He even managed to get down the curb cuts by rolling the device down the slope. Neighbors who were washing their cars, doing gardening, painting lawn chairs looked up and waved at Matt. Even though Matt had known them for years, he looked up with *a who are you expression* on his face. After a straight two block walk, Caroline thought it was time to turn around and go home. Matt protested, "I don't want to turn around and go home now." Caroline nudged Matt, helping him slowly turn himself around with his walker and headed back toward home. He could be manipulated as easily as Bari Lynn could manipulate the vacuum cleaner. As soon as Matt and Caroline walked up the path, Bari Lynn and Nicole were waiting inside of the living room by the front door, watching as Matt made his way up the driveway ahead of Caroline. Bari Lynn and Nicole were all smiles as though they were watching a live sports performance. Bari Lynn opened up the front door and the screen/storm door as Matt glided up the path and into the house. "Bravo!" Nicole and Bari Lynn cried as Matt maneuvered himself over to the sofa and sat down. Thinking about Matt's accomplishment, "How do you feel?"

"I have to go to the bathroom," Matt replied. Nicole and Bari Lynn lifted him up on both sides so he could use his walker. He headed for the hallway where the bedrooms were and walked into the bathroom. He walked into the bathroom without turning on the light or closing the door. Bari Lynn walked by and noticing Matt standing over the toilet bowl, she closed the door. Bari Lynn shook her head thinking that she wondered if Matt would ever remember to close the door of the bathroom. In a few minutes Matt walked out of the bathroom. Caroline happened to be in the living room. She walked over to Matt and felt his hands. They were bone dry. Caroline led Matt back to the bathroom. Caroline turned on the light to see Matt had urinated without lifting the seat. Her son had forgotten to flush the toilet again. With her left hand she flushed the toilet, grabbed a moist nap from a cylindrical plastic container and wiped up the toilet seat. With her right hand she held on to Matt's rolling walker. Caroline walked towards the sink. "I want you to wash your hands."

"I don't want to."

"Yes!" demanded Caroline. "Turn on the water," she placed Matt's right hand on the cold spigot. He turned the lever on. Caroline placed Matt's right hand on the hot one and he turned it on. She placed his hand under the soap dispenser on the wall and he pressed against it allowing an amber soap jell into his hand. He started to rub it into his left hand. "Place some of it into your right hand and rub them together like I showed you this morning." The soap was drying on Matt's hands as he rubbed them together. "Place them under the water and rub. You'll see it lather." Matt placed his hands under the water as he rubbed the soap into his hands. The soap had dried too much to lather because he didn't rub his soapy hands under the water immediately. Caroline grabbed a hand towel and gave it to Matt. He looked at the towel as though it was something he had never seen before. "I showed you this morning. Rub your hands with towel." Every time Matt went to the bathroom, no matter how many times Caroline went over the ritual of using the bathroom, Matt just didn't seem to get it. Caroline wondered if it was Matt's brain injury or if it was his new attitude. Caroline wondered if he would ever get back to the proper bathroom behavior which he had before the accident.

Caroline walked into the kitchen to check on her crock pot of beef stew to see if it was ready. Bari Lynn helped Caroline set the table. "Mom, can Niki join us for dinner?"

"I suppose so," Caroline said weakly. "She really should call her mother and see if she doesn't mind."

Nicole sat down at the kitchen table and pulled out her cell phone. She called her mother, "Mom, Bari Lynn and her mother invited me to dinner." Nicole paused for a moment and then said, "Thanks Mom, you rock." She pressed the end call button on the phone and then the pressed the power switch. She placed the phone in her pocket again.

Bari Lynn sat down at the kitchen table with Nicole. "The driving teacher at school says that I'll be ready for my driver's test on Saturday."

Caroline brought the crock pot of beef stew over to the kitchen table. "If you are asking to go out with your driving teacher on Saturday, it is alright."

"How did your visit with the biology teacher go?"

"Good news," Bari Lynn said as she cut up her brother's serving of beef stew in very fine slices. "He said that I could enter his class. So, the teacher wrote me a note and I took it to my guidance counselor. She wrote it on my roster and now I can makeup my C from biology." Matt, sitting on a kitchen chair at the table, took a spoon and scooped up some beef stew to feed himself. "Everything seems to be going well for you then," Caroline said after she swallowed her beef stew. "What about your math?"

Bari Lynn started eating her own beef stew. Between bites she said, "My math grades are fine."

"It looks like both of my children are making a lot of progress," Caroline smiled.

The tittering buzz of the phone sounded. "I wonder who this is at dinner-time." Caroline got up from the table and answered the phone.

Nicole and Bari Lynn listened to Caroline's side of the phone conversation. It was Sue Daniels on the phone.

Bari Lynn moved almost so close to Nicole she almost sat on her friend's lap. She whispered to Nicole, "It's Matt's would be mother-in-law on the phone."

"Oh. Move over you are almost sitting on my lap."

Bari Lynn moved back over to her seat.

Caroline went back over to her seat. "That was Mrs. Daniels. She and her husband want to come over tonight to show us a video."

"Yeah?" Bari Lynn, Nicole and Matt cried in unison. They were getting as excited children on the last day of school and the first day of summer vacation. "What kind of video?"

"They are looking at one of those retirement developments and they want us to see it."

Matt squinted and looked as though showing such a video were absurd. Bari Lynn and Nicole's mood dropped like the air pouring out of a balloon. "Mom, can I go over and spend the evening over Nicole's house?" asked Bari Lynn.

"I want to go, too!" protested Matt.

"You'll miss a nice little video."

"Oh, what a shame. I suppose I'll have to wait until they play it on television," quipped Bari Lynn.

"Very funny," Caroline said as she started gathering the dinner plates. "Girls, I want you to help me clear the table before the Daniels get here." Nicole and Bari Lynn started collecting the plates, bowls and glasses, bringing them over to the kitchen counter. Nicole went back to the table to find Matt hardly touched his dinner. "You barely touched your food," Nicole commented.

"Just leave it there. Matt always eats like that," Bari Lynn responded.

"So when will it be alright to take his dinner plate away from him?" asked Nicole.

Returning to the table, Caroline said, "I think I'll give him until the end of dessert."

"What about him eating the coffee cake?" asked Nicole.

"He rarely wants anything after dinner," replied Caroline. The mother went over to the hutch and opened up the bottom drawer, taking out a white linen table cloth. It was the good table cloth. Underneath it she found the flag which draped Harvey's coffin. She hadn't looked at it in over ten years since the funeral. The Desert Storm widow didn't bother to unfold the flag which was so nicely folded in triangular, the point of the fold alternating right and then left. She held it in the palm of her hand and then she placed it back in the bottom of the drawer The mother of two hadn't used this table cloth in ten years.

"What do you have for dessert beside coffee cake?" asked Nicole from the kitchen

"I was thinking that with the Daniels coming over, maybe I should have the after dinner treat in the living room. I can set up some trays and put some napkins out on the coffee table."

"Since we don't want to see the video, can we have our dessert in here?" asked Bari Lynn, fearing a rejection from Caroline. "We have rice pudding or Jello. What about fruit cup?"

"I forgot to buy the fruit cup."

"Where is Shauna when you need her?"

"Do you really want to miss the video?" asked Caroline.

"Let me put it this way, Mom. If the closest movie theatre in town was showing that video, would you pay money to see it?"

"Probably not. I think that the purpose of this video is so that people who come to that retirement development will see what they have to offer. Then hopefully people will buy homes in that development."

"Do you want to live in a retirement development?" asked Bari Lynn.

"Not right now. I have a few years or more left of work before I retire."

"I thought the Daniels were still working?" asked Bari Lynn.

"I don't know, that's what she called it. We'll find out what it really is when they get here."

"You mean you will find out. Nicole and I aren't ready to retire yet. We are still in high school."

The doorbell rang. The couple entered the Cobel home as though they were attending a reunion. The Daniels embraced Caroline. "Oh yeah, here is the video," said Sue Daniels as she whipped it out of her purse like a rabbit out of a magicians hat. "I can't wait for you to see it." Caroline took the video and walked over to her VCR as Nicole and Bari Lynn stood there in the living room rolling their eyes.

"Where is Matt? I heard you brought him home to stay," inquired Mitch.

"He's in the kitchen," said Caroline,"wait till you see him. Have we got a surprise for you?"

"Look, I'm sorry we have a test for tomorrow and we really must start studying," said Bari Lynn.

"Not on the second week of school you don't," answered Caroline. She turned on the floor model television set, inserted the video and pressed play. The screen was very snowy."

"Oh dear what a shame," responded Bari Lynn, "I guess we'll have to miss it."

"Oh no you won't. I found the problem," Caroline turned the channel slightly. "Someone had my television set on the wrong channel for the VCR." Bari Lynn and Nicole shrugged their shoulders. As the video came on Nicole said, "Mrs. Cobel, my mother told me to be sure to come home right after dinner." Bari Lynn sneered at Nicole thinking she was being deserted at her hour of need.

"Sure Nicole. It was nice having you," said Caroline.

"See you in school tomorrow, Bar," Nicole said as she headed for the front door. Bari Lynn gave her an icy look as though she were planning to stab her at the next convenient opportunity.

Caroline slapped Bari Lynn on the shoulder, "Don't give me any trouble young lady," she whispered to Bari Lynn, "Now take a seat somewhere in this room and watch the video. Where is your brother?"

"In the kitchen where we left him." Matt suddenly made an appearance with his rolling walker. The Daniels clapped and gave Matt a standing ovation as though he were a nightclub act.

Matt looked at them as though they were wearing some sort of odd clothing, "Huh?" he asked. He moved so close to Sue he ran over her foot.

Seeing that, Caroline said, "What do you say when you run over someone's foot?"

"Move it."

Caroline said, "Matt, why don't you find a seat?"

"I don't feel like it," he moaned.

"Are you tired?" asked Caroline.

Matt nodded his head.

"O.K. then you can go back and get ready for bed."

Bari Lynn gave Caroline a look and spoke as loud as she could with a whisper, *"Mom!"*

Caroline answered, "Bari Lynn you can go back with Matt and help him get ready for bed."

"Gee thanks," Bari Lynn answered sarcastically.

"Be sure to come back when you are finished so you will at least see some of the video," said Caroline.

Bari Lynn gave her mother one of those knifing planning looks for a second and then followed Matt into the bedroom wing of the house, via the adjacent hallway off the living room.

A lanky suntanned man in his fifties, wearing a hat, a short-sleeved polo shirt, shorts and sneakers looked as though he were ready to go out and play golf. He stood outside brand newly constructed town houses all painted grayish blue with white trim. "Welcome to Keane Heritage Village. I'm Ernest Fields and I am here on this video to show you why you should buy one of our homes." Mr. Fields walked over to one of the homes and entered. "This is Mr. Twist who lives in this particular home. What do you have here?" the tour guide asked.

"It is all on one floor," the resident answered. "I have a one-bedroom, but these town houses can have up to three bedrooms. Over here is a cozy little kitchenette. I don't have to eat all my meals here. There is a cafeteria in which I can have one meal per day. I usually have my dinner there with the other residents."

The video goes on to show people in the cafeteria lined up with trays at a buffet style set up. In the film, Mr. Twist went up to the man who was carving the rib roast. The man put a thin sliver of meat on the plate. "May I have some more please?" The man behind the craver looked at Mr. Twist as though he would like to carve him up next, **"More. You Want More!"**

Backing away a little, Mr. Twist said, "Well on second thought, I probably do have enough as it is."

The video went on to show Mr. Fields leaving, "Thank you for showing us your home, Mr. Twist."

The tour guide does a voice-over as the video shows the activities. "We have a lovely clubhouse, for parties and socializing." There is a table of four playing poker shown. There are some retirement pension checks lying in the center of the table. One person takes both of his hands, scoops the retirement checks up and moves them close to the end of the table where he is sitting. "I win. Want to play again, anyone?" The other three are seen starting to get up out of their seats.

The video goes on to show an aerial view of the tennis court and the swimming pool. "We have tennis, swimming, and by the way, after this tour I am going to play some golf in our twice as much fun golf course, with thirty-nine holes." The video shows the golf course.

Two paramedics with a gurney show up. "Have I forgotten anything?" He looks and sees the paramedics with a gurney. One of them excuses himself and says he needs to get in to see the resident of the house which Mr. Fields in standing in front of. "Oh sure," Mr. Fields steps several doors down. "We have a medical clinic and hospital right on the premises in case one of the residents needs some medical attention." A frail white-haired lady, strapped down on the gurney is taken a few minutes later out of her home. "What's wrong with this patient?"

"We are pretty sure she has either had a heart attack, angina attack, or maybe even some food poisoning."

"This place has all the conveniences. What would this lady do if we didn't have our medical clinic on site here? Sometimes when a person needs medical attention, minutes are very crucial. It can be a matter of life or death if quick medical attention isn't given. Keane Heritage Village understands. Keane Heritage Village also understands people like to get out and go places." There are some still pictures shown of some people standing and posing on the capitol steps in Washington, and other people posing in front of New York City's Statue of Liberty. "We have day trips to places like New York City, Washington D.C. and other trips. We also have shopping trips for people who want to go clothes shopping or buy groceries, but don't drive. If you feel you don't need that big house anymore and want to find a nice convenient place right here in Bergen County, you give us a call at this number 201-555-1212 and be sure to ask for Ernie Fields. I would be glad to help you."

"Wasn't that a great video?" asked Sue Daniels.

"Bergen County?" asked Caroline as she went over to the VCR and removed the video tape. "What about the tour of the homes. I didn't see any of that."

"You've seen one townhouse you've seen them all," said Sue.

"If I were moving into a community like that, I would like to see a tour of the entire house, even pictures of the homes."

"They have all of that in the brochure and I guess they didn't want to duplicate it on the video. We'll be neighbors; won't that be great?" sounding like an excited schoolgirl

"Is this a retirement development?"

"Yes it is."

"Are you and Mitch planning to retire?"

"No. I don't think that just because we are moving into a retirement development that means that they can control how my husband and I live our lives. If we want to work, we will."

"Oh, I see. I think before you move you ought to check that out with the management, don't you think?"

"Here is the best part. I cut back my interior decorating a bit. I work with the little people exclusively."

"How sweet of you," Caroline placed the video into its plastic box and snapped the lid shut. She held the video in one hand as she tapped it up and down into the palm of her other hand. "How many bedrooms are you getting?"

"I thought I told you that Mitch and I are getting a one-bedroom. That house is way too big for us now."

"I thought it was way too big for you before."

"The best part_____"

Caroline walked over to the Daniels to return the video. "I thought that you already told me the best part."

"I left out the really really best part."

"What is the really really best part?" asked Caroline who stood before them with her arms folded across her chest.

"We'll be able to help you with Matt, you know, take him off your hands every now and then."

"Do me a favor if you do take him to visit you."

"What is that?"

"Don't take him into that cafeteria for any meals."

"Mitch and I would probably take him out to a restaurant."

"It looks like I am going to have to find some outpatient rehabilitation to help us with Matt."

CHAPTER 26

▼

SOME KIND OF A WINTER.

It was seven in the morning as Caroline sat on the sofa in the living room, looking out the window as the first big snow storm of the season fell on the lawn. Ever since the winter of 2001, Caroline asked herself what she was going to do to get through the snow. Usually some neighborhood boys, from the local junior high school would come over asking Caroline if she wanted her walkway and driveway shoveled for a few bucks. She wished now she had gotten their phone number, so she could call them up and ask them to come help her with the shoveling. Now, it was too soon because it would not be worth scooping out when the snow was still falling. She knew the snow had to stop falling before any clean out could take place. Ever since the winter season of 2001 Caroline had a fantasy which took her back to March of 1996, five and half years before the World Trade Center disaster. Five and half years before that airline not only destroyed that twin tower, but also destroyed the Matt who Caroline used to know. It was the twin tower tragedy which took the Matt whom Caroline used to know and left her with a Matt whom she needed to get used to. People told her she was lucky Matt survived the calamity, but sometimes Caroline wondered. Everyday, even though Matt did make some strides to improve and return to his old self, Caroline wondered if she really was lucky Matt survived the disaster. She looked out the window of the 2002–2003 winter snowfall and went back in her mind to March 1996. Ten-year-old Bari Lynn was thrilled as she came down the hallway and into the living room, announcing t the radio mentioned her school had a snow day. She could go sledding down a neighborhood hill with her friends. Matt was a senior in high school who also had a snow day. Even though in 2002, Matt was still in his bed asleep, it was like the Matt of 1996 were a memory of someone who had gone away for good, never to return. It was if the Matt she had loved and raised had perished in the crisis. Now she was forced to live with a stranger who tried each and everyday to become more and more like the Matt she used to know, but coming up short every time. Eighteen-year-old Matt went up to Caroline in her fantasy. "What are you doing all dressed?" she asked. "Aren't the schools closed because of the snowstorm?"

"Yes, but I know that you have to go to work today," answered Matt.

"But the snow hasn't stopped falling yet," said Caroline.

"I figured that I would clear l out the driveway for you so that you can get your car out," replied Matt who headed outside, leaving the front door opened, as he walked to the garage in order to the shovel. In Caroline's mind she heard the creaking of the garage door as it went up manually. She looked out onto the driveway and saw only her Geo Metro sitting there wearing a coat of thick white snow. Matt came back out of the garage with a heavy shovel and a scraper with a brush at the end, "Mom," he called out. "Would you like me to see if the car will start?"

"Just a minute, Matt, I have to get my purse." As Caroline got off the sofa and headed into the dining room area where she left her purse on the table, Bari Lynn bounded past her in a blurry streak of pastel pink. As Caroline reached into her purse to take out her car keys, she could hear Matt and Bari Lynn quarreling outside by the garage. When Caroline took her car keys and closed her purse. She headed for the door, noticing Bari Lynn dragging her sled down the driveway. Caroline grabbed her pale blue down jacket from the coat closet, put on her snow boots and adjusted the hood of the garment. "**Bari Lynn**," Caroline called out. **"Isn't it a little early to go sledding?"**

"Don't you remember the deal?" Bari Lynn called back.

"What deal?" Caroline asked, as she slowly headed down the path leading from the house to the sidewalk.

"You know, Mom. If there is a snow day, then I am supposed to go over to Nicole's and spend the day there because you still have to go to work."

"O.K. Bar, have a nice time. Don't fall," Caroline called out. Bari Lynn didn't seem to hear Caroline, as Bari Lynn trudged along the unshoveled sidewalk towards Nicole's house. This was the very same Nicole that Bari Lynn was still friends with now in high school. Matt met Caroline at the end of the driveway, "Mom, you didn't have to come outside, I would have gone back to the house."

"Here is the key you wanted," replied Caroline, handing the key over to Matt.

"Now, we'll see if this car will start." Matt walked over to the driver's side of the car and took the brush end of the combination scraper/brush, dusted off the newly fallen coat of snow which was on the car. He dusted the door, the driver's side window, the windshield and just about any part of the exterior of the car covered with snow. He was a gem and Caroline still missed him. When Matt was finished, he found he could open the car door with the car key because the lock had not yet frozen up. Matt started the engine and it purred. Matt called out, "I'll let the engine run a little, Mom."

Caroline said, "You know, I'm still in my nightgown. I think I'll run back into the house and get myself dressed. The Caroline of 2002 fast forwarded in her mind when she was fully dressed and ready to go outside to Matt, who was shoveling the snow around the car while the motor was still running. She remembered how he used to take chances like that. The mother remembered how she used to worry about what would happen if her son was standing behind the car and the emergency brake gave way, allowing the car to slide down the driveway. Caroline in 1996 couldn't imagine the real terror which lay in store for her boy in five and half year's time. Caroline remembered walking outside, going down the path and making a right over to the driveway. She walked over to the driver's side of the car, opened the door, closed the door and strapped herself in. The mother of two remembered how warm and toasty her car felt back in those days. In recent years, she was lucky if the heat was working by the time she was half way down to the salon. Caroline remembered seeing Matt making his way, up and down the driveway, on both sides until Caroline could back the car out of the driveway and go to work. Caroline rolled down the window, "What are you going to do all day while I'm at work?"

"I have some studying to do and then I'll fill out some more forms for college. I have plenty to keep me busy. Have a nice day, Mom."

She was jostled back to the year 2002 by a rap on the door. A man, bundled up and holding a clipboard stood at the door. Caroline screamed when she noticed the woolen scarf wrapped around his nose and mouth.

"Lady, I am here to pick up your son."

CHAPTER 27

▼

THE CLUBHOUSE

It would take about a half an hour to get Matt to the Bergen County Rehab Clubhouse. A tall, striking, reed—thin freckle faced, frizzy red-haired woman came to the entrance to greet Matt as he came in escorted by the Para Transit. Her name was Rosalie, twenty-seven years-old and working towards her PhD in rehabilitation therapy. "Hey guy," she said "where is your jacket?"

"I don't remember?" answered Matt.

"Hey, wait a minute!" Rosalie called out to the Para Transit driver as he was about to leave the building.

"What is it? The driver asked, turning around in his tracks.

"Was Matt wearing his winter coat or any coat for that matter when you picked him up at his house this morning? Maybe he took it off in the van because the heat was on high?"

"No he wasn't." The driver turned around and walked out of the door.

"Tell me something," Rosalie said as they stood in the vestibule by the coat closet.

"What?" asked Matt.

"Did you lose your coat?"

"I don't remember."

"Who got you ready this morning?"

"My sister."

"How old is your sister?"

"She is fifteen."

"When was she born?"

"She was born on September 4, 1985."

"What year is this?"

"It's 2001."

"How old are you?"

"I'm twenty-three."

"When were you born?"

"I was born in 1978."

"You don't realize that in about a month it will be 2003?"

"Yeah?" Matt looked at her as though she were putting him on.

"Yeah! You come in with me and I'll get you a cup of coffee," said Rosalie. Matt followed Rosalie into the room. Some of the other members were in wheelchairs, some had single canes, quad canes, walkers, and some needed no assistance to walk. There were people with severe problems and others with mild problems. Rosalie went over to the kitchenette, poured Matt a mug of coffee and brought it over to him to drink. Matt screamed flinging his hands up in the air, "Take it away! Take it away!" He nearly knocked over the entire mug of coffee, splashing some of it on the table. The young man looked at the small pool of coffee as if it were the first time he'd ever seen the liquid.

"It's just coffee."

"I can't stand the smoke. I can't stand the smoke," he yelled jumping up and down.

Remembering Matt's condition, Rosalie took the mug away and placed it behind the counter. Matt calmed down."Oh. Well maybe if I let it cool down a bit so that it doesn't steam, will that be alright."

Matt nodded his head. He said "If you cancel the plan before two years you have to pay a penalty of $175.00"

Rosalie replied, "Well that's nice to know even though I have no idea what you are talking about."

*   *   *   *

February 2003. It was the day after President's Day.

The county was getting over a very big snowstorm. Caroline's meeting was supposed to be a week before, but was postponed because of the heavy series of snowstorms which had occurred one right after the other. Matt's mother luckily managed to drive the minivan to the meeting. The mother walked through the vestibule, past the wall long coat closet which was on one entire wall of the vestibule. She was greeted at the door by Rosalie, Matt's therapist, who offered to take Caroline's coat and hang it up for her. Caroline declined the offer. Rosalie signaled with her right hand for Caroline to follow her. Matt followed behind them with his walker. The room the threesome walked through looked like one big dining area with square cafeteria-like tables and chairs, and a kitchenette. It was a full house that day, mostly thanks to the help of the Para transit service which most of the members used to come to the Clubhouse. There was another therapist and a few members at the kitchenette, preparing lunch for the members. The entire room had a pretty soft white and light blue décor which made it a cheery place to be. Other members were busy setting out the placemats, silverware, while others were off working with the computers in another part of the building. There was a hallway beyond the kitchenette. The hallway was lined with two bathrooms on the right side, and cabinet and closet space on the left. The hallway led to another room with an elevator and a staircase beside it. Rosalie, Matt and Caroline got aboard the elevator which took them down to the basement part of this basically one story building. It took seconds for the elevator to deposit them in a non basement looking office setting. Around the corner there was one door which led to an office room. It had Formica white office space for each of the four people who helped out at the Clubhouse, the three therapists and the manager. At each office setting was a computer and a telephone able to handle three lines of phone calls. In the back of the room was a long white Formica table with enough chairs for about seven people. As Caroline removed her coat, she started to feel a chill and put her coat back on. "I'm sorry it is a bit chilly in this room. We'll definitely have to check the vents," said Rosalie, as she took a seat across from Caroline. Matt took a seat beside his mother. "We'll only be a moment longer. Our manager and the manager of the program at the main rehab center will be along shortly," Matt's therapist said, speaking to Mrs. Cobel. Walking by, Rosalie sneaked a wink at Matt, who acted as if he had no idea what she was doing. Rosalie got up out of her chair and walked over to a bookcase, along the wall of the office and behind some of the therapists' desks. The bookcase shelved thick black loose-leaf books which contained the personal information of every client who attended the clubhouse. She quickly rifled through the collection of loose-leaf books, as though she were rifling through encyclopedias trying to find a particular volume of the alphabet. She stopped at a large thick book which had the name *Matthew Cobel.* The name was *printed* with a black ballpoint pen on an index card placed in a laminated pocket on the binder of the book. Rosalie removed Matt's book and placed it on her desk. She opened up the side upper right drawer, of her desk, and took out a white lined legal pad from her desk and a pen. She placed the pad on top of the loose-leaf book, the pen in the right side pocket of her faded blue jeans and carried everything to the table. As she headed for the table, the other members of the meeting came into the room. There was one black man, one black woman and one white woman, all somewhere in their thirties and all neatly dressed in office attire. Caroline sat straight up in her chair with her back pressing hard against the back of the chair. She looked at them silently as they took their seats around the table. She thought to herself, she felt like she was in the principal's office for misbehaving in class.

Or maybe it was as though she were in a judge's chambers about to get her sentence doled out to her. One by one the three other people, held their right hands out to Caroline, introducing themselves to her, shaking her right hand and then taking their seats. Only Rosalie seemed to be enjoying herself. Matt seemed to be staring ahead at a Chagall painting of stained glass which hung on the wall behind the three managers. *His mind took him back to springtime 2001. A young man in his thirties came over to Matt's cubicle with Laura. "This is Laura. Laura this is Matt who is probably one of the best reps in the section if not the entire room. "Matt worked in a cubicle which had all type of papers over the sides of it. There were promotions for April. Go to a Verizon in Baltimore, MD and call this 800 number for a free cell phone upgrade when you sign up for a two year phone plan.*

"Oh I am not", Matt responded. "Hello Laura. Nice to meet you," he said with a snicker in his smile.

"Hello," she said with a large smile which almost giggled.

"We just take your head phone and plug it into this part of Matt's headset. Would you take off your headset for a second? Does anyone know where I can get an extra chair?" A young rep with a pierced earring in her tongue found a chair at a cubicle where the rep was absent for the day. "You can use this one. John is out today." She moved it over to Matt's cubicle right beside his chair. Laura sat down and nearly banged her knees up against his desk drawers. The supervisor spoke, "Now Matt is going to log in and get some calls and you will listen to how he conducts his calls so you can get an idea of how it's done." After the supervisor walked away Matt and Laura broke into laughter. "It's so funny that you are in this department now. He didn't even suspect that we knew each other from before. What brought you here?"

"Someone from the corporate office came to visit and I was so nervous that I messed up something. The phone rang and I forgot to answer it and I was dismissed. I think it must have been kismet to bring us to the same department."

"Seeing you at work and dating you just isn't enough for me."

"I never lived with a guy before, well except for my father. That was different."

"How did you know I was going to ask you that?"

"You already asked me to sleep with you. I figured that would be the next step."

He grabbed her knee and started to rub it.

"Don't do that they will think you are sexually harassing me." She looked around to see if anyone was watching.

"I already did that last week, finally. Move in with me, Laura."

"Not here. Ask me over lunch or over at your apartment some time."

Matt was back in February, 2003. "Laura! Laura!" Caroline's attention was averted to Matt. "Shhh. You're interrupting the meeting!" Matt started to stare down at his black shoes which were fastened with leather straps and Velcro.

"So, have you given this some thought Mrs. Cobel?" asked Rosalie.

Caroline felt a rush of fear going through her entire body, and the managers were in a serious mood which could only make Matt's mother seem as though she were about to get really bad news. The manager from the main rehab center spoke first. "Mrs. Cobel, once a month, or, so we like to have meetings with the family members of our clientele, and our clients to discuss the improvements and the problems which we notice. We will, of course give you our recommendations for further improvement on various things concerning your family member, in this case, Matt."

"What do you recommend for Matt?"

"I think that Rosalie should talk to you about Matt since she is his direct therapist."

"Well, Mrs. Cobel, I really think that Matt's progress depends somewhat on your attitude."

"What do you mean?" asked Caroline.

Rosalie opened up Matt's loose-leaf notebook and flipped through the first section of pages. Rosalie separated the rings and took out a form which Caroline had originally filled out when she enrolled Matt. Rosalie handed Mrs. Cobel the part of the form in which Caroline filled out goals she wanted met for Matt. The concerned mother read the goals which read she wanted Matt to be completely cured and back to his original self. "So?" she asked.

"We need to discuss this matter, Mrs. Cobel."

"Why didn't anyone ask me about this when I originally enrolled Matt?"

Berlinda, the clubhouse manager, replied, "I thought maybe you were under stress or something when you filled out this form. I didn't want to upset you with it."

"What's the problem?" asked Caroline, who felt as though she were being backed into a corner by some schoolyard bullies.

Rosalie said, "You see," she sighed, "This is not exactly a goal we can work with."

"Are you telling me there is nothing you can do to help Matt?"

"No. I'm not telling you that. It's like Berlinda may have told you at the beginning. Members of this clubhouse, our clients, are in charge of keeping the clubhouse in order. They are in charge of everything, from typing up letters for the family members to making lunch every day for our members. The idea is that we are working to rehabilitate our members so that they can eventually go back to work."

"Do you really think that Matt may be able to go back to work?"

"Eventually, but that's not the point that I am making," said Rosalie. The therapist was quite aware that Matt's job was to set the table for lunch and he usually acted like a mechanical toy on weak batteries. He had to continually be coaxed in every move he made, but she didn't say anything about it to Matt's mother because it was no news for the family.

"What just is your point?" asked Caroline in a more relaxed state.

"You see, Mrs. Cobel," Rosalie sighed again, "I'm afraid ... I don't want you to take what I am to say, the wrong way."

"Yes?"

"Even though we can work with Matt and eventually help him to lead a productive life, I'm afraid that Matt is never going to become the person he was before the accident." She opened up Matt's book, "We have assessed that he has problems with executive function which means he has trouble planning, organizing, abstract reasoning and making judgments. If he does go back to work he won't be able to do the work that he used to do."

Caroline started to pout and then she went down from there in a gradual emotional landslide which descended with every word. "Why is this happening to me? First it's Harvey. A regular job wasn't good enough for him. He had to be a soldier. He couldn't work in an office. What am I saying? He couldn't work in a safe job. My son's would have been father-in-law is a car dealer and his wife doesn't even appreciate that. I wish Harvey had been a car salesman" She looked over at Matt who not only had no emotional reaction to what she was saying, but was staring out the window looking up at a bird feeding a worm to one of her babies, considering they were in the basement. Caroline cried harder as she spoke of her late husband. "I wish he were here right now. After the war, I had Matt to lean on and do all the chores around the house which Harvey used to do for us."

"You didn't do anything wrong to deserve anything bad. It's just bad luck," answered Rosalie.

Caroline calmed down a little, opened her purse and pulled out a tissue.

"Have you seen someone to talk to, a professional, about Matt's accident?"

"I work five days a week and I have spent all my free time running around and seeing Matt. I just haven't had the time."

"What is your schedule like?" asked Rosalie.

"I work Tuesdays through Saturday and I am off on Mondays."

"Now that Matt comes to the clubhouse five days a week, you now have time to see someone."

"Why do I need counseling?"

"You see, when someone has an accident in which brain injury has taken place then there needs to be a grieving process. I know that you are thinking that since Matt didn't die you probably don't need to grieve, but you do. The Matt you knew before the accident is dead_____"

"Wait a minute!" Caroline held up her right palm like a traffic cop trying to stop traffic at a busy intersection. "I think that I have grieved and I am still grieving."

"Then why did you say on the form that your goal for Matt is to make him the way he was before the accident?" Rosalie asked accusingly, standing up and waving the form in Caroline's face as though Rosalie were a bullfighter and Caroline were the bull.

"I don't know. The funny thing is that I told my daughter that Matt wouldn't ever get completely better. I must have lost my head when I heard about the work that you do here. I have started to believe for a moment that maybe it was possible for Matt to actually become whole again."

"I had a feeling," replied Berlinda, "I must have picked up on that when I first met you."

Vicky worked at the main rehab center and was the head of the brain injury department there. Vicky spoke up and said, "If you would like the name of someone reliable that you can talk to about Matt, I know a good person."

"Oh, I don't know," replied Caroline.

"Don't be embarrassed. It is a normal thing that you are going through. In fact, some of the patients in our program at the rehab hospital actually celebrate the anniversary of their injuries."

"I'm afraid the whole country is going to remember the anniversary of Matt's accident. I can't even begin to wonder why anyone would want to celebrate the injury of a traumatic anniversary."

"Well, for those who enter their second year since their accident, they can look back and see all the progress that they have made. They can also look ahead and hopefully plan to make some improvements in time for the second anniversary."

"I suppose I do sometimes remember what Matt was like a year ago, make that almost a year and a half ago. I smile when I think of how much he has improved since the incident."

"But do you also think about how Matt was the day before the accident and compare him to that?"

"I suppose I do, even though I told my daughter not to."

"In the three months that I have worked with Matt, I have seen a few little strides in improvement. You need to bury the Matt from September 10, 2001. Comparing Matt now to the way he was then is like comparing Matt to another man. It is like saying you need to live up to this ideal. I think you can understand how it can feel to be expected to live up to achievements of another person."

"I didn't know it was like that because he really is the same person when you look at it."

"He still is the same person except that he has some injuries done to part of his brain that will never be able to heal. What we do here and are hoping eventually to be able to do, with Matt, is apply strategies."

"Strategies?"

"Another way of doing something. It is like if you have two people going to the market to shop. One person may be able to create a list in their head and stick to it. The other person needs a list to help. In both cases they are both competent and able to do the grocery shopping. One needs special help and the other doesn't."

"I see."

Rosalie started to speak, "We want to help Matt be able to live and function as normally as is possible. He will only improve so far and then he will need strategies. Just because I am telling you this doesn't mean that he will ever be the way he was before the accident. Until you accept that, it will make Matt's future progress harder."

"Ms___"

"Just call me Rosalie."

"Rosalie, you don't have to keep hitting me over the head with this."

"I think that I do. My job and my desire is to give Matt the best future possible. I'll strive to fight any battle I have to in order to do it, even if it is you," said Rosalie.

Vicky reached inside her purse for a business card.

"Are you giving me your business card?"

"No, this is the business card from the doctor that I want you to see." Vicky handed Caroline the card. Caroline looked at the white card with black lettering.

"Does he give you commission for every patient you recommend?"

"No he doesn't," answered Vicky, "I send a lot of family members of my clients. The only difference is that they usually make their first appointment just after the accidents."

"I told you that I couldn't help it because I am a widow and I have to work," Caroline's throat was getting tight. "I have a teenage daughter to care for. I had a teenage daughter to care for and now I have a grown son to care for as well. It just isn't easy. Anyway, nobody even came to me and suggested that I attend counseling sessions."

"I didn't mean to hurt your feelings, Mrs. Cobel. I hope to see you next month and I promise we won't be hard on you."

Everyone at the table rose up. Matt even got up from his chair and reached for his walker, which stood on his right against the wall.

Caroline had that worn out *I hope not* look on her face.

"You will go see him, won't you?" Vicky begged.

Caroline nodded, as most of them walked towards the door. Rosalie stayed at the table, quickly putting the form back in Matt's loose-leaf book and then she quickly walked to the door entrance. She quickly re-filed the book as she left the room with the others, closing the door behind her.

CHAPTER 28

▼

CAROLINE'S EXORCIST.

The doctor's office was located in the main rehabilitation center, the same place where Matt spent a few months at after he left the hospital. When Caroline entered the main entrance she went over to the receptionists' desk. The receptionist smiled at Caroline in recognition. "Hi Mrs. Cobel. How are you?"

"I'm fine."

"How is Matt doing?"

"He is doing great. We have him in the—a community entry rehab."

"That's wonderful and what brings you here?"

"I have a doctor's appointment," Caroline removed the business card from her purse and handed it to the receptionist.

"The reason that we have him here on the site is because it is very convenient for our clients."

"Really?"

"He is here, basically, for family members of those who have severe injuries that will cause life changing effects for the family members as well. You just walk down that entry and take the elevator up to the fourth floor," the receptionist pointed towards her left. "Then you make a sharp left turn and it will take you to a passage with some offices and hospital rooms."

"I hope I can remember all that."

"I'm sure you will. Just sign your name on this chart," said the receptionist, "and don't forget the time of your appointment and the doctor's name." The receptionist handed Caroline a pen.

"I think all of this is coming back to me. I suppose that I am also supposed to pick up a visitor's badge, or don't I?"

"Come to think of it, you probably don't because it is your appointment."

Caroline headed down the hallway towards the elevators. Passing by the offices and the snack bar brought back all kinds of memories for Caroline who had last been here only several months ago. As she walked by the snack bar, the cashier and his assistant waved to her and shouted her name. Walking down the hall to towards the elevator, Caroline felt like some sort of a celebrity for the first time in her life. It felt good Caroline had made so many new acquaintances in the rehabilitation center. The whole positive recognition thing sort of gave her a buzz, and she started to wonder if she really needed the counseling sessions or not. She entered the elevator. For the first time in all of her visits, the elevator was not only empty, but went straight up to the fourth floor without stopping on any other floor. She wondered to herself if this could have been some kind of an omen.

The elevator door opened up on the fourth floor and a young man dressed in white scrubs walked on the elevator, pushing a two level cart with trays of medication. The white little pills and capsules were in small corrugated white paper cups which looked like what fast food restaurants used for mustard and catsup. She wondered if this young man could have stopped by Matt's room to give him drugs when he was in the rehab. There was also a pitcher of ice water. It looked for a moment as though, the attendant was going to block Caroline from exiting the elevator as he tried to maneuver the cart around what little space was available. Caroline made her way around the man's right side and out of the elevator. The door closed and took the attendant down to the third floor where he was to make his rounds. Caroline became distracted as she noticed a group of pictures with captions together in one large frame. She nearly "lost it" as she looked at the pictures and captions were under them. It turned out to be a display on how to put on a prosthesis after amputation of either the arms or the legs. It showed the sock which went over the stump and then into some sort of a rubber cup and then it all fit into a hollowed out plastic arm or leg. There were instructions on when to tell and how to prepare the stump for the procedure as to how to wear the prosthesis. "Dear God," Caroline said as she walked away. "I'm so glad that Matt didn't have to go through any of that. I felt so good today until I had to see that display." She walked down the hallway which resembled the one Matt's hospital room was located just six months before. Caroline knew that Matt's room was on the second floor. The mother knocked on the closed door of Dr. Torres, Psychologist, PhD. A young Hispanic man in his early forties opened the door. "Are you Dr. Torres?" asked Caroline.

"Yes I am. You must be Mrs. Cobel?"

Caroline nodded and the doctor gestured for Caroline to enter the office. The office was rather small. The office was just big enough for two people. Caroline was grateful at least there was a window. The white horizontal blinds were half-way up and the window was slightly open on a cool early March, 2003. "I tend to hyperventilate a little in small rooms. If the room is too cold let me know and I'll close the window," the doctor spoke in an accent which reminded Caroline of television's Ricky Ricardo. Caroline sat across from Dr. Torres with his large desk between them. "I don't know whether or not you were told that I am the resident psychologist around here for family members of the patients who need to talk about the family adjustments."

"I was."

"Tell me about yourself."

"I feel cursed. It was a war between the United States and Kuwait over the oil crisis. We were getting our heating and gasoline oil from Kuwait. My husband, Harvey Cobel, was one of the first to ship out in August, 1990. The war was officially underway in January 1991 and would only last one month. Some people believe that the senior George Bush was anxious to prove he wasn't a wimp by challenging Saddam Hussein on his own soil. We have been getting our oil from Kuwait from the Regan years if not longer. The war really lasted a month from the middle of January to the middle of February and he would be home. It turned out that he would only last a week before he was killed in one of the Kuwait blasts. If he could've made it just until the middle of February, who knows what might have been."

"Was he a career man?"

"He started his army career in the early sixties as a private in Viet Nam. He became a Lieutenant when he joined the army to get some money in order to attend college as an engineer. It was the middle sixties by the time Harvey enrolled as engineering major. It was only one of those special programs that lasted about eighteen months. On the weekends he worked with ROTC (Reserve Officers' Training Corps), mostly classes. Harvey believed that if he had his foot in the army maybe they would continue to pay for it. He happened to stroll into one of those beauty schools that cut and washed hair for a fraction of the traditional beauty salons and barber shops. The student who waited on him was me, Caroline Jennings from West Orange, New Jersey. I had a few months to go before graduation. While I worked on him shaving, shampoo, cut and blow dry we talked. By the time I whipped out a hand mirror so he could see how I did the back, he had asked me out. "Maybe tomorrow during my lunch break."

"I have another class in two days. How about if I stop by then around noon?"

"Fine."

"How romantic."

"The rest of the relationship developed just as quickly. In a year we were married and by 1969 we had a mortgage. It lasted beyond Desert Storm. I ended up having to struggle by my self to continue paying off after her husband's death.

In less than twenty-five years, a marriage and two kids later he would be gone and I would be a single mother. He was only forty-six years old and I was barely forty-five during Desert Storm. What would I do with a five year-old daughter and a thirteen year old son?"

"Why didn't you ever get married again?"

"I never had time to balance my job and raising children with having a love life. It was easier with Harvey because I was in beauty school and I didn't have to raise any kids or make a living."

"Is there anything else that you feel you want to discuss?"

"That picture outside on the wall about prosthesis."

"I have spoken to many family members about their loved ones who are being fitted for prostheses. Is that the problem with your son? I was informed that you have a son who is healing from a brain injury."

"Well, no, Matt doesn't have any need for prosthesis of any kind."

"Then you would rather talk about the prosthesis display on the wall so that you don't have to discuss your son?"

"I was told that I need to give up the way Matt was before the incident, but I don't know how."

"O.K. What have you done about it so far?"

"I suppose I mourned for him. Sometimes I would cry myself to sleep at night."

"That's good."

"Is it?"

"It is a start. When someone dies you need to go through the grieving stage before you can go on."

"I don't really see this as a death. When I went to the meeting at the clubhouse to discuss Matt's progress, the people I met with mentioned that I was going through some sort of death."

"I know it sounds kind of strange, but you see_____"

"They told me that I was dealing with two Matts, in a way. I guess I was mourning the way Matt used to be before the accident. They told me that in a way it was as though one Matt died and I am left with another Matt."

"Yes, strange as it seems that's the case. You know, I think we are conditioned throughout life that time heals injuries and that our loved one is going to be as good as new."

"Matt's doctor told me that he really couldn't tell how much Matt could improve and that it was possible that he could completely recover."

"When did he tell you this?"

"A year and a half ago right after the tragedy."

"I would think that things change after eighteen months. We seem to get a better idea of a prognosis even after a year has passed."

"I suppose. I secretly hoped that Matt would completely recover, well except for what I told the rehab therapists."

"If we're lucky maybe that happens. Unfortunately, that doesn't always happen and it can screw up the order of life. May I ask if he is on any type of medication?"

"They have him on Ritalin."

"Do you think it is working?"

She shrugged her shoulders. "There is another problem, but with me."

"Yes."

"I sometimes think maybe I have some sort of brain injury myself because whenever Matt's doctor talks to me about his condition all that terminology seems to go in one ear and out the other. Should I remember all those things he's said to me?"

"Not unless you are medical doctor. All you have to do is follow the doctor's orders in how to care for Matt. You don't have any problem with that, do you?"

"No."

"Do you worry a lot?"

"Yes. I suppose," Caroline said looking down and at her right hand, her fingernails drumming the arm of the chair. "Then there is that wants to be this mature adult and I tell my daughter that Matt will never be the person he was before and we have to be grateful for whatever improvements he has made."

"That makes you uncomfortable?" the doctor asked as he looked at Caroline looking down at her fingernails drumming the arm of the chair.

Caroline looked up appearing like a frightened little girl. "Am I a hypocrite or something? I don't know what to think. I know in my heart that I want miracles and instant cures and then I tell my daughter something else."

"That is a step in the right direction."

"O.K. I really want Matt to be completely healed of his brain injury and return to the way he was before the accident. I learned since then that brain injuries don't completely heal. The part of the brain that is injured dies and scars. I suppose Matt will have to compensate and learn how to deal with his injury. I was told it is like if one person can remember an entire shopping list in her head and another person needs to physically write down a list to follow."

"Yes, it can be like that."

"Nobody really knows how much more improvement Matt is capable of. I just saw something on television about Christopher Reeve. Did you know that he can move his pinky and he is starting to have some feeling in his hand? His improvements were made more than a year after his accident. I must be a crazy person. I keep saying two different things. I'm like two different people in one and two different personalities and ideas since the tragedy."

"I saw that program too, but you can't use Christopher Reeve's progress as a way to measure Matt's progress. I would strongly suggest that you don't go that route."

"Matt has made a lot of progress in the first year of his recovery. He can feed himself and he can walk. He needs a walker, but at least he is out of his wheelchair."

"Nobody really knows how much Matt can improve even more than a year later. You are doing the right thing. He needs therapy and stimulation if he is going to progress any further."

"You actually admit that you don't have all the answers. That is really refreshing."

"In my practice I have seen far too many doctors misjudge their patients' abilities. I even remember doctors saying that Christopher Reeve would never regain feeling in his hands again and those doctors were wrong, too. Just keep Matt's brain stimulated and be patient. It could take months …"

"You sound like Matt's surgeon. Did you say Months?"

"Or years."

"Years?"

The hour was up and Caroline was asked to come back the next week. Caroline made an appointment to see Dr. Torres on March 10th at the same time.

*   *   *   *

Monday, March 10, 2003. 10AM.
Caroline sat in Dr. Torres' office. "I'd like to ask you something."
"That's why we are here."
"Could I be responsible for Matt's brain injury?"
"Were you in any way involved in the terrorist attack?" asked the doctor with tongue in cheek humor.
"No I wasn't and I don't think that it is funny."
"I'm sorry, but why do you ask such a question?"
"I was looking at that hideous picture of the prosthesis demonstration on the wall. I said 'DearGod' and a woman told me that when I say the Lord's name in vain that I open up the possibility of bad things happening. She actually accused me of causing my son's brain injury simply by saying 'Dear God'."
"Oh that!" the doctor said practically brushing it aside.
"What do you mean?"
"I mean that I know quite a few Atheists and Agnostics who are having tremendously good fortune in their lives. If that woman were correct in assuming that the mere saying the Lord's name in vain were to cause bad luck to happen, then, I must also assume that the Lord have even worse in store for the person who either doesn't believe in the existence of God, or isn't sure whether he exists or not."
"I suppose that makes some sense."
"I believe that anyone who supposedly created this entire universe in one week, must be smart enough to know that you mean no real disrespect when you utter, 'Dear God,' at something that distresses you."
"That makes me feel much better."
"Is there anything else you want to talk about?"
Caroline was silent as she tried to figure out what she had come for in the first place.
"Caroline. If you tell me what it is that you want to talk about today, perhaps I can make you feel better about that, too."
"My daughter is graduating high school in June and I'm nervous about that."
"Why does that make you nervous?"

Well, I'm afraid that when we celebrate her graduation another tragedy might take place."

"That is a perfectly normal reaction. You are saying that there was a celebration going on around the time of Matt's accident."

"Yes. Bari Lynn was Sweet 16 three days before the accident. I was thinking about what tomorrow is."

"What does tomorrow mean to you?"

"Tomorrow is eighteen months since Matt's accident. It seems much longer to me."

"Would you like to tell me about it?"

"Before the accident we were planning to have a bridal shower. You see, Matt was engaged and last spring he was going to get married, and now ..." she reached into her purse and took out a folded bundle of tissues. She removed one, put the rest back and dabbled her eye, one at a time. "I can't talk about it. It is too sad."

"Go ahead and talk about it. Get it out."

"We were thinking of having the shower at the Windows of the World restaurant where Matt and Laura met. Then I thought, she mentioned she wanted the wedding reception at Windows of The World. So, we were thinking of holding the reception at La Jolie where Bari Lynn's sweet 16 was held. Laura really liked La Jolie and we could have had a surprise bridal shower there."

"What about the ceremony?"

"She mentioned something about St. Patrick's Cathedral. It's a big gothic structure over on the corner of 5th Avenue and 51st Street."

"Oh that is some place."

"She's catholic and wanted to have a catholic wedding?"

"I suppose. Her mother was a big Kennedy-Bouvier buff. I don't know if she was born and raised a catholic or converted to it. It was going to be one of those weddings where the bride's maids wear white gowns and red gowns to signify the blood and body of Christ."

"Was that where President and Mrs. Kennedy were married?"

"I don't know, but I heard something to the effect that Bobby Kennedy's funeral was there. Laura's funeral was a graveside service."

"Could she get red gowns for a spring wedding?"

"She was going to get them when the winter gowns went on sale right around Thanksgiving."

""How are you and her parents coping?"

That's all over and done with. We had a funeral for her instead of the bridal shower, baby shower, and the wedding."

"Tell me more."

"When Bari Lynn and I learned about the accident we were about to start planning a bridal shower for Laura."

"You just told me that you were planning the bridal shower."

I haven't been myself in the last six months thinking of what might have been. She was going to be my daughter—in-law."

"So I figure."

"I just spend time sometimes thinking about what might have been and I feel bad about what is."

"Go on."

"We would have asked them the next time we saw them. Then the next thing I knew it was several days later, I was watching television, one of those morning talk shows. There was a news interruption. I never got the chance to discuss it with them." The tears streamed down both cheeks, creating medium beige tears. Caroline looked embarrassed as though she were caught with her hair in curlers in front of a hot date. Caroline dabbed at the tears and makeup on her cheek. "I'm sorry," sounding like a child who had broken the kitchen window with a baseball. "I would tell you more about the shower plans, but we didn't even get beyond making an incomplete guest list. I was also thinking about the baby shower. When would we fit that in, too. I guess I could have had that at Matt's apartment. There was Bari Lynn, her schooling, her cheerleading, which she eventually gave up after the accident, and I had my work. We didn't even really get beyond starting the guest list. When we learned about the accident, I decided to stay home from work that day and Bari Lynn took the day off from school so that we could go down to New York City. Look at me; I'm falling apart right before your eyes."

"Don't be sorry. Everything we talk about will stay in this office and be between us."

"It is strange, but talking about Laura's engagement party is starting to make me feel better." Her tears stopped falling and she flashed a smile as wide as an upside down rainbow. "I shouldn't feel bad about my son's injury, because at least I still have him. He will be going to the graduation."

"I don't understand."

"It's Laura. She was killed in the accident and it is ironic, but her parents seem to be coping a lot better than I am."

The fifty minute hour was over and Caroline made an appointment for March 17, 2003 at the same time.

When Caroline strolled down the hall she thought of Laura. It came back to her the day after the Sweet 16. *Laura went over to Caroline in her bedroom. "Now that Matt is packing up the car I would like to talk private to you."*

"What is it?"

"I seem to be spending all my time with Matt and sometimes it gets on my nerves. Do you think it would be a good idea to transfer out of the customer service?"

"I can't answer that for you. What about that team leader position you mentioned?"

"I haven't really had the time to look at the position description. If it is the other side of the room, I suppose I'll put in for it. It doesn't mean that I'll get it. Besides that I really don't feel that well. I'm always running to the bathroom to pee or throw up and that might be a strike against me."

"What does your obstetrician say?"

"How did you know?"

"You know I've been through it myself. How far along are you?"

"I'm entering my second trimester and I haven't seen my mother in months. I'm getting nervous and I know that I am going to have to tell her."

"Do you know the sex of the baby?"

"They are going to do an ultrasound on me Wednesday, that's September 12th, to find out."

"Do you want to know or do you want it to be a surprise?"

"I'm not sure. It would help to know the sex because you know how to decorate the nursery. On the other hand I like surprises. I feel mixed because I am nervous about giving birth. I wonder if I'll be able to handle the pain."

"Women were built for this and if you couldn't handle it your doctor would have said something to you. I'd like to ask you something else. Does she know you are engaged?"

"Yes she does and I don't want her to find out when I am showing through my wedding dress. What a dilemma. Do I have the wedding before I start to show which means I better do it before the end of this month? Do I have the wedding when I am still showing? Do I wait until the baby is born and bring it to the wedding? My mother will have a stroke. She believes that the baby should come before the wedding and not after the wedding. If she didn't have those archaic ideas of hers things would be so easy. I wish I could talk to her the way I can talk to you. I wish she were different because then I could find out what the baby's sex is and she could help me decorate the nursery."

Caroline seemed to magically end up on the first floor. She nearly walked into an orderly who was pushing an empty gurney down the hall. He stared at her as though she had blue hair. "I'm sorry," said the grieving almost mother-in-law to be. "I have a lot on my mind."

✳   ✳   ✳   ✳

Monday, March 17, 2003 10AM.

The first thing that Dr. Torres wanted to know from Caroline was how March 11th went. "Alright, I suppose. I just got up early and helped Matt get ready for his day. I nearly forgot that it was March 11th. I remembered to send Matt out in his coat, not like I forgot a few months ago. The Para Transit driver even came a few minutes earlier than scheduled to pick Matt up. I took it as some kind of an omen that maybe I didn't have anything to worry about."

"Well that is good to hear. Often when we worry about the next day, we find we have worried for nothing."

"I suppose. It was even one of better days at the salon. Sometimes we are very backed up schedule-wise, and the customers have to wait maybe up to a half an hour past their appointment in order to get served. Yesterday, things went well. I even took some of my customers before their scheduled time."

"I suppose things work out like that, sometimes. Anything else happen that day?"

"I received a phone call from Sue Daniels. She would have been Matt's mother-in-law."

"How long have you been friendly with this woman?"

"Since we learned about Matt and Laura's engagement."

"You've become very friendly, then."

"Well," Caroline hesitated to answer. After a few seconds she replied, "I was invited to see their new place that they moved into. It is one of those retirement villages. I went down to see it. It was a two bedroom and a den in what they call a townhouse these days."

"You don't sound delighted."

`"I guess I'm tired," she sighed.

"I'd like to ask you a personal question, may I?"

Caroline nodded.

"Do you really like the Daniels?"

"I don't know. Getting together with the Daniels is more like a habit that I do. I don't think about whether or not I like them or not."

"I think that your assignment for next week is to think about why you are friends with the Daniels."

"Is it wrong for me to be friends with the Daniels?"

"Next week I would like you to give me that answer yourself."

Caroline left Dr. Torres office with her thoughts in her head spinning around of what to do about her relationship with the Daniels family. She knew she and the Daniels family only got together for the sake of Matt and Laura. Caroline walked down the hallway of the rehabilitation center towards the elevator. She opened her purse as she walked, her hands fumbled around the purse as though she were blind, trying to find the parking valet ticket. Matt's mother grabbed onto the pale blue ticket with dear life as though it were a winning lottery ticket worth millions. Caroline was jolted into reality. She had to wait for several disabled people in wheelchairs and with canes exit the elevator before she got on. Alone in the elevator, she thought about the Daniels. Are they really clinging to each other because of the terrorist attack? The door opened up at the fifth floor because Caroline didn't bother to see she took the wrong elevator. A doctor wearing blue scrubs entered the elevator. He pressed the button for the main floor. He noticed Caroline in thought. "Is something wrong?"

"I just left counseling and my head is spinning."

"So you have a loved one who was injured?"

"How did you know that?"

"All the counseling sessions here are for people who were either injured or are related to someone who is injured. You don't look injured to me so you must have a loved one who has been injured."

"Well now he is getting some outpatient therapy, and maybe from there he will be able to find some work."

"Well, I am glad to hear he is coming along."

"I feel as though he is making far more progress than I am," Caroline said as she still pondered over her relationship with the Daniels. *"I wonder if they are using me as a way to cope with Laura's death."* After she exited the elevator, Caroline walked towards the exit thinking t maybe she had made up her mind about the Daniels. Next week she would ask Dr. Torres how to handle the situation.

Meanwhile: The individual square tables were assembled to make one long table. Matt, the only person at the table with his chicken sandwich from lunch and a can of Sprite, stared at the half sandwich left on his plastic plate. Rosalie sat at the head of the table, "Welcome back to our monthly lunch menu meeting. Since we are entering spring we will be having less hot meals and more cold meals" A young woman with long dark hair typed into what looked like a small laptop computer on a tray attached to her wheelchair. She was a beautiful young woman that many people still compared to Jennifer Love Hewitt, *Party of Five*. Matt always called her, "Laura." The young woman didn't care. Rosalie looked over at her, "It looks like Rachel is getting ready for our lunch menu session." Rachel's head bobbed up and down like one of those objects people put in the back windows of their cars. "Should we start with you?" Rachel smiled and then cooed like an infant as saliva dripped down her chin and onto a napkin she had tucked in her shirt. She sat between two small pillows that kept her in place. Rosalie continued, "Name two things that you would like to have for lunch." All Rachel did was a press a button on her key pad using a finger from the one hand that she could still use. A voice that sounded like the one you get when you dial a wrong phone number, spoke from the laptop. "Caesar Salad and tuna sandwich."

"Thank you Rachel. Matt?"

"I want to go home."

"Dave spoke up, "You always say that no matter what our meeting is about."

Rosalie spoke, "Why do you want to go home?"

"Because people are always yelling at me during lunch to eat. I eat when I want to. I eat when I want to." He picked up the half a sandwich on his plate, took a bite and placed it back down, chewing the sandwich with his mouth open for everyone to see him masticating."

Rosalie tried to control herself, "O.K"

Still chewing Matt got up out of his seat.

Rosalie grabbed his shoulder and pressed downward as Matt eased back into his chair. "Nobody bother Matt during lunch."

"You know how silly this looks," said Dave. "Every time we have a meeting, Matt is the only who is still having his lunch. When we had our unit meeting last time, he gave the update of the kitchen unit when he still had some hotdog and roll in his mouth."

"That's enough! I won't have any fighting at this table."

*   *   *   *

Wednesday, March 26, 2003.

When Caroline arrived at Dr. Torres' office, she noticed the door was closed and locked. Caroline stood there looking down at her watch. Dr. Torres walked over to Caroline, "Sorry I am a little late. I had an emergency with one of my patients." He took out a key and placed it into a lock which was built into the doorknob. Caroline followed him into the office and sat in front of his desk. She looked to the right of him and noticed a framed picture of his wife and young baby, placed on the lowest level of the book shelves mounted on the wall. Dr. Torres looked at Caroline as though he were a confused little puppy dog.

Caroline turned back to him. "I've been figuring out a lot of things about my life in the past week."

"Such as?"

"I think that the Daniels and I are clinging to each other more out of the 9/11 disaster than for any other reason. The problem is that I don't know how to go about bringing the subject up with them."

"Maybe you could call her up right now and invite her to lunch today," the doctor suggested.

"I suppose I could call her when I get home."

"If you wait until then, you will probably put it off," the doctor said picking up the receiver of his multi-line phone. There was a series of buttons beside the cradle of the receiver. The doctor pressed the one marked *line one* and handed the phone back to Caroline, "what is her phone number?"

*   *   *   *

12:30PM Monday, March 24, 2003

Caroline walked down the freshly snow shoveled walkway at the strip mall. She stepped off the curb and walked over to the Jetta that was parked at the end of the first row. The car was parked near a large white mountain of snow, standing there ever since the last snowstorm which fell over a week ago. She got into the driver's seat and sat there for a few seconds. She felt as though she were being made to go on this meeting as though Dr. Torres had been performing some sort of magic. She hoped he wasn't another Shauna. Caroline didn't think she felt like this since she was a child and under the rule of her parents. Now she was an adult and under the power of Dr. Torres. "*What will he do if I decide to chicken out and cancel the lunch? What will he say if I cancel next week's appointment? What if I never go back and the staff at Matt's clubhouse find out that I am no longer keeping my appointments with Dr. Torres? Am I selfish enough to risk getting Matt thrown out of the whole clubhouse?*" Caroline started the engine and drove the auto out of its space. She backed up and swung her steering wheel to the left, straightened out the wheel and then pulled out. She made her way through the light traffic in the parking lot. She then waited at the traffic light until the go arrow told her she could move into traffic.

Caroline walked through the double doors of the restaurant. She very carefully hung her coat up on a wooden hanger at the coat rack in the front of the restaurant. She very cautiously fit the triangular part of the hanger through the shoulder part of the coat as she slowly and warily placed the garment and hanger up on the rod. Caroline gradually turned around and strolled down the aisle which had two long hot pink upholstered couches for those waiting to be served. There were a few people sitting on one of the couches waiting for takeout. Caroline went up to the hostess, a lovely young Chinese woman with long black hair tied back in a ponytail. "One person," the hostess grabbed a menu.

"I'm waiting for someone. She has short blonde hair …"

"Come with me," the hostess signaled with her right hand and led Caroline into the dinning area. She made a sharp right turn and guided Caroline to a booth where Sue Daniels was sitting and taking a sip of ice water from a small glass. Caroline slid into the booth across from Sue Daniels. Silently, Caroline watched as Sue Daniels put down her glass of water and reached for a small floral porcelain tea kettle. "Caroline, would you like me to pour you a cup of tea?" she asked without expression. With equal lack of expression Caroline said, "Yes please." She moved a teeny tiny floral porcelain cup over so t Sue Daniels could pour her some tea. "Thank you," Caroline answered frowning. Caroline tried to pass some time taking one wide fried noodle from the plastic bowl and dipping the end into some amber colored sauce-duck sauce. After she dipped the noodle, she brought the noodle up to her mouth and ate it. Caroline and Sue tended to alternate eating noodles and duck sauce so their mouths would be too full to discuss anything. After they nearly consumed the entire bowl of fried noodles, Sue Daniels spoke. "I was about to call you up about meeting you for lunch, but then I got your call."

Caroline was silent. "I told my marriage counselor about you and your family and he asked me to make a date with you to discuss things."

"I am seeing a counselor too."

"Really?" in surprise.

"I told you that Matt is in some type of rehabilitation program in order to gain skills so that he may one day reenter the workforce."

Sue Daniels nodded her head once in understanding.

"They seem to think that I am stopping Matt from making progress by expecting him to recover back to the way he was before the accident."

"And are you?"

"I suppose so. I told my counselor about you and he was the one that insisted that I make a luncheon meeting to see you."

"Did your counselor ask you to consider a three month separation period for our families to see how things go?"

"You know something? That's not a bad idea. I feel a lot better about our meeting. The truth is that my counselor wanted to me to figure out things for myself and all he suggested was the meeting itself."

"A three month trial separation period for friends. What would you expect from a marriage counselor? You know something, I really like you better than that Maureen from my support group. Ever since I met her I have appreciated you a lot more."

"That's nice to hear that you appreciate me."

"I thought she was mad at me for awhile because I made her get rid of that telephone answering tape she had been listening to all day. A few days later she was back and more grateful to me than ever."

"Did she ever do anything for you?"

"I got rid of all of Laura's clothes from the apartment."

"You told me about that. I remember. Are you still going to that support group?"

"No I don't need to. In fact, not only was I able to get rid of those clothes, but I had a yard sale before we moved. We got rid of all the baby furniture and I feel just great. It was just an unhealthy obsession to keep Laura in my mind, but that is silly. I'll never forget her and I don't need things to help me remember. Why hang on to my grandson's things as part of a museum shrine, when I can sell them to someone who could really use them?"

"That's great!"

"The couple who bought the stuff was not even as well off as Mitch and I. They were moving into a two-bedroom apartment straight from her parents' house and were expecting their first child."

"Tell me about you and Maureen."

"She follows me around whenever I go to the hospital."

"You don't go to the meetings there anymore. When did you stop the meetings?"

"I had my last one about a week ago."

"Does she know where you live and have your phone number?"

"She knows where we used to live and she had that phone number, but not the new one."

"You don't have a problem anymore."

"If I hear about one more bake sale at Rebecca's school and those original cakes that she used to bake for them!"

"Maureen or Rebecca?"

"Maureen of course. What if I meet her on the street?"

"Just say hello and act like you are on the way to a pressing engagement. She won't know the difference," Caroline suggested.

"Thank you. I feel great! Want to order a couple of platters and share them between us?"

"Why not?"

"Sounds fair to me. See you in June. I did want to ask you something personal."

"What's that?"

"Are you able to talk about Laura without crying?"

"Sometimes. I get misty at times when I think of what might have been. Her wedding would have been this spring."

"I thought it would have been last year."

"No. We checked with Saint Patrick's Cathedral and they told us we had to book it one year in advance. I called up as soon as I learned about Laura and Matt. It was too soon for a spring, 20002 wedding."

"Oh."

"Don't be surprised if I don't break down and cry at Bari Lynn's graduation party, because Laura's wedding was going to be right around that time. I suppose I would have consulted with you and scheduled it so that it didn't interfere."

"It would have been a busy month."

"Laura really wasn't sure exactly when in the spring it would have been, but she knew she had to wait an extra year. That's all over now. Mitch and I have to go on as a childless and grandchild less couple I suppose. We aren't the only ones who have lost a child and a grandchild."

"I still cry sometimes."

The busboy came by and refilled the small glasses of ice water.

The two managed to smile. "To June," Caroline and Sue Daniels raised their glasses in a toast. "I'll invite you to Bari Lynn's high school graduation and then will we'll evaluate this separation period."

Sue's final word was "Thanks for giving us Matt's computer."

"You're welcome," Caroline said in a monotone voice.

CHAPTER 29

▼

WHAT A DIFFERENCE A
YEAR MAKES

It had been a year since Matt joined the clubhouse. Caroline remembers that spring day well when she and Bari Lynn first met Rosalie who greeted her at the door. "I'm in charge of kitchen prep. All the members are responsible for keeping up the clubhouse. They are part of the menu planning and meal preparation. We have three therapists on staff here to oversee things."

"Do we pay for lunch daily or is it part of a monthly plan?"

As Caroline talked with Rosalie, Bari Lynn looked around. She saw a guy washing the table with a sponge. Occasionally this beer belly burly fellow who wore only a short sleeve T shirt and jeans would replenish the sponge by sticking it in the dish pan. He looked up, "Hi baby!" Dave looked like one of those beer and nuts can of guys you find hanging out in the local bars.

Bari Lynn rolled her eyes. ".I'm still a minor. I could turn you into jail bait."

"What's wrong with you?"

"Are you kidding?"

"I'm colored blind."

"That's no reason to be in a place for brain injured people."

"You ever see a black and white photograph or watch black and white television shows or films like *Raging Bull* or *The Elephant Man*?"

"You mean you don't see any color at all? How do you know those films weren't in color?"

"I saw them before my seizure. I can't even tell what color outfit you're wearing."

"Bari Lynn!" Caroline called out. "We can start a tour now."

Rosalie talked to the guy who was washing down the table." Dave, why don't you give these ladies a tour of the place?"

Bari Lynn thought to herself, *"Does he have to give the tour?"* "Alright!"

"This is the kitchen area." The two women noticed a young woman with use of one hand wearing one of those transparent kitchen gloves. She was placing tomatoes on top of cold cuts and cheese inside a long roll. "This is Marie who is one the greatest cooks here. Marie this is Matt who will be joining us, and his mother and sister."

"Over here as you saw you were in the dining area where we do everything. We have our lunch here and our meetings. This sort of a combination living room and dinning room area." Dave led them into the computer/communication room where everything from the newsletter, the menu, special notices and fund-raising reports are created. A young woman with reddish-brown hair and freckles turned around from typing the minutes. "What do you do when you want to make the letters capital?"

Dave replied, "Press the shift key. For the left side of the keyboard you press the shift on the right side and for the right side of the keyboard you press the shift on the left side."

"Could you show me, whatever your name is?" Dave continued to conduct the tour. "This Cindy who types up the minutes of the weekly meetings. We both came here about a year." The words were hand printed in a black and white marble covered notebook which she copied from. Cindy suffered head injury in a car accident which she and her boyfriend were in after he had too much to drink and was supposedly driving her home. She survived and was in a coma for about a month.

"A whole year? What is your name? Is it Frank or Ted?"

"It's Dave," he said wearily. "She does this everyday."

"I do?" she replied. Cindy turned back to doing her typing. She knew what to do, to indent and create space in the document, but she needed someone to turn on the computer and bring up the MS Word document in the Word 97 program. The clubhouse got their computer and programs from the rehabilitation hospital when they were done with them and decided to upgrade to Professional

Millennium of Office 2000. The computers were 386s when the rehab hospital upgraded to 686 computers. "We have kitchen detail, computer typing detail, and cleaning and maintenance. Whatever anyone's specialty is. "Next to Cindy sat Rachel in her wheelchair. She typed up the weekly menus on another computer. Her boyfriend was drunk one time too many, New Years Eve 1999–2000, and beat her head against the wall one night causing her to go into a coma for a few months. She had just joined the clubhouse over the summer of 2001.

Caroline replied, "Matt worked with computers when he was a customer service rep. I must tell you that two months after the accident he had a problem using the keyboard, but I haven't had him tested since."

"The person in charge of the communication department is Peggy and she will try him out. Perhaps she will start him with typing up the weekly menu."

A tall forty something black woman entered the room, "I'm Peggy. I just overheard that your son knows something about computers. We could certainly use some help in this department."

Caroline replied, "You mean that the members are responsible for keeping up this establishment?"

"Yes because many of them are going to go back into the workforce in many areas like maintenance, cooking, clerical. We even have a transportation unit for booking rides that one of our members looks after. Another member is our receptionist. She answers phones and will call up people if they are absent when they should be here."

"I get the idea"

"If we had a staff do things for them then they wouldn't be able to work on the skills that they will need to bring to the workplace one day."

"So there is some hope for Matt."

"Oh yes, we had a member who was in a wheelchair, couldn't speak or use his hands and we found a data processing job for him. In fact, his leaving opened up a space for Matt to come in.

Caroline is back in March, 2003. Dr. Torres asked, "So what happened when they tried Matt out on the computer?"

*   *   *   *

Matt went to the clubhouse everyday He sat at the desk top computer which sat on a long table in the communications room. Peggy turned on the computer which took about a minute to warm up. The computer ran on a Windows 95 operating system. The desktop page came up with a greenish-blue background.

Peggy moved the mouse around on the mouse pad until the white arrow was over the MS Word 97 icon. She clicked the left side of the mouse and it seemed to take another thirty seconds for the word program to come up. Matt kept staring into space or staring through the computer. "Now Matt," she opened up a black and white marble designed notebook to a page with the newest menu to be typed. "All you have to do is type up what is on this page."

Matt stared and the screen for a few seconds and then gazed at the keyboard. He started banging on the keys, as though he were playing an organ, creating a string of letters "mliewrjkmckewik, mcioewdinif" and wide spaces that didn't make up any words at all. Peggy came back to see what Matt was doing. "I guess computers are no longer your thing. I think we can find something else around here for you to do."

*   *   *   *

Back in the doctor's office, "And that was how Matt ended up in the kitchen working with Rosalie."

"Did you ever get him to try to shovel snow for you again?"

"I told you about the time that we forgot to put Matt's coat on him when he went to the clubhouse."

"That was the day that you fantasized about the 1996 snowstorm."

"After Matt was picked up, I got dressed and walked down to the bus stop to take that form of transportation to work. I was a half an hour late, but nobody cared because everyone understood when you consider those kind of days. By the time Matt arrived home, I was there to welcome him with shovel in hand. The weather had warmed up to about 42 degrees and the ice on the sidewalk was turning into little ponds. I escorted Matt into the house and made him some tea, making sure it had cooled down. He has this new aversion to food with steam coming up from it."

"I understand."

*   *   *   *

"Come on Matt," Caroline said grabbing her coat.

"Where are we going?"

"Outside. I'd like you to shovel the driveway for me. The snow is sloshing up and I think it should be easy to remove now."

"It's cold out. I don't want to go out."

They walked out of the kitchen door and over to the driveway. Caroline's personal shovel with the plastic orange scoop was leaning against the garage door. She grabbed it, "Now look at how I am holding this shovel." Matt just gazed at the ground. "Matt, look at me!" Caroline called to him. She thought to herself, *"Oh please be able to do this. I know your days of working at a computer are over, but please be able to do this"*

Matt grabbed onto the shovel as though he were trying to hold onto a railing and started to tap the softened snow.

"No Matt, not like that. Give me the shovel and let me show you how."

"No!" He pulled the shovel away and held it behind him.

"Matt please. I just want to show you how to shovel."

"I want to go in." He threw the shovel on the ground and started to walk towards the kitchen door. Caroline reached out and took a hold of his coat sleeve, tugging on it slightly. He turned around and headed back to the driveway. The ice on his boots resembled a spilled slurpee before the syrup was added. Matt watched the "flavorless colorless piece of slurpee" quickly turn into water on his foot. "Matt please help me shovel, "Caroline begged, tears in eyes, her face getting red from the cold. She picked the shovel up from the ground and started to shovel the slush away from driveway. "See what I am doing?"

Matt watched, "Uh huh!"

She picked up the shovel and dumped the debris on the snow covered lawn. "See what I am doing?" She started moving the edge of the shovel under the slush, scooping it and then lifted the shovel and dumped the contents onto the lawn. "Can you do that?"

"I can't do anything anymore!" Tears started to come down Matt's cheeks. At first it was a little hard to tell if it was water from melted snowflakes that fell against his cheek. Matt took the shovel, anyway, and gently started to scoop the slush, but he ended up moving it up the driveway and layers of the slush broke a part and began to lay on top of the next area of ice sludge. "Give me the shovel," Caroline said, broken hearted.

"I want to go in," Matt insisted.

"Go ahead, "the defeated mother cried. As Matt headed for the kitchen door, he climbed the steps and opened the steamed up storm door, going inside. Caroline remained outside. *"I want my son back. What will he ever be able to do now?"*

*   *   *   *

Dr. Torres handed Caroline a tissue since the other tissue was all rumpled and torn.

"Thank you," she whimpered

"How is he doing in the kitchen area?"

*   *   *   *

Nobody seemed to work at cleaning out a muffin bin slower than Matt Cobel. "Come on Matt," shouted Dave, as Matt seemed to stare at a crumb. He started to move his right hand wiping out the crumbs from the container. That would only last for a few seconds when he would again stop to stare at something be it another crumb, the square plastic structure, or something. Again Dave would coach him on, "Come on wipe it." What may have taken a moment or so to wipe out could be stretched to five or ten minutes if you included dipping the sponge in the dish pan and sopping up the hot soapy water, "It's hot," Matt cried as he quickly removed his hand from the container. Removing his hand was probably one of the few quickest things he did at the clubhouse. "It's not that hot, it's just a little hotter than warm. You won't burn yourself." said Dave. "They wouldn't do that to anyone," the co-worker said with a gentle laugh.

"No?" Just seconds after Matt removed his hand from the water, his hand started to feel cool.

"They wouldn't. Would you like to continue to wash these muffin bins out?"

"No!"

"Why don't you dry them?"

"All right," said Matt as he and Dave traded jobs. Once again, Matt had to be prodded along in order to finish his job, but he completed it to everyone's satisfaction. Soon it would be time to see if Matt could be promoted to table wiper.

*   *   *   *

"We are getting somewhere," Dr. Torres said to Caroline.

"What kind of job is that?"

"You told me about the Sweet 16 you had last year for your daughter. What would you do if the table wasn't cleared away between courses or tables were dirty when you sat down because nobody would clean them?"

"I always thought these were like jobs held by students who were trying to make some extra money while in high school or in college."

"In some cases yes. In others, no. Matt's slowly finding things that he can do and succeed at. There is no telling if he will have those level jobs or be able to do something that requires more skill. He needs to have some success in something regardless of how little value you put to it. If he doesn't start having some success in something, he will give up and do nothing."

"I see."

"Did he ever try Dave's job?"

✶   ✶   ✶   ✶

The following week they decided to try Matt out on cleaning the four square tables off for lunch. Rosalie came over to him when it was time for the chores. Dave and another member were assigned to clean out the muffin bins. She held her left hand in a scooping position under the edge of the table, while she wiped the crumbs off the table onto her hand. Matt looked away at Dave and another member washing and drying the muffin bin. It wasn't that he wanted to do that job instead; it was just that it was not at this table. "Matt, look over here at what I'm doing," called out Rosalie. Matt turned his attention to Rosalie, "Do you think you can hold your hand like this and wipe the dirt from the table with your other hand?" Matt nodded his head. Once again he had to be coached and prodded along in order to continue the motion of wiping the dirt off the table into his other hand. Sometimes he seemed to be going through the motions of pretending to brush invisible dirt off the table and onto his other hand while avoiding some real crumbs or maybe all the crumbs were scooped up off the table. Matt didn't realize he was finished. He had his left hand filled with crumbs and the first few times he had the job, he moved his left hand away and opened the palm of his hand looking at the crumbs and wondering what to do next. The first time or so he turned his hand over and dumped the debris onto the floor. "No Matt, "Rosalie said as she rushed over to the table from the kitchen. She grabbed the trash can from the kitchen area while the member preparing lunch complained that she didn't have any place to put her potato peelings. "I'll think of something," Rosalie replied, moving the trash can over to Matt. "For now you should dump the crumbs in here. Next time I think you should walk over to the trash can and dump out the crumbs. I need a broom right now." Dave left his area to retrieve a broom for Rosalie. "Matt," Rosalie said, "Can you sweep?"

Matt shrugged his shoulders.

"I'll demonstrate." Rosalie dabbed at the crumbs on the floor, pushing them together until they were in one neat pile. "Can you do that?"

Matt nodded his head. He took the broom and started to sweep the pile of crumbs, flattening and spreading them out. "No, don't do that. There must be other crumbs on the floor. Wait," she rushed to the closet where the cleaning tools were kept and grabbed a dust pan. Matt stood like a statue until Rosalie returned. "Matt," he looked at her, "This is a dust pan and you place it on the floor. After you make the piles of dirt, you push them into the dust pan with the broom. I'll demonstrate." The therapist demonstrated how to sweep the dirt on the floor into the dustpan. "Now when the pan is full like this," she squatted and lifted the dustpan to eye level, "You simply take this and," she turned over the dustpan until the contents fell into the trashcan. "You think you can do that?" He nodded.

By the end of the week, Matt could clear crumbs off the dining tables as well as he had learned how to dry and wash the muffin bins. Next he was ready to learn how to wash down the tables.

*   *   *   *

"They tried to teach Matt how to wash down the tables."
"How did that go?"

CHAPTER 30

▼

GRADUATION
JUNE 2003 AFTERNOON

Nicole and Bari Lynn walked several blocks towards Bari Lynn's home. They hauled their graduation gowns on hangers, over their shoulders "I'm really going to miss you, Nick."

"I am not leaving until the end of August."

"I don't start Bergen County Community College until September."

"I know, they accepted you into their undergraduate therapy program."

"What are you going to major in?"

"Business, but it is all my mom's idea. She says that a degree in business will always come in handy no matter what I decide to do in life. I figure I'll major in that until I come up with something else."

"How about the senior prom? Who are you going with?"

"That boy from chem class who picked up my text book when I dropped it coming into the classroom last fall. Are you going, Bari Lynn?"

"I've been so busy with Matt lately that I forgot all about the prom. Matt is the reason that I want to stay in the area. At least I am not forgetting about graduation day."

Matt came to the front door with his quad cane in hand. "Hey Matt, look at you," Nicole smiled looking at his quad cane for the first time.

"What?" he asked.

"The last time I saw you, you had a walker and now you have a quad cane. I think it is wonderful."

Matt moved away from the door and allowed Bari Lynn and Nicole to enter.

"Where is Mom?" asked Bari Lynn.

"She's in the kitchen," answered Matt.

Caroline came out of the kitchen and into the living room, smiling. Nicole draped her gown over a nearby chair while Bari Lynn hung her gown over the coat closet doorknob. "Why don't you put on your gown so that I can see how you look in it?" suggested Caroline.

Bari Lynn removed the gown from the coat closet doorknob, detached the gown from the plastic. She placed the gown over her clothes as though it were a jacket. "Put on the cap so that I can get the entire effect," said Caroline.

Bari Lynn put on the white graduation cap. The cap had white and maroon tassels. Large golden colored metal digits *03* dangled from the cap, along side the tassels.

Caroline stepped back as far as she could without banging into anything. "Come on Nicole and Matt, take a look at her. Isn't she lovely?"

Matt nodded his head once and Nicole smiled.

"I guess we are all set for tomorrow, then."

"I think my own parents would like to see me in my gown, too. I hope I look as lovely as Bari Lynn does," Nicole said as she took her gown off the chair, flung the gown over her shoulders, down her back and walked over to the front door.

Caroline got up and said, "Let me help you with the door."

"Thank you, Mrs. Cobel." Nicole walked out of the front door and down the path towards the sidewalk. Caroline thought to herself it couldn't be possible twelve years had gone by so fast. She remembered she said the very same thing when Matt graduated the same high school five years before.

"Are you looking forward to the graduation, Matt?" asked Caroline.

Matt nodded his head.

Bari Lynn frowned. "I was only able to get enough tickets for you, Shauna, and Matt."

"That's O.K. we'llmake it up to the people when they come to your graduation party this weekend."

Sunday night.

Matt was out back at the picnic table. Matt set the table picnic table out back. He is shaking a little and has to anchor himself by holding onto the table. The napkins are crooked and cockeyed but they are folded and the plastic ware and the cups are in the proper places. Caroline stepped outside to put some salad on the table and screamed as though she had seen a rodent. "Matt!"

He jumped, "Huh!"

Caroline grabbed him and hugged him.

Just then a woman petite woman with curly auburn hair walked into the yard. Caroline turned around with a blank expression on her face. The woman said, "I'm Lorraine Brenner, don't you remember me from the Christmas Party at the center?"

When Caroline walked over to her she noticed the lady was pushing a folded up red framed wheelchair. "Mrs. Cobel, I'm Rachel's mother."

"Right I spoke to you on the phone. It's just that I don't remember meeting you."

Just then a man with thin graying balding hair and a pot belly carried Rachel in his arms like a groom carrying his bride over the threshold. Lorraine placed her hand in the middle of the wheelchair to open it as her husband placed Rachel down. "Don't forget to put the straps on so she won't fall out." Rachel sat in her chair as though she were a rag doll in a little girl's toy stroller. Sam secured the seat belt. "Mrs. Cobel, I was very surprised to get your call. Rachel hasn't been on a date since that awful New Years Eve party at that Frat house. That reminds me." She put her right hand into her pocketbook and took out a small gift wrapped box. Lorraine asked, "I have something for Bari Lynn. It's one of those sapphire toe rings. I hope she likes it. Rachel picked it out. I'll keep it until I see her."

"Rachel was in her freshman year and she hadn't even declared her Childhood Education major yet. Ever since the summer of 2001, she has been just one pleasant surprise after another. It was the best decision we ever made since that incident. Sam, will you take Rachel over to the picnic table where Matt is?" Lorraine spotted Bari Lynn and headed over to her.

Sam took his youngest child and only daughter over to her friend. "Would you like your liberator?"

Rachel bobbed her head.

"O.K. but I can't get it for you until after you are done with your meal. We don't want to ruin it. In the meantime," he took out a sheet of paper in a document protector. The sheet had the twenty-six letter of the alphabet, number 0–9, and some common words that Rachel often used. "We can use this." He sat down on the bench, right of Rachel. "This is so she can talk to people without using her liberator."

Matt placed his head down near his neck and raised his eye balls. "Laura,"

"No Matt this is Rachel," her father corrected him.

The fingertips of Rachel's useable hand eased across the paper. Word by word, letter by letter, Sam figured out that his daughter told him it was alright and that he should let him be. Rachel quickly moved her hands over the laminated paper, "I know he calls me Laura …"

"Slow down," her father said. After he moved Rachel's plate and cup into the middle of the table, he handed her the liberator and Rachel quickly typed in her message and played it back in a monotone voice, "I know he calls me Laura, but I don't care. Besides he's cute!" She gave a Cheshire cat smile.

One of the guests happens to be a notary republic who looked over at Caroline. "He set the table. He set the table." Caroline cried.

The notary republic looked at her as if she had jumped on the table and started to dance and wasn't supposed to. "I'm sorry." Caroline apologized. "It's just that …" "You don't understand. It's been almost two years since he was injured. He hasn't been able to do anything like this in almost two years."

The man smiled.

"I'd like you to meet someone. I have an extra car that I'm giving to someone and I wanted to make it official, Can you come into my kitchen for a moment?"

✳   ✳   ✳   ✳

Caroline was loading the dishwasher full of dirtied casserole dishes and bowls from the end of the party. By the kitchen door there was a bulging black trash bag filled with soiled plastic ware and soiled paper cups, napkins and plates. Shauna said, "I really need to go now." She embraced Caroline and then she embraced Bari Lynn. "That was some party!" "And you, Matt."

"What?" he asked.

"You made the most progress of all," Shauna hugged him.

Huh?" Matt replied.

Shauna backed away and said, "You know it's not a good idea for one to stay around longer than one is needed."

"If you can just stay one more day, I have some time tomorrow. We can go over to the license place and get new tags for the car."

Shauna removed a pen from the pocket of her long skirt.

"Just sign your name here," pointing to the place where the new owner should sign. Shauna with her pen in hand signed the title. "I really have to go now. I'll be in touch. I will head for the license place before I go anywhere." Shauna took the car key and the title out of the front door of the house. She headed down the path and headed towards the driveway. Shauna got into the driver's seat of the Geo Metro, started the car, turned on the head lights and backed down the driveway into the street. She turned and headed east down Morrow.Caroline, Bari Lynn and Matt stood by the storm/screen door as Shauna and the car got smaller and smaller and vanished from their sight.

CHAPTER 31

▼

SECOND SEMESTER.

Bari Lynn was in her second semester of college in her English 102 class. The class is doing workshop. She read the paper and began to shriek as though the school building were under attack. Bari Lynn raced out of the classroom, ripping up the paper into tiny pieces. The professor ran out of the room until he reached the ladies' room, door, swishing through the torn pieces as though they were fallen leaves. He stopped.

The student who wrote the paper had a "what's the matter with her" look on her face as she reached into her knapsack, grabbing another copy of her report. She handed it over to the female classmate who sat on her left, shaking her head.

On the way to the Psychologist's office, Bari Lynn passed by some bicycle racks filled with probably more bikes of every size, style and color than one would find in a bicycle store. When she crossed the street on the campus mall, she noticed an electric blue colored Geo Metro with beige and black New Jersey tags parked outside the student services building. She walked into the lobby and followed the sign with the arrow on it, towards the counseling area. Bari Lynn found the door was opened and a lady with red shoulder length hair was stooped over a book case. She had her back to the door. Bari Lynn looked over on the desk and found a picture of from the graduation party. It was of her brother and Rachel sitting next to each other at the graduation party.

The End.

Afterword

As a writer, I am supposed to give credit where credit is due when it comes to researched material. I don't want to give you the idea that everything I told you is out of my head and my personal experiences. Here is the following information that I have pulled off of various websites from the internet.

1. The personal experience of the World Trade Center Tragedy comes from some of the websites created by survivors who have actually worked at the WTC. There is also some information there about the Empire State Building.

2. The businesses in the World Trade Center are from a website that lists which businesses are on which floors in both the South Tower and the North Towers.

3. There are several websites about Windows of The World restaurant which also include photographs.

4. Brain Injury information came from several TBI websites.

5. Information about the Bombing of Pearl Harbor came from several websites dedicated to Pearl Harbor Day.

6. References to Catholicisim come from Catholic websites, St. Patrick's Cathedral particularly.

7. Various websites about Muslim culture.

8. The Waco Stand off with David Koresch.

9. The World Trade Center bombing 1993.

10. The Tulsa Oklahoma crisis April 19, 1995 with Timothy McVeigh.

11. A website that gives lyrics to popular tunes like *I Don't Know How To Love Him.*

12. Tower records for the 2001 *NSYNC Album.

13. Cheerleader uniform website.

I hope I didn't leave anybody out.

14. Einstein-Moss Rehabilitation Research Institute. (Employment).

15. From Revolution to Reconstruction—an .HTML project.

What few tidbits may be left after that came from actual news reports that I had seen, heard or read back in the early 2000s and also my own personal experiences.

978-0-595-42635-5
0-595-42635-2

LaVergne, TN USA
02 November 2009
162746LV00004B/89/A